PLAY THE GAME

PLAY THE GAME

GAME

CHARLENE ALLEN

KATHERINE TEGEN BOOKS
An Imprint of HarperCollins Publishers

Katherine Tegen Books is an imprint of HarperCollins Publishers.

Play the Game
Copyright © 2023 by Charlene Allen
All rights reserved. Printed in the United States of America.

Library of Congress Control Number: 2022917574
ISBN 978-0-06-321279-4

Typography by Joel Tippie
22 23 24 25 26 LBC 5 4 3 2 1

First Edition

For my grandparents, Margie and Clauzell McCombs and Ancella Allen, and my parents, Hazel and Charles Allen. Thanks for the most amazing family ever.

LIGHTNING STRIKES TWICE IN BROOKLYN PARKING LOT

Phillip Singer, the Brooklyn civilian who killed Black teenager Ed Hennessey last year, was found dead early this morning. Singer's body was found in the parking lot of Yard restaurant, the same Brooklyn location where he shot Hennessey. Investigators stated that Singer died of head trauma inflicted by a blunt instrument.

Singer, who was white, was not prosecuted for killing Hennessey, a decision that caused an uproar from the Black community and other activists. Black leaders are now demanding an independent investigation into Singer's death, raising concerns that the local police will unduly target members of the Black community as suspects. The NYPD has issued a statement that the investigation will be thorough, and justice will be served.

The Girl and the Game

"I got a plan," Jack says, falling in step beside me as I come up out of the subway. "For tonight. You understand what's going down tonight, right?" He drops a lanky arm across my shoulder. Classic. Ambushes me at the subway, and now I'm supposed to ask what's going on, so he can go off on one of his Jack-rants. I shove his arm off me. The sidewalk's crowded with people sorting through racks that've been pulled outside stores now it's April and the weather's decent. Any other time, I'd be pumped, going to work on a nice day like this. The way it is, I'm jumpy as hell about walking into Yard for the first time since Singer got killed. And I don't need Jack making it worse.

"What do you know, Jackson?" I ask, sidestepping a dog walker who's got half a dozen yappy dogs on too-long leashes. "Or think you know?"

"More than you, buddy," he says, flashing a grin at a bunch of girls coming out of a diner. He's turned up, got himself in a state. "Listen. The cops told Ms. Fox she shouldn't reopen the restaurant yet. Some shit about an *active police investigation*, which means they're gonna be up in our business when we reopen tonight. Well, I say whatever they want, we don't do it. Teach them to settle the hell down."

"Right," I say. Roll my eyes at the thought of Jack telling somebody else to settle down. "Ms. Fox knows what she's doing," I say. Which is true. Ms. Fox's been running her restaurant forever without help from him.

We turn a corner. There're no stores here, less people. Jack slows down 'cause he gets his juice from an audience. Has since we were kids. Jack, the outgoing one. Ed, the goofy geek. And me, the guy in the middle. With good sense. The thing is, though, now I'm seeing Jack, there's something I want to tell him. So I try to shake off being irritated. But, of course, Jack doesn't stop.

"Just roll with it, all right?" he says. "If the cops start asking questions, we tell 'em we already gave our statements, we don't have anything else to say."

When I don't answer, he shoots me a side-eye, accusing, ugly. "Still going with Easy VZ, huh? Still can't get up off your ass and do what people ask you?"

Just like that, four months of irritation walks between us. Because the whole time since Ed died, Jack's been dogging me to be like him and go at the cops, join the protests, make noise in the streets to get Singer up on charges for what he did to Ed. I don't

4

say what's obvious, that you can't bring a dead guy up on charges, so give it a rest. I don't need another Jack-rant about how it's the principle of the thing. What I do is, quit walking. "Know what?" I say. "Go on ahead. I gotta make a call."

"No problem." He strides off down the block.

It's not like I don't get it. Not rocket science, why Jack wants to take on the cops. But he should've believed me when I told him I couldn't go out there and yell about Ed. In December, when it first happened, it was hard even getting that it was real. Some random white man actually killed Ed. I stayed in my room all day, stuck as fuck, doom scrolling online and especially in my head. But Jack acted like I was just blowing him off—and Ed, too.

Stepping back into the closest doorway, I watch his back, thinking of what happened this morning, before I left home. The way Jack's been acting, he mighta given me shit, anyhow, if I'd told him. Even though I didn't ask for what happened. Was just trying to get out of the house on time when Ed's ma showed up at the door, with her little intense self. And the next thing I knew, she was shoving Ed's red laptop at me, telling me she had to give his stuff away since the cops were back in their business, now Singer'd got killed.

"Have it," she said. "You knew this part of him best."

I took the thing because no sane person argues with Ed's ma. But I didn't want it. After she left, I zipped it into my backpack and walked the streets, feeling like I had a shiny red corpse on my back. And, of course, it wasn't even true, what she said. I never bothered with the game Ed was making on the laptop, even though it was his best thing. I'd get irritated when he came barging in—any hour, since our families lived on the same floor—going on about some puzzle he could use in the game. I remember the last time he did it, a Saturday morning. Me toasting waffles in my kitchen, Ed leaning on the counter holding up his phone—red like the laptop.

"It's called a rebus puzzle," he said. "You use lateral thinking on these, thinking outside the box. Otherwise, your brain'll see what it expects to see and you won't be able to solve them." He lowered the phone. "How I do it is, close my eyes and wipe my brain like it's a chalkboard. Then I open them and stare at the puzzle. Don't even blink." He scrunched his eyes shut, to demonstrate, his round cheeks bulging. Then he opened his eyes and put the phone back in my face.

"Have a waffle," I said, sliding a plate to him.

"Just try!" he said. The screen had a bunch of letters in different colors: an orange *U*, a red *E*, and a black *YET*.

"Yeah," I said. "No clue."

"*Come on!* Close your eyes."

I rolled them instead. Got the syrup down. Ed moved on to his favorite part, explaining the thing in detail. "Okay, watch. The *U* is orange and the *E* is red, right? So, if you *see it like that*, it's *orange-u red-e*. Or *are-n't you read-y*. See? Then on the last part, *Y-E-T*, the color doesn't matter, it's just the word *yet*. *Aren't you ready yet?*" His grin broke loose, taking over his face. "So cool. You think letters just spell words—you don't think the color of them can be part of what they're spelling."

I poured my syrup, started eating. Ed picked up his whole waffle on his fork, raised it overhead, and lowered it into his mouth. With one long arm in the air over his big head, the other bent on the counter, I remember thinking he was shaped like a stick-figure drawing. And I was impressed, too, with how his brain worked. Like a scientist in a fifteen-year-old body. I just didn't bother saying it. I wonder if I'd remember the puzzle at all if Singer hadn't done what he did. How do you even make a memory when you aren't paying attention in the first place?

"And, by the way!" The shout comes from the end of the block. It's Jack, who should've been long gone by now. "I got Ms. Fox to make it all-hands-on-deck tonight," he says. "Diamond's gonna be there."

"What? *Oh . . .*" I try not to let it show, but if Diamond's gonna be there, the night can't be all bad. She wasn't on the schedule to work, another reason I wasn't feeling going in tonight.

"You done with that call?" Jack asks.

I take my time catching up to him, doing my best to let the Ed-thoughts go. When we hit the next corner, we can see the green neon letters under the blinking yellow palm tree. *YARD, Caribbean Home Cooking and Song.* A cop blocks the restaurant's doorway, framed in the gold lights Ms. Fox uses to decorate. Police tape and wooden barricades section off most of the parking lot. Just like when it was Ed.

Jack lets out a heavy breath. "This, right here?" he says. "Is what you call a mindfuck. Singer could've got killed anyplace in the whooole city. And we get him here."

We trade looks. No question, we agree about this, at least.

7

The usual homeless guy's digging through the dumpster by the restaurant's side door. Got on his checkered suit jacket over a sweatshirt and pants. He lifts his head, mutters in the cop's direction.

"He messing with you?" Jack asks.

"Ain't about me," the guy says. "That woman deserves better."

Also true. The whole neighborhood's over these cops messing with Ms. Fox. It's bad enough that she was the one who found Singer's body. The cops don't have to keep asking her about it. I grab a breath. Remind myself Diamond's inside that restaurant. Jack and I walk by the cop, a Black guy who's been here before, and go inside. She's the first thing I see. Diamond, in the middle of the dining room, spreading out a red tablecloth that matches her tight skirt. She runs over in her low boots, bare brown legs too sweet to be real. Pulls me into a hug that's all softness.

"Glad you're working tonight, VZ," she says.

I am, too, now. I tell her that, and when she doesn't move back I tighten my arms, rest my head on hers, my hands right where her bra cuts under her shirt. She's so little; she only hits my chest. Is barely half as wide as me. The girl-lotion smell of her mixes with the curry scent in the air, the low-volume soca music, the orange walls. For a minute, it's all good.

"So much for Easy VZ," Jack whispers in my ear as he passes by. Then louder, so Diamond can hear, "Just better hope I don't tell Fisk."

"Fisk knows I'm friends with VZ," Diamond says. But she pulls away from our hug.

Jack heads to the stage to hook up the sound equipment, and

Diamond goes back to putting flowers and silverware on the tables from the cart beside her.

"What can I do for you?" I ask, picking up a pile of napkins. She grins like I meant more than I meant to mean. The air melts between us. Like it's been since Ed. We're more than just flirting; there's something real here. But she still won't say she's leaving Fisk.

I take the stack of silverware she hands me. We move to the next table, me watching her. She's always focused. *Intentional.* Even doing something as simple as setting a table.

"Ms. Fox is having nightmares again," Diamond says, glancing at the kitchen, where Ms. Fox does her magic.

I know she thinks of Ms. Fox like a mom, but there's so much feeling in her eyes, I wouldn't mind her looking at me that way. "I've been sleeping upstairs to keep her company. She wakes up screaming, then comes down here and cooks for the rest of the night, just like she did after Ed." She half laughs. "I end up studying all night, so at least it's good for something."

"You want a break?" I ask. "I can finish. You could play your Switch before we open." This gets a grin, dimples and all. She shakes her head, but just thinking about it seems to cheer her up. She's like Ed, the way she loves her gaming.

I put down my silverware. Pull off my backpack, unzip it. Stare at Ed's laptop.

"What?" Diamond asks, noticing.

I check the room. Jack's caught up in the soundboard, and there's still ten minutes before Fisk needs to be here. I grab Diamond's hand, pull her into the stock closet, heart racing from what

I'm thinking and what I'm doing. My idea's batshit, but I still think it's right. *A chance to do something for Ed.*

I have to leave the door open so Ms. Fox doesn't get on us, but it's still private, the two of us stuffed beside the table we use to measure spices. It smells like ginger and cloves.

"Ed's ma came over this morning," I say. Tell her the quick version of the story. "You got how much he loved the game he was making, right?"

She lets out a sad laugh. "You know that day I helped him with his coding class? I kept telling him he wasn't bad at code, he just had to take his mind off the rest of it for a minute. He had this whole complicated story. And the puzzles had to be hard enough to make people work but still fun. He was so into the *experience* his players would have."

"Yeah, good," I say. "And this contest—it was like every ounce of his game love went into this contest. He worked his ass off and finished the game so he could submit it. But then . . ." The next part's hard to say. I take a second and start again. "Even though he finished it, Ed never got to play the whole game through. Because he was waiting for me. He'd entered it in this big contest for game makers, and before the competition I was supposed to play it with him—you know, like consumer-test it—so he could find the glitches, clean everything up. He wanted to win *bad*. I promised I'd help, but I wasn't in any hurry. And then . . ."

"I get it," Diamond says, soft-voiced.

"You don't, though!" I tell her, getting excited again, now that I've said the hard part. "That contest hasn't happened yet. *And now I've got Ed's game."*

My hands shake when I take out Ed's laptop. I set it on the spice-measuring table. "I can play it like I was supposed to, fix whatever needs fixing. Then show up at the contest and win the thing."

The more I talk, the more I realize the idea's been coming together in my mind all morning—I just needed Diamond. And here she is, acting like I haven't lost my mind trying to get a win for somebody who's dead. I keep going.

"Just one problem," I say. "I'm the guy who quit video games in seventh grade. I'm gonna need backup from a serious gamer."

Diamond's smile comes with a worried forehead crease, but before she can explain it, the front door opens. And, damn it to hell, it's Fisk, sliding in on his stupid electric scooter. Diamond's smile turns guilty, and she bolts out of the stock closet. I lick my lips, swallow back the hurt. Watch Fisk slip an arm around Diamond's waist, almost white-boy confident. That's his thing. Him and Jack are older than me, but Fisk's the one with the nice clothes and gear. All the time turning on the charm, like he's too good to have problems like the rest of us.

I leave the closet but stay in the back of the room, Ed's laptop pressed to my chest. Diamond goes to the table she'd been working on, adjusting stuff that doesn't need it.

"That cop still out there?" Diamond asks Fisk, eyeing the front windows.

"He says he'll come in when his partner gets here," he tells her. "They getting to you?" He looks all concerned. "Want me to take

11

you home? I could cover for you."

"Yo, Fisk! Give me a hand over here?" Jack shoots me a look, tells me he's getting this Fisk fool out of my way so I can finish my conversation with Diamond. But too late.

The front door opens again. In walk the cops.

You Gonna Be Next?

In comes the Black cop who'd been outside, a short white woman behind him, steel-gray hair popping out from under her cop cap. Fisk pulls Diamond to him. I cuss my crap luck at losing my chance to talk to Diamond. And Ms. Fox bursts through the kitchen door, filling up half the room in one of her huge African-print dresses. Her sweaty round face is tight with stress, but she smiles when she sees us. Since I'm in the back, closest to the kitchen door, I get wrapped in three hundred pounds of coconut-smelling hug.

"In the kitchen, the whole of you," she says, going extra hard on her Jamaican accent for emphasis. When she reaches Jack, he gets a thick finger in his chest along with his hug. *The whole of you.* Don't trouble yourselves, these officers won't be long."

Jack throws the cops a side-eye, but I hustle him into the kitchen, glad Ms. Fox got on him. The kitchen's warm and steamy and smells like the coconut cake that must be in the oven. Diamond, Fisk, Jack, and I stack up, one head over the next, to look through the crack in the kitchen door. Ms. Fox matches her dining room, bright warm colors from her skin, clothes. The white cop, who's stepped up to her, looks pale as paper, compared. She's got her shoulders back and her chest thrown out, like she's trying to make herself bigger.

"We'll get right to it, ma'am," she says. "We're wondering if you've reconsidered your story about the night of the murder. You said you saw the victim fall, but you didn't see the person who hit him. And we all know that doesn't add up."

Ms. Fox laughs. "Wanting a new song won't make me change my tune," she says.

"*Ma'am.*" The white cop doesn't miss a beat. "If you're protecting a member of your staff . . ."

In the kitchen, we trade looks. Protecting her staff? Is that what they think? I get the sick stomach I got when the cops first came asking questions. Tell myself it's stupid, I wasn't even here the night Singer got killed. In the dining room, Ms. Fox pulls a chair back from one of the tables. Drops into it. Sighs.

The Black cop widens his legs. "The only way this ends, ma'am, is with an arrest," he says. "A murder was committed here."

Ms. Fox sucks her teeth. "Goodness, for true? You think I forgot the man dropping dead before me eyes?"

"Which makes you our only witness," the white cop snaps, not feeling the humor. "And, of course, it's the second incident on your property, isn't it? Given the young man Singer shot last year."

"Killed," Ms. Fox says, quieter. "Mr. Singer didn't just shoot. He killed that sweet boy."

"That's not the point!" The white cop grips the edges of the table Ms. Fox is sitting at. Takes a long breath, gearing up for another round.

"Nah, leave her alone!" It's Jack, pushing through the kitchen door. I'm right behind him, because Jack's too big an idiot to go out there on his own. Diamond and Fisk come, too. The three of us stop when the cops're right in front of us. Hands on their guns. Up close, I can feel their tightness. Ready for anything.

Jack doesn't stop with the rest of us. He goes up behind Ms. Fox, puts his hands on her shoulders. He's facing the cops now. I feel Diamond and Fisk go stiff on either side of me. We all know how Jack can be when he gets going about the racist system that let Singer off for killing Ed. None of that can happen in front of cops.

"The only way this ends is with an arrest?" Jack mimics the cop's words. He's got one foot in front of the other, leaning over Ms. Fox.

I can't see his face, but I know it's screwed up, red heat burning through his light brown skin. "How you gonna fix your face to say that?" he asks. "It didn't end that way when Singer killed our friend. Now, Ms. Fox told you she doesn't know anything, all right? Hell, wouldn't nobody tell you if they did!"

"Really?" The white cop raises her brows like things just got more interesting. "What's that supposed to mean?"

"It means, get a grip!" Jack says. "That Singer fool came at somebody with his piece? Everybody knows what he can do with that thing. No one's gonna blame anybody for going back at him."

15

Aw, hell. "Jack . . ." I say his name as calm as I can. He ignores me.

"And you know that, how?" the white cop asks.

"Know what?" Jack sounds confused.

"Young man, where were *you* the night Mr. Singer was killed?" the Black cop asks, getting in it. "You said you weren't here that night, correct?"

"You know that," Jack says.

"Tell us again where you were."

Jack takes a breath, blows it out through his nose. "My neighborhood," he spits out. "By where I live."

"Jack . . . ," I try again.

"And what were you saying before?" the white cop asks. "What were you saying about Mr. Singer and his gun?" While she talks, the Black cop moves closer, crowding Jack.

"Back the hell up!" Jack shouts.

"*Who* has to back the hell up?" The Black cop's face-to-face with Jack now.

Ms. Fox stands up, but Jack and the cop step to the side, blow her off. The cop's as tall as Jack, and bigger, broader. I catch Fisk's eye. We trade *It's about to go down* looks, because I feel it, even though I don't get *why*. Why mess with Jack this bad? Then I remember what they said about Ms. Fox covering for her staff. Did that mean Jack? *Did they come here to question Jack, not Ms. Fox like we thought?* Cold fear cuts through my chest. Out in the lot, a car rumbles to a stop, the engine cuts. In my mind, I beg whoever's there to come in and stop this. Right now.

"*Back. Down.*" The Black cop says it real soft.

There's a beat of quiet. And then Jack does the stupidest thing I've ever seen him do. He throws up his hands. It's because he's fed up, I know that. But the cops don't seem to. In a heartbeat, they're on him.

What comes next hits me in pieces, slow motion, while a loud pounding beats in my ears. Because it's the thing I always knew could happen—to me, Jack, any of us. But tonight? Here? Now?

"*. . . under arrest.*"

"*. . . interfering with a police investigation.*"

"*. . . failed to follow orders.*"

There are voices out in the parking lot. Car doors slam. When the Black cop talks, I feel a shiver on the back of my neck.

"I'm gonna give you two choices," he says to Jack. "I can pull out the cuffs, *or* you can cooperate while I pat you down. Then you can walk out of here between us, no cuffs. What's it gonna be?"

Ms. Fox holds up a hand, and relief explodes in me because she's finally gonna stop this. But all she says is, "Do what them tell you, son. Don't make them come with no shackles."

Shackles?

"Jack, what the fuck?" I hear myself say, stepping toward Jack. "You can't let them—"

The Black cop moves so fast I barely see it. He sidesteps Jack, grabs my arm, and twists me around so my back's against his chest. Ms. Fox shouts, Jack too. Maybe even Diamond. But I barely hear. Slow motion's gone to no motion. Everything still. The cop's breath on my ear and Ed's laptop still in my free hand.

17

"You gonna be next?" the cop asks. I swallow. I know the answer, 'cause I've always known it. I can't say it, though. So, I shake my head.

And the whole thing falls the rest of the way to hell.

The cop lets go of me. Pats Jack down. Chest, ass, legs. I clench my own muscles to not flinch. Jack squares his shoulders. Throws us a look, playing like he's fine. And then they walk him out the door. And I stand there, knowing we're so not fine.

In Other Worlds

"Ms. Fox wasn't playing, huh?" Diamond says. "You saw how she shut down those customers who were acting like the cops perp-walked Jack outta here after some kind of dramatic takedown." She locks the restaurant door behind the last customer, turns, and slides down the wall, movie star–style. Fisk collapses against the wall by the kitchen door, and I pull two chairs together, one for my ass, one for my feet. Somehow, we got through the night with a house full of gossiping customers, one less staff, and the three of us whipping our heads around every time the door opened. But no Jack. No news to keep me from picturing him in some dirty cell, fingerprints, body search. The whole nine.

"Don't be adding *few-el* to the *fiya*," Fisk says, in a spot-on imitation of Ms. Fox's accent.

We all laugh, which feels like a shock to the tightness I've been holding in my belly all night.

Fisk straightens up. "Y'all sit a minute," he says. "I'll go see if she's heard anything."

He heads into the kitchen, and Diamond shoots me a *See, he's not so bad* look. "I know you're worried about your boy," she says, when Fisk's gone.

"I'm cool," I say, because I can't stand talking about it.

"I know," Diamond says. Like she gets it. She crosses her feet and stands up, no hands. "You want to get back to what you were talking about, before?" I give her a big-ass grin because Ed's game's exactly what I need right now. I get my pack from the back and pull out the red laptop. Can't help glancing at the kitchen, hoping Fisk stays in there a while.

We head to a bare table, and I open the laptop. Feels weird as hell, pulling up the game. Ed should be doing this, showing off the whole wacky Ed-i-verse he made. He worked on it every day after school, belly-down on my bed on the days he came over. Laptop open and a pad beside him to draw stuff out. I watched comedy videos, maybe did some homework, while he worked. But I knew how big a deal it was. How it was supposed to make up for shit that wasn't working in his life.

"You ever see the cut-scene?" I ask Diamond. "This animated video Ed made to show the setup." When she shakes her head, I start to hit play, but I'm getting nervous all over again. "I mean you helped him with code, but did he actually tell you the story and all?

Because it's Ed. So, you know, mutants and monsters, shit like that. And the puzzles are *wack . . .*"

"Yeah, I know," she says, like it's a good thing.

I relax. Bring on the Ed-i-verse. There's organ music, *duuum-duuum, duuuuuuum.* On-screen writing tells the backstory.

A tsunami crashed into Brooklyn. The East River flooded, and the city swam in a sickening soup of radium and roach killer, KFC and car parts, drugs and dead people. When it was over, mutant humans got strange powers along with tails or claws or giant body parts.

In the river, the biggest water bug in Brooklyn mutated into a three-headed mega-monster. It decided to take over the city. No one was a match for it, except the coolest mutant of all. His name was EDRIC THE GREAT.

The screen comes to life. A mutant Black kid stands on the Brooklyn Bridge. He's got huge muscles in his arms and legs, a scrawny middle, and kinky green hair cut exactly like Ed's. His skin's like leathery brown hide. An alligator tail grows out of his ass.

Underneath him, the three-headed bug-monster rears up from the water. It's twice as big as Edric, with a diamond-shaped back, red eyes on all three of its heads, way too many legs. Edric the Great faces it, makes an *o* with his lips, and shoots black sludge at it. The bug dodges. Shoots puke-green gunk from its middle mouth. The gunk hits Edric square in the face. A puke-green seal forms over his lips. He struggles but can't open his mouth again.

The title of the game appears across the screen.

Edric the Great vs. SirBugUs
The Battle for Brooklyn

I hit stop, check on Diamond. She looks like she's in it, waiting for more. I let some breath out.

"The animation's good," she says. "And I love that it's a point-and-click game. Simple and classic. Even if it is about a giant three-headed water bug in the East River."

"Gross was one of Ed's specialties," I say. "Couldn't stand water bugs, so he picked one for his villain. Did you get the joke? Sir-BugUs, the three-headed water bug, after that three-headed dog, Cerberus, from Greek stuff?"

"Well, yeah," Diamond says. "Of course."

So much for that stereotype, I think. Hot as hell and a real-deal geek. I hit play again, for the last setup screen:

Welcome to SirBugUs's Castle

Play: You are Edric the Great. You have to get through four levels of SirBugUs's Underwater Castle in order to reach the evil bug and defeat it before it takes over Brooklyn.

At the end of each level, you have to unlock the door to the next level.

Screw up a puzzle and you're back to the beginning of the level.

Hurry up! You're the only one who can save Brooklyn.

SirBugUs Powers: Mini minion-bugs that do whatever he wants. And **bug sludge**, nasty sticky stuff that hurts and can seal up body parts.

Edric the Great Powers: Smarts. Also, **deadly discharge** that can cut through exoskeletons and **kill.** Except, of course, his lips have been sealed by SirBugUs.

"So, the four floors of the underwater castle are the four levels," I tell Diamond, pausing the game. "Each one's got these different mutant creatures you have to get past. The final level's the big boss bug. So, we've got four levels to play through. And the contest, it's called JersiGame 'cause it's in frickin' New Jersey, is Saturday after next."

Diamond does the math. "Not much time," she says. "It'll be tight if there's coding problems we have to fix."

All I hear is the word *we*. I'm thanking her when Fisk comes back from the kitchen. The look on his face smacks me out of the Ed-i-verse. Back to the real-life shit-i-verse.

"Ms. Fox called everybody we could think of," Fisk says.

"Nobody knows a thing. It's like Jack went into the precinct and got swallowed up." He trades a look with Diamond that sends a shiver down my neck.

"What?" I ask.

"It's like in Ed's game," Diamond says. "People go in that place, and it's a whole other world in there. Who knows how they find their way out?"

Double Dad Madness

"Victor! Finally picked up, eh, son?"

"Pop?" I'm blinking in the dark of my room. Did the alarm go off yet? And was I really stupid enough to answer the phone without checking who was calling? I push myself up on my pillows. My hand smacks Ed's open laptop, and the screen lights up. It's Tuesday, I remember. And, far as I know, Jack's in jail.

"Look, son, your mother told me what happened to Jack," Pop says. "Terrible. Tragic. But it lets us know that restaurant's no place to be, now doesn't it?"

I'm waking up for real. His extra-tight voice tells me the Jack thing's got the stick even further up his ass than usual.

"It's my job, Pop," I tell him. I pull Ed's laptop toward me and try to remember how far I got last night before I knocked out. The screen shows the top floor of the castle. I'm still facing the first set of creatures on level one.

Pop gets louder. "Can't underestimate the emotional toll from this type of thing," he's saying. "You're still fragile from what happened to your friend. Losing a friend that way? You're in a delicate state. . . ."

I put the phone on speaker, lay it down on the bed. Get up and open the shade for something to do besides listen to him. It's gray out. I wonder if Chela's up yet.

"A young Black man can't be too careful," Pop says. "Working in a place like that, at a time like this . . ."

"You really need to stop," I mutter.

"Come again?" Pop asks.

"You know what?" I say. "Ma thinks it's good for me to keep busy, stay at the restaurant." I say it to shut him up. He hates when I one-up him with Ma. And it's not a lie. Ma gets that the restaurant and Chela's place are easiest for me, right now.

"*I'm* the lawyer in this family," he snaps. "I've seen these so-called investigations. They're like dirty dishwater; they slop all over everybody that's near them. Your mother wouldn't know that, now would she?"

I don't bother reminding him that he's a dial-a-lawyer, doesn't get a lot of murder cases. The room's getting lighter, showing my tangled sheets half off the bed.

"I'm telling you, son," Pop says. "That place is poison right now. Let's make a deal. If it's over, fine. But if the cops come back there, or if it goes any deeper with Jack, you'll quit that job."

Quit? Right. With Diamond there, Ms. Fox, and . . .

I ignore Pop, check my phone to make sure I didn't hear from Jack. Nope. I'd woken up a bunch of times, checked then, too. Now I'm mad. Fool can't be bothered to tell anybody if he's in some cell in Brooklyn or on Rikers Island, or what?

"Victor?"

"I'm here, Pop."

"Do we have a deal?"

I pull on a T-shirt and message Chela. *You up?*

"Can't make any deals, Pop, but I'm sure it's over, okay? I'll be late for school. Gotta go."

I hang up quick. Can't win with Pop, though. He's always so sure of what he's saying, it gets under my skin. End up with a nauseous thing going in the pit of my stomach. Pop-sick, brought on by too much Pop. I head down the hall, past the wall of family photos. Grin, like always, at the one of my baby sister, Sammy, sleeping on my head.

Bald Bennett's in the kitchen, chopping zucchini and looking over the breakfast bar where he can see Sammy and the living room TV. I already know I'll see a bald Black guy when I look at the TV. Bald Bennett's good at finding bald Black guy movies. No complaints, though, having the TV on and Sammy in the room makes life easier with the 'rents right now.

"Smells good," I tell him, heading over to Sammy in the living room. Bennett's got all four burners going in the kitchen like always on his days off from taking X-rays on the night shift. His eyes follow me, suspicious.

"I'm already starting on tonight's casserole," he says. "You okay this morning?"

"'Course," I say. Like it's completely normal for me to toss him a compliment and have a seat on a Tuesday morning, just for the hell of it.

"All right, then." Bennett gives his head a single pump. "I can whip you up some high-protein pancakes."

I agree, even though Bennett's a shit cook. The call from Pop got me, and I need intel only Bennett can give. Sammy's on the floor bouncing to the movie music, surrounded by toys.

She shrieks, "Veezwee!" when I plop down on the couch behind her. Can't see the girl and not wonder how a two-year-old can look just like Bennett, giant jowls and all, and still be cute as hell. But my baby sister pulls it off.

"John Shaft," Bennett says, nodding at the bald Black guy on the TV screen. "The *original* cool detective. Puts me in mind of your pop, big guy like that."

I shake my head. Poor Bennett, can't see the guy on the screen looks ten times better than Pop. He's got a worse case of Pop-sick than me, half-scared Ma'll go back to him some day. Doesn't get how far that ship's sailed. The good thing about Bennett, though? He likes to play the wise old Black man so much he'll tell you anything to keep talking.

"Pop called, just now," I tell him. "Ma told him what's going on with Jack?"

"Told him more than she needed to in my opinion," he says. "She'd gone all this time not saying how bad it was back around Christmas, when your friend passed. But now that boy's got arrested, she up and tells him everything. I told her you'd be fine.

28

Got that little girlfriend and everything, right?" He wide-pops his eyes and I know he's hoping for some intel of his own about this imaginary girlfriend.

"What'd Ma say?" I ask again. "What'd she tell Pop, exactly?"

Bennett grunts. Drops his gaze and chops some more carrots before answering. "She told him how you wouldn't leave out your bedroom, back then," he says. "Never slept at night. Didn't wanna go nowhere. She's worried it'll start up again now, with this arrest. 'Specially since you—"

"Since I what?"

"You know your ma'd like you to be home more. Take some meals with us."

"She also says she wants me to keep busy," I remind him.

"Well," Bennett says, nodding. "It could get worse if they bring charges on Jack for killing that racist." He puts down his knife, gives me his wise-old-Black-man look, straight in the eye. "That happens, you're gonna need your ma. I've known young men to snap for less."

"Well, that's not happening, this time," I say. "So, don't sweat it. Jack just got arrested 'cause he wouldn't shut up." Somewhere in the night, I'd decided that had to be true. The cops were trying to scare some sense into his silly ass, that's all. "Pop doesn't need to hear all that."

Not that they got it right, anyhow, about how it was after Ed. Wasn't that I couldn't sleep. It's that my dreams were real as shit. Ed doing regular stuff, walking to the subway, laying on my bed with his nose in his laptop, or telling stupid jokes. Or I'd be in Yard's

29

parking lot, and it would start out regular, too. Except I'd know something was wrong. And I couldn't figure out what it was till I caught sight of the stretcher, always out of nowhere, right in front of me. And I'd wake up at the exact second I saw the blood. After that, how was I supposed to go to school? Deal with everybody talking about him?

"Come here, waddlecheeks," I say, pulling Sammy on my lap and planting kisses on top of her head to help me calm down. She keeps her eyes on the screen, settles back like I'm her favorite chair. Bennett looks at me sheepfaced.

"Your pop said if it doesn't blow over soon, he wants you to go to his place. Could be before school even ends."

"*What?*" I'm on my feet. "I'm not going to Atlanta!"

"Fly me!" Sammy says, thinking I'm gonna play airplane with her, since I got up so quick.

"Not now, Sammy-ka-lammy," I tell her. I'm realizing why Pop's voice was extra-tight. He's got shit up his sleeve.

"I told your mother." Bennett holds up a hand. "I said, what happened is bad, sure. But we can handle it right here. Maybe some more of that therapy you had, or a new one, somebody you can talk to when that mood takes hold of you."

I close my eyes, try to keep it together. A gunshot rings out on the TV. Shaft chases a guy across a rooftop.

"There's nothing to handle," I tell Bennett. I put Sammy on the floor with one last kiss and get the hell out of there before I lose it.

The Burner

"Jack was probably too pissed at the cops to talk to anybody," Chela says. She's on her living room couch with me on the floor in front of her, scooched back between her open knees. Afternoon sun slides through flower decals on the windows, hits piles of clothes on all the chairs and the cat-pee-smelling gold carpet. None of that makes the place any less good. Because nobody here gives a shit about judging you. And the after-school food rocks. Chela stuffs a handful of homemade s'mores popcorn in her mouth, wipes her hands on her jeans, and pushes my head forward to get at a loc in the back. The crackle of static from her ma's old-school car service radio comes from the back of the apartment.

"I mean, what a shit show, getting picked up behind this whole Singer bull."

"Huh-uh, no excuse!" I complain. "He gets let out and can't

even tell me? I don't see how that works." Irks the hell out of me that I had to hear from Ms. Fox that they'd let Jack go. That was this morning. Now it's after school and I still haven't heard from the fool.

"Not about you," Chela singsongs. "People deal with shit in different ways." She gets on her knees to get at the top of my head. "What say you stress about something you can actually do something about? Like getting yourself laid."

I relax, 'cause we're done talking about Jack.

"'Scuse you? Who needs to get laid?"

"At least I'm trying," she says.

I roll my eyes. Wonder where to start.

"One," I tell her, "being too picky for all the people who wanna get with you *is not* trying."

Chela's convinced everybody who likes her's just into her "type": biracial with browned-butter skin and curly hair. Queer, wears Doc Martens. Actually, people like her 'cause she's bold as fuck without being a show-off. Hot, but with this off-center face that makes you wanna stare at it. Probably saves her that she can't see all that, but still.

"And number two," I say. "You're also not trying because you're over here drooling after a grown-ass woman who'd have to commit a felony to be with you."

"You don't worry about Ronnah." Chela doesn't miss a beat. "At least I'm not chasing people who're already taken. *And* got bad weaves."

I twist around, give her a stank-face. Should've known we'd end up here. Chela's always got something to say about Diamond.

She yanks a loc, settles back into twisting while I eat more popcorn. "Speaking of Ronnah . . . ," she says. Her fingers curl tighter in my hair. "You're still gonna do it, right? Tomorrow, at school?"

She sounds so pitiful, I don't even mess with her.

"I'll be there," I say. Though I'd rather be tied to the subway tracks, there's nothing else for it. Chela's been the best kind of friend since last summer, when I took driving lessons with her ma. She'd sit in the back seat, go from teasing to serious in a heartbeat if she caught on to something real—like how hard it was with Ma and Bennett back then, when Sammy was in baby mode and they had time for shit else. She asked questions that were tuned-in but not irritating. Was all about my hanging at her place. And that was even before Ed died.

Besides, she'd shocked the shit out of me when she told me what happened last week. I twist to the right, let her get the side of my head. Think back to the scene, that day at school. Chela walking into the student lounge for our free period together. Right off, I knew something was wrong. She had her lips tucked in, like she does when she's stressed.

"Don't say anything till I'm done talking," she said. "I gave a teacher a black eye—don't say it!—and now I have to do a discipline process with Ronnah. And you have to help me or I swear I'll fucking lose it."

"Don't lie," I said.

Yeah, she was upset, but I still didn't believe her. Chela's not the one to be popping off at teachers.

"Not lying," she said. "It was because of this." And she pulled something out of her pack.

My eyes snagged on it like clothes caught on a nail. An eight-by-ten photocopy of *the* picture—the one of Ed in his blue-striped shirt with the dumb look on his face. The picture that'd been all over the internet, on ten million protest posters. Across the photocopy, someone'd written in black marker, "AT LEAST THE SCUM WHO DID IT PAID."

My stomach turned. I spent my life trying *not* to think about what Singer did to Ed, and here it was again. Chela told me the story. This kid who was next to her when they saw the flyer didn't like the "scum who did it paid" comment. Said, "Whoever wrote that oughta be expelled." And Chela went off on him—said people had a right to righteous anger and he shouldn't censor it. Got so mad she'd slammed a classroom door open and it smacked a math teacher in the face. So now she had to do some disciplinary process that'd be led by her counselor crush, Ronnah.

Chela's fingers go tight and still in my hair. "Ronnah said I could be her intern next year," she says. "I don't need her knowing how bad I lost it. I actually hurt Ms. Doyle because of what fucking Bruce Walendorf said. And now *Bruce* gets to call *me* out in front of Ronnah, when he's the one who started it. How's that fair? Anybody would've done something crazy if they'd heard what Bruce said. Even you."

I don't bother answering. We both know it's not true.

"Oh, right," she says, getting her sarcasm back. "You woulda acted like you didn't hear him and felt even worse in the end."

"Yeah, pretty much," I say, hoping to make her laugh. We'd been down this road plenty, Chela telling me I need to "deal with my feelings about what happened to Ed." Me telling her that not dealing is how I deal.

"Anyway," she says. "Tomorrow's prep session's gonna be rough. I've only ever been in RJ circles as Ronnah's helper. Now it'll be all about me."

I know RJ stands for *restorative justice*, which sounds like a load of all-about-feelings crap I want to stay the hell clear of. But it's Chela, so . . . Her cat, Walter, jumps on the couch next to her, and she pets him one-handed, still holding my hair with her other hand.

"Ronnah!" she groans. "God, she's so amazing. What if I act like a total idiot in front of her?"

I open my mouth to answer, but she pushes my head to one side with a vicious shove.

"Never mind," she says, yanking a loc. "Don't start." I jerk out of reach, glad the mood's lighter. My phone buzzes. It's Diamond. Even though I know it's her, her voice gets me. The way she says my name—like it matters to her.

"Yeah," I say, trying to sound normal. "What's up?"

"Listen, VZ. I found something. I'm not trying to make a big deal, but I want to show it to you." She sounds stressed.

I stand up, get a grip on myself. "What do you mean, you found something?" I ask. "What kind of something?"

"It has to do with . . . Singer," she says. "Him getting killed. I just left the restaurant. Can I come over?"

Can she come over? I glance at Chela, who's staring right at me

35

with an *I know who you're talking to* look.

"Only thing is, I'm not home," I tell Diamond.

Chela gets up, presses her head next to mine so she can hear.

"Oh," Diamond says. "Could you meet me somewhere?"

Chela points to the floor, meaning Diamond can come here. I hesitate, but I don't want to pass up a chance to hang with Diamond—which I've never done outside of work.

I tell her, "Okay," hang up, and send her the address. Start to think about what just happened.

"She sounded spooked," I say, pacing the shabby gold carpet. "What's it even mean? She found something to do with Singer? What could that be?"

Chela smirks. "All I know is, she's about to see you with your head all lopsided. That should be fun."

I put a hand to my half-done hair while Chela cracks up. Goes back to the couch, points for me to sit in front of her. When I do, she takes one of my hands, presses it into my own hair.

"Know what?" she says. "You should start twisting yourself. It'll lock faster. And it's something you can do with your hands instead of balling up your fists all the time."

I look down at the hand that's still on the floor beside me. Balled up tight.

"That's a thing?" I ask.

"All day long," she says. She puts two of my fingers around a loc of hair. "Just keep twisting," she says.

I do. And there's something calming about twisting hair while I stress about Diamond. I wouldn't tell anybody, but I like picturing how I'm gonna look when the locs grow out. Chela says it's a good look for my build. *Chub looks good in locs*, is how she put it.

Twenty minutes later, when the bell rings, she pats down my head. "You only look half-stupid," she says, heading to the intercom to buzz Diamond up.

My stomach drops, because now I'm picturing the three of us in a room together. Those two don't really know each other, but they never got along.

Diamond comes in, wearing tight jeans, a bright blue top under her jean jacket. Her hair pulled on top of her head. Good as she looks, I can tell she's stressed. Got her brow knitted up, arms wrapped around her chest, hugging herself.

"Thanks for letting me come over," she tells Chela. Her eyes dart around, take in the mess.

Chela doesn't seem to notice. Just says, "Sure," and leads us back to the couch.

I go for the floor, to give me some distance from the two of them. Diamond sits all the way to one side. She takes off her jacket, reaches in the pocket, and hands me something. Fast, like she couldn't wait to be rid of it. It's an old-school flip phone. Smudged and dirty.

"This is what you found?" I ask.

"It's a burner," she says. Stops me when I start to open it. "I need to tell you something first."

She scooches forward so she's sitting on the edge of the couch, elbows on her knees. She smells like girl soap. "This all happened last night," she says. "What I'm about to tell you. Fisk and I stayed

37

with Ms. Fox after we closed, so we were still there when Jack called, at like two in the morning. Ms. Fox told him to come by, so she could feed him and see he was okay."

I've got no clue why she's telling me this. It must show, 'cause she says, "VZ, you remember what people were saying at Yard, right? That Jack didn't get taken in just because he was giving the cops a hard time. They think he's a . . . a suspect."

"For what?" I try to act surprised. Diamond looks at me like I'm pitiful, so I say, "Okay, I know what people were saying, but that's just 'cause they're idiots."

"Could you just listen?" Diamond asks. "So, Jack came by, and after he left, Ms. Fox asked me and Fisk to take the compost out. Fisk's bag broke, and we had to hunt around to clean everything up. And that's when I found that phone under the bushes. Right by the recycling, which Jack had taken out before he left." She leans forward, even further. "I think *Jack* dropped it. Because today, before we opened, he came back talking about he'd lost his keys. And he was definitely feeling a kind of way when he couldn't find them. I think it's bull. This burner's what he lost."

I wonder if she knows she's not making sense. Who cares if Jack dropped a burner phone? I want to ask her how he was acting, if he said anything about what happened while he was in there. But she points to the phone, impatient.

"You'll see," she says. "It's not locked, go ahead and open it."

I do. Chela leans over me so she doesn't miss it. There's only one text: *J-man. You got the jump on him. Didn't think you had it in you.*

38

I read it a couple of times, confused. "You think . . . *J* means *Jack*?" I ask.

Nobody says anything. Chela breaks the silence, talking real slow.

"If you think *J* means Jack," she says to Diamond, "then you think . . . Jack's boneheaded enough to not just *kill* a guy but to tell somebody who'd text him about it?" She looks disgusted. Chela doesn't know Jack that well, but she's always liked him.

"I didn't say that!" Diamond snaps. "I just thought VZ should know, because he and Jack were tight."

I don't miss that she said *were* tight, not *are*. And also, what kind of logic is that? Because Jack and I are tight, I need to know why she thinks he could've killed somebody?

"Don't you think it's strange?" Diamond asks. "Jack got all freaked out when he couldn't find his *keys*." She puts air quotes on the last word. "There's the *J* message on the burner. And now Jack's MIA. Not even Ms. Fox has heard from him, and she left a bunch of messages asking him to do a shift tonight. What are we supposed to think?"

"You're supposed to think he needs a minute!" Chela snaps. "The man just got arrested, for God's sakes."

"Yeah, and he acted really stupid with the cops," Diamond says, going stubborn. "You have to wonder why, don't you? Even Ms. Fox said so. And this is awful for her. It was already bad enough, without Jack making it worse." Her voice gets stronger when she talks about Ms. Fox.

I don't know what to say. I get that Diamond can't deal with mess and confusion, especially around Ms. Fox. But how come she has to make it Jack's fault? It's quiet a minute. Chela's mom's radio clacks in the background.

"There's somebody else here?" Diamond asks.

Chela says it's just her mom, but Diamond stands up, anyhow, like she's ready to go. She points to the phone. "What should we do with it?" she asks. "Fisk says to leave it alone, but I don't like having it around."

"You should take it back to the restaurant!" Chela says. "A customer could have dropped it, for all you know."

"I'll do it." I stand up. Pocket the phone, mostly 'cause I don't want Diamond to have it, thinking what she's thinking about Jack. She shoots me a smile.

"I promised Daddy I'd cook him dinner tonight," she says, heading for the door. "I took a car over. I don't really know this part of Brooklyn." She turns, looks at me with eyes that are soft and bright, the color of maple syrup. I stand there, taking them in, until Chela kicks my leg, and I get the hint.

"Oh, right!" I tell Diamond. "Lemme help. Show you the way, I mean. Get you home for supper."

I can feel Chela rolling her eyes as she closes the apartment door behind us. Right away, I feel dazed—me and Diamond alone on the dark, narrow stairway inside the building. This random burner phone in my pocket. At the bottom of the stairs, Diamond stops and I almost run into her. She turns my way, standing close. Reaches up, plays with a few of my locs, which sends waves all down me.

"She does your hair?" Diamond asks, glancing up toward Chela's place.

"Not without a price," I say. "Got some sadist in her."

Diamond doesn't laugh. She looks at me sideways with those sweet, clear eyes.

"I don't really have to cook for Daddy tonight," she says. "But—I had an idea. I know where Jack might be."

"Jack?" I've got no clue where this is going. Don't care, either, as long as I can stay this close to her.

"My friend Jasmine," Diamond says. "She lives next door to me, and she's into Jack. They've been meeting up at Coney Island, and she told him last week that she was going tonight. So he'll probably be there. And if we show up, too, we could ask him what's going on. And this whole thing can stop feeling so weird."

"You mean, go to Coney Island?" I ask. "You and me?" Doesn't make a whole lot of sense since she's the one that just said Jack had disappeared.

"Not if you don't want to," Diamond snaps. She shoots another look up the stairs, and I wonder if she's actually jealous of Chela. If maybe Jack's not the real reason she wants to go to Coney Island with me tonight.

"No, I want to," I say. "It's a great idea. Let's go look for Jack."

Boardwalk Karaoke

The subway angels are feeling us, and we get corner seats. Life's better than it's been in a while, sitting beside Diamond on the little bench. Knowing we'll be alone together for the whole ride and, at least at first, once we get to Coney Island.

"You know what Ms. Fox told me?" Diamond asks, cocking her head and shooting me a smile. "She said she's proud of you."

"She says that all the time," I say. "About all of us."

"She meant because you figured out how to come back to work, get back in your routine and everything. After Ed."

I feel myself go stiff. Why's she bringing that up now?

"It's nothing to be proud of," I say. "Can we talk about something else?"

She sighs. "It's not like I wasn't there with you, VZ. I saw how hard it was for you."

42

For the umpteenth time, I wonder what it was like for her, the night Ed died. For the umpteenth time, I push the question away, along with the pictures in my head. The train screeches to a stop.

"I know you were there," I say. "But talking about it doesn't help." Some idiot white guy gets on the train, stands right in front of me, his knees bumping against mine with the motion of the train. I glare at him, and he gives it right back. When the train stops again, he gets off.

"You could've just asked him to move back," Diamond says. "Why can't guys just have a normal conversation?"

Our eyes meet. I know she still wants to keep talking about the night we lost Ed. But then her face goes soft. She grabs my hand.

"How about if you catch me up on Ed's game?" she asks.

"Good!" I say, liking that she let it go so quick. I take out the laptop, slide an arm around her to pull her closer to the screen. And everything's better. We're in a moving theater, the train rocking side to side and Ed's game just for us.

Diamond studies the screen like Sherlock Holmes checking out his best clue. The viewpoint's first-person, so all you can see of Edric are these long-fingered leathery hands making their way around SirBugUs's underwater castle. Orange zombie fish—looking crazy against the acid-green water—swim around with mini three-headed minion-bugs. Under a sign that says River Booty, all kind of shit's piled up: bikes, jewelry, books, furniture, food. At the far end of the screen, there's a door with a lock on it.

Diamond clicks the mutant hands and drags them to move around the screen. Right away, the zombie fish block her.

"Feral goldfish," I tell Diamond. "They're based on a real thing—not the zombie part, but Ed found out there're these giant bloated goldfish in the East River."

"Mmm," Diamond says, pointing to the screen. "See that one out in front? He's the first NPC—nonplayer character—so he's probably got information for you." She mouses over the fish and a speech bubble pops up:

> We Feral Golds are clever, so you had best be leery.
> To get the gear you'll need, come correct to all our queries.

"Ed had a whole app on his phone just for rhyming shit," I say.

"Okay, but you get it, right?" she asks, all business. "He says there're queries, that means you'll have to mouse around to find a way to answer questions and win inventory items. Then you can use the inventory to fight the fish and the minions."

I try mousing random stuff all over the screen. Nothing, till I click a rusty set of scales in the pile of river booty. A question pops up.

> Which is heavier, a pound of bricks or a pound of pillows?

There's a blank line afterward so I can type in the answer.

"The whole game better not be these stupid riddles," I mutter. I can feel Diamond watching me, thinking I don't know the answer. But I'm not an idiot. I get that the obvious answer, *bricks*, probably isn't right. So, I type in *pillows*.

EHHHHH!

Diamond cracks up as the mutant hands freeze, crumble, and I have to start over.

"At least you were thinking out of the box," she says, throwing encouragement in with her shade. "Going with the pillows. The trick with puzzles like this is that they're visual more than anything. Which, in this case, means the answer's in the question. See?"

She pulls up the speech bubble again, points to the word *pound.* Which is heavier, a *pound* of bricks or a *pound* of pillows? And of course, I get it.

"Time for one more," Diamond says, checking the electronic sign that tells us what stop's next. She clicks around and gets a question in yellow-brown type.

> Find what's common between these two treats
>
> Potato
>
> Banana

"Ooh!" Diamond says, excited. "This is clever."

"Yeah?" I say. "So, nothing obvious, like that they're foods, or yellow-brown colored. What, they're both carbs? Or, I don't know . . . you can make bread out of them? Because my steppop's actually made both, banana bread and potato bread."

"That's why it's clever," Diamond says. "It's apophenia."

"Apo . . . ? You making this up?"

"*Look closer*," she says. "He's relying on your seeing a connection—a pattern—that isn't actually gonna get you to the answer.

It's a thing people do, called apophenia. You think it's gonna be about food, right? So that's the connection you'll look for. But that's wrong, there's actually a pattern in the *letters*."

I stare at the letters in the two words. "Yeah . . . *no*," I say.

Diamond lays a finger on the *p* in *potato*, then slides her finger to the end of the word. "If you move the first letter of each word to the end, you can spell the same word backward." I check out *banana*, put the *b* at the end, and see that it works.

"The point," Diamond says, "is if you wanna beat Ed's game fast, you need to start thinking like he does. He's good at this kind of thing, making you see things that don't matter, while the real clue's right in front of you."

"Who thinks like that?" I ask.

"People like Ed and me," Diamond says.

Her laugh's a little sad, but it's still so damn cute. Best subway ride ever.

"It makes you forget everything," Diamond says a half hour later as we cross under the archway to Luna Park, where all the best rides are on Coney Island.

She throws a side-eye to the barkers who're calling her out by her clothes ("Sweet girl in that tight blue top, come on and get you a teddy!"). Rap music blares. Smells like hot dogs, cotton candy, ocean. Pure Coney Island, even if it's not hot enough yet to catch the serious scent of BO.

"Right?" Diamond says. "Whatever's getting you lets up when you walk in this place."

I'm about to answer when somebody yells and we both turn.

About a dozen kids are going at it by the Tickler ride. White kids, this one ginormous guy whaling on everybody else.

"Right," I say. "Definitely makes you forget." Diamond grins. Cops run over, and we get out of the way, but not before trading looks. The cops are white, like the kids. Can't help but wonder if anything'll happen besides telling them to quit it.

"When Daddy was a prosecutor," Diamond says, as we pass under one of the tunnels, "they did a whole thing out here. Trying to equalize the arrests. Show they weren't discriminating against Black and brown kids."

"It work?" I ask.

"It was stupid," she says. "They just arrested everybody, even the guys peddling nutcrackers on the beach and the game scammers. But none of that was hurting anybody, so the whole thing fell apart."

"Those games hurt *me*," I say. "Jack couldn't keep away from them when we were kids, kept trying to win stuff to impress girls. Blew his allowance every time and I'd end up having to share mine with him."

Diamond shoots me a grin but not just a *That's kinda funny* kind. There's something way sweeter, the way her eyes stay on mine.

"Which is why Jack's probably here tonight," Diamond says. "Jasmine's pretty hot." She points across the park to the boardwalk. "She's into karaoke. They usually meet up there."

We weave through the crowd, searching for Jack. What's true is, even though I came here to be with Diamond, I can't help hoping we find Jack. I want this whole mess with Singer off my mind, and seeing Jack being his regular girl-dogging self would help. The crowd gets thinner as we climb the steps to the boardwalk, which stretches as far as you can see on either side, lit up by food stalls, game booths, people on bikes and scooters. The ocean's straight ahead, but it's so dark you can barely see. More about the breeze coming off it, the crashing sound of waves.

Diamond grips my arm, leads me to the karaoke setup, stuck between a Nathan's hot dog stand and an Italian-ice cart. There's a mic, a screen that shows the lyrics, and a guy wearing a T-shirt that says "EMCEE," taking names of people who want a turn at the mic.

"Let's sign up," Diamond says.

"What? I thought we were just looking for Jack."

She catches sight of my face, and her eyes go double-wide. "Don't tell me you're chicken? Karaoke's so fun. I'm great at it."

"Here's the thing," I say. "And hear me out on this." I scrunch up my face like I'm thinking how to put it. "No way am I doing that. As in, no way in hell."

This gets me a laugh, making me feel pretty good. Diamond signs herself up, then holds up a *Be right back* finger and moves down the boardwalk. I watch her slip through the crowd. Wonder again if she really thinks Jack'll show, or if this is about her and me. I mean, she's right, Jack does love this place—music, hot girls, ocean. But the more I look around at the crowd, the more I doubt he's coming.

"Here you go," Diamond says, next to me again. She's holding two red plastic cups. "My friend's selling on the sand tonight. No big deal. I know I look twenty-one."

"You don't," I say. I don't like that she's a year older than me, let alone thinking about four. I gulp some of the drink. It's bright orange. Tastes like a Popsicle soaked in booze.

"Best nutcrackers on Coney Island," she says. The little dimple pops out in her cheek, and I don't tell her I don't know what a nutcracker is. We head to the back of the crowd so we can watch for Jack. It's darker here. Waves crash behind us, and the breeze is fierce.

"You cold?" I ask.

"No," she says. "Listen, if we see Jack, let's just ask what happened, why he's not answering his phone. I don't want to tell him I found the burner—I don't want him to think I'm accusing him or anything."

"No problem," I say, and start to worry that she only wanted to come for Jack after all. The boozy Popsicle thing's working for me, though. Touches me where I wish Diamond would.

Onstage, somebody busts out with Bruno Mars's "Marry You." Diamond pulls me backward so we can talk over the music.

"I'm sick of that song," she says.

"You and everybody else who's not a twelve-year-old white girl," I say.

She gives me a half smile. "I hate to break it to you, but my fifty-eight-year-old dad's planning this for his wedding song next month."

"Damn, your pop!" I say. Because Diamond's pop is a legend. "For real? Who's he marrying?"

She sighs. "*Her*," she says. "Justine."

I try not to laugh, but I do anyhow. Diamond's pop can't seem to get it right. Poor guy got elected to city council this year, but every time he's in the news it says how he *once got caught sneaking out of a hotel with Justine Banks*—who, at the time, was the mayor's wife. And now he's going on to marry her.

Diamond twists her lips into a sour face. "The year all that happened is when I started staying by Ms. Fox," she says. "She had just moved in across the way and being home was too hard. I've been going over there ever since. Ms. Fox listens. She pays attention. She's a better mom to me than he is a dad. That's just the truth."

I take a drink, liking that she's telling me all this, even if I don't get why she is. "I never knew what happened to your ma," I say.

"Cancer, same as my grandma. I was real little when my mom died."

"Sorry," I say.

"No, I'm all right," she says. "It's just rough now, with everything." She turns her back to the stage, faces the ocean. "Sometimes I want to walk straight into it. And never stop. Not like a death wish or anything. I mean, it makes me feel powerful, like I could do that and be okay. When I get out of school and become a businesswoman?" She shoots me a side glance. "That's how I'm going to feel all the time. On top of my empire."

"Look out, universe," I say, feeling way turned on by the way she looked at me, what she said. I drain my cup. "If Jack shows, he'll hang around awhile. We could walk down to the water and be back in time to catch him."

"I'd like to," Diamond whispers. I feel how close we are. Reach down, take her hand like it's something I do every day. Her fingers curl into mine, and we walk, my sneakers sinking into the sand. I calculate how long it'll take to get to the water. It'll be a while. And maybe I shouldn't wait that long. Because it feels right now. I tug Diamond's hand, pull her to me. Lower my head and kiss her warm soft lips. She kisses me back, presses into me, opens her mouth. I raise my hand to the back of her head, pull her harder against my mouth. Breathe her in.

"And next is . . . Diamond from Crown Heights!"

Diamond breaks our kiss. Turns toward the boardwalk, and it hits me that the emcee guy just called her name. I cuss myself for not getting us out of earshot before I made my move. Already, she's pulling off her jacket, handing it to me, running. I'm throbbing in all the places our bodies touched as I follow her, and the first notes of Ciara's "Goodies" are blasting out of the speakers. Diamond grabs the mic. She starts to move, rocking her top, side to side. Sexy as hell and killing me. I get the lyrics, too—how her goodies are gonna stay in the jar—and I wonder if they're staying in the jar when Fisk's the one pulling the lid. Guys in the crowd don't care about the lyrics, though, or that her singing's half-assed. They whoop like fools watching her move. I step to the side, make sure she can see me whooping, too. But she's not looking my way.

She works every second of it. Loves being up there, in control of the crowd. When it's over, she struts off the stage to crazy-loud clapping. But she doesn't come back to me. She waves for me to come up front, with her. Doesn't catch my eye when I tell her how good she was. Or seem to notice when I put my arm around her. I get it. There's no going back to where we were before they called her name. I don't ask. Don't need to hear in words what she's saying every other way. The rest of the singers go by in a blur. There's no sign of Jack. When the show's over, we go home. Give up on finding Jack tonight. But still. Maybe starting a whole other something.

That Night in SirBugUs's Castle

I'm belly-flopped on my bed. Laptop open, Pringles can I grabbed on my way past the kitchen next to me. Doing my best to be like Ed, let the game make me forget. Think about three-headed mutant water bugs instead of where Diamond might be right now. And who she might be with. And if she's doing with him what she was doing with me. Except more. I stare at Ed's screen, move the mouse around. But all I can think about is Diamond.

Why is it so hard to get her away from that Fisk fool? So what if he's older, got more money. Ten thousand jobs, so he can buy her nice things. Diamond's not like that. She's just loyal, doesn't believe in breaking her promises. But doesn't mind flirting like hell with other people. Kissing them on the beach, then chucking them to the curb . . .

I get up, kick the bed. Pace. It's not fair, how getting girls's never been easy for me. Not like Jack. Or probably Fisk. I pick up a stone horse from the fancy chess set Ma got me in sixth grade when I was kicking chess-ass. Until people started beating me and it wasn't so fun anymore. My whole room's full of shit I was once good at. The plaque from a third-grade writing contest. The purple tae kwon do belt, my big thing till I turned ten and started liking food more than practice. Ma was too big a wreck that year to get on my case about it. Just said to find the thing that works for me. So I figured out that Easy VZ works. Keeping it chill when my friends lose it. Making sure there's respect, good grammar for the adults. It's not a bad gig. Except now I think, maybe I got lazy—didn't have to work at anything. Maybe that's why I'm not getting anywhere with Diamond.

I slump back down on the bed. Feel Diamond's kiss. The girl used tongue, so I know I wasn't kissing alone. Had to be good for her, too, right? The way she pressed against me . . . I get under the covers, finish the job she started. Relax a little. The house is quiet, not even any Sammy sounds. I pick up the red laptop. This time it feels better, sinking into Ed's world.

I'm still on level one, with the feral fish. Thanks to Diamond, I've got a decent inventory. And I'm close to the locked door at the end of the level. Just gotta get past one last fish. Ed was getting fancy with the artwork, because this fish's got on a T-shirt that says "See." Its speech bubble reads:

> We feral fish can't see ourselves, so we must make a fuss.
> We need your help, so we can gaze at fishies beauteous.
> We suggest you learn to cipher, it's more than a request.
> Blow off our good advice, and you'll be our long-term guest.

I get that I have to "cipher" or else I'll be a "long-term guest," which means not getting to the next level. But I don't know what ciphering is, so I pick up my phone, look it up.

Cipher: A secret or disguised way of writing; a code.

No help, yet. I drag around the stuff in the junk piles, see if anything happens. It doesn't, except for giving me chances to solve puzzles and win more inventory. I spend another hour collecting stuff. Finally, my sore eyes find their way back to the fish in the "See" shirt. There's something off about the lettering. I remember what Diamond said about the game being visual. So, I read the clue again, thinking of that.

> We feral fish can't see ourselves . . .

There's a mirror in the pile of junk. *If you can't see yourself, a mirror would help* . . . I click the fish wearing the "See" shirt, then the mirror. And there it is. The mirror image of the shirt pops up on the screen. *S e e* turns into *9 9 2.* Which must be the code . . . which is the combination to the lock on the door!

A sweet feeling pours through me, like when you nail the thing that's on the tip of your tongue. A minute later, I'm clicking the lock, typing in the code. The door swings open. I even get a silver sword and shield as a reward.

Outside, a garbage truck rolls by and I hear the guys jump off the back, start tossing cans all over the place. It's 5:00 a.m. if the truck's on its usual schedule. And I'm wide awake.

To wind down, I scroll down my texts. Chela's reminded me we've got a prep session for her circle with Ronnah after school later today, plus we're meeting first period to study for our sixth-period ELA test. I smack my pillow. No problem. Maybe I'll just find Jack, too, in my spare time.

Half-Truths, Secrets, and Lies

It's right before last period. I'm still at my locker, trying to figure out just how bad the test went and how I'll drag my ass through another class without snoring in the teacher's face. I wake up, though, when Diamond's name comes up on my phone.

Diamond: I told Fisk

Me: Told him what?

Diamond: If you don't know . . .

But . . . why would she tell him we kissed—does she want to break up with him? Should I ask her that? Another text comes through.

Diamond: He's upset

So . . . does that mean she's with him right now?

Me: Where are u?

Diamond: Yard. We're both on prep today. I have 2 go.

I stare at the screen, try to think of something that won't sound stupid. Too much time passes. The hall around me goes quiet. I send—

Me: Still there?

And, of course, no answer. I hate that they're at Yard together, hate that they're both out of school—Diamond taking college classes and Fisk working however the hell many jobs he's got, while I'm still stuck here. I look around the empty hall, make my decision.

Slam the locker shut and head for the doors.

On the way to Yard, I stress over Diamond and Fisk. But it's the first time I'll be at the restaurant since Jack got arrested and I can't help wondering if he'll show for his regular shift. Pissed as I am, it'd be a relief to not have to search for his ass. And know he's all right.

When I get there, Ms. Fox is squatting in her garden by the side door. She waves me over, and I worry she'll ask why I'm not in school. But she's got other stuff on her mind.

"It's hot as the devil's bam bam in there," she says. "Come! Make I test your smeller." She straightens up, slaps a cushiony-warm hand over my eyes. A second later something brushes up under my nose. "Guess the ingredient" is Ms. Fox's favorite game. No such thing as not being in the mood for it.

"Mint," I tell her, sniffing the fresh, sharp scent.

"Which kind?"

"That black stuff you like?"

"Incorrect! Spearmint. And this one?"

"Basil."

"Purple or green?"

"I don't know, Ms. Fox. Come on." I'm jumpy from cutting class, half-sick wondering what Diamond and Fisk are up to. I can't be standing around in this garden right now.

"Hmph," Ms. Fox says. "A man can't love food like you love food and don't know how to cook it." She keeps her hand where it is, shoves something new under my nose.

"Okay, I know this one!" It smells delicious, like good food and good weather at the same time. "That lemon thyme stuff," I say.

"So, Mr. Smarty, what am I making?" Ms. Fox asks.

I think a minute, put all the herbs together. "Corn fritters with Yard sauce," I say, my mouth already watering.

Ms. Fox moves her hand, and I open my eyes. She looks me over, runs her thumbs under my tired eyes—which is a thing of hers. Pats my cheek.

"I told Jackson to bring him best tunes," she says. "We're opening the dance floor tonight. Remember how we did last summer?"

"Jack's coming?" I ask, already looking through the kitchen door for him.

"The boy's too smart to give up him job," Ms. Fox says. She's not quite looking at me, and I wonder if she believes what she's saying. Which scares me, because if Ms. Fox thinks there's something bad going on . . .

"Go on," she tells me. "Measure spices for Yard sauce, please. And bring up carrots and cabbage from the cellar for me stew." It comes out *cyarrots* and *cyabbage*, which makes me smile.

I'm feeling better by the time I go inside. And there they are, Diamond and Fisk, standing by the door to the dining room. Diamond's got her arms crossed over her chest, and Fisk's got his hands shoved in his back pockets. Not a happy couple, which thrills the hell out of me.

My phone buzzes, but I ignore it. "Ms. Fox said for you to bring up carrots and cabbage from the cellar," I tell Fisk.

"No problem," he says. Comes off chill, but I know better. When he's gone, I follow Diamond into the dining room. Just the sight of her gets me going. Bare arms and legs, her apron hugged tight around a little white dress. I wish to hell I knew how to play this.

Diamond heads to the cart in the back that's covered in a jumble of just-washed silverware and a clean white cloth. She picks up a fork and starts to polish it.

"I know why you're here," she whispers. "And just so you know, I told Fisk I kissed *somebody*. I didn't tell him it was you."

"You . . . *what*?" I say. "Why would you . . . ?" I don't even know where to start. Why would she . . . *erase* me like that?

"It *happened*," she says. "So he had a right to know. And I didn't say it was you, because we don't need any more drama around here. You don't think we've got enough?"

"Are you breaking up with him?" I ask. Hold my breath, waiting for the answer.

"Not right now, at least." She doesn't take her eyes off the silverware.

My phone buzzes again, and I reach in my pocket to shut it up.

"Are you just—playing me, Diamond?" I ask, swallowing back the lump that wants to take over my throat. "Is that what's going on?"

"If that's what you think of me, VZ . . ."

"Then tell the truth!" I half shout. And I'm glad my voice sounds pissed instead of hurt. She puts down the fork, finally looks at me. And her eyes go soft. Like she's remembering the kiss. Like maybe she's gonna tell Fisk after all, break up with him. Like anything's possible.

Footsteps from the cellar stairs. I only break eye contact with Diamond for a second. But she heard it, too.

"Come on, Diamond!" I say, hoping to hell his timing didn't wreck everything. "Let's tell him now." The steps are coming closer. My fucking phone buzzes again.

"I'll think about it," Diamond says.

"Or I could just do it!" I say. "I could tell him right now."

"Then I'll know you don't respect me!" she hisses. "Because you can't let me do things my way."

The cellar door opens, Fisk comes in.

"Answer your phone, VZ," Diamond says. Fisk tosses us a look, then backs into the kitchen with the boxes of vegetables. It'll only take a second to put them down, and he'll be back.

"*Please, VZ, go answer your phone*," Diamond says. "Give me a minute to think." There's a threat in her quiet voice. I step away from her, scared. To keep from having to look at her, I glance at my phone. Four messages from Chela.

2:26 Where r u?

2:27 Hurry up! I have something 2 tell u b4 she comes

61

And I remember. I'm missing the meeting with her and Ronnah to prep for the disciplinary thing. Cussing at myself, I dive into the spice closet, call Chela.

"Emergency, I'll explain later," I say, wondering what the hell I'll tell her. "I'm not near school, though. Can't we do it on the phone?"

"The phone? Victor!"

"I'm sorry. For real."

"You're killing me. Lemme ask her."

I wait, breathing fast. I can't be letting Chela down like this. Especially when it's for nothing. Because, what the hell is Diamond thinking? Is she just trying to make Fisk jealous? Is that all it is between us?

My phone rings in my hand, freaks me out. Chela's cut our call, called back on FaceTime. Except it's Ronnah's dark brown face that fills my screen. I've seen her in the halls at school, know her rep for keeping it real, for a school-counselor type. But close up she's a lot, intense black eyes that kind of grab you right through her bright blue cat-eye glasses. She introduces herself, and I apologize again for missing the meeting. Try to muster as much teacher charm as I can while I'm hiding in a spice closet with Diamond and Fisk doing who knows what outside the door.

"Life happens," Ronnah says, in a tone that lets me know it can't be happening all the time. "We'll see if we can make this work. Hold the phone so I can see your face, though, please. This process is all about connection."

Now we're in it, I remember all the reasons I didn't want to do this. I lift the phone.

"And we're off!" Ronnah says. "Tell me what you know about the situation that led to tomorrow's circle."

"Oh," I say, "Uh . . . Bruce Walendorf was being a . . . a racist you know what. And Chela called him on it, got so mad she slammed a door and hit Ms. Doyle by accident."

"Mm-hmm. And what do you think your role is, as Chela's support person?"

That's an easy one. "I'm there to have Chela's back," I say. With my foot, I nudge the closet door open so I can hear what's going on out there.

"Not bad," Ronnah says. "And not quite. The circle is a repair process to support Ms. Doyle, to help everyone understand what happened, and to determine how best to move forward. Part of how we do all that is by holding Chela accountable in a way that Ms. Doyle finds helpful. You'll be there to support Chela because being held accountable usually isn't easy. So far so good?"

"Sure." Outside the door, Fisk and Diamond are talking faster, louder. But Ronnah's face on the screen grows bigger and more serious.

"Then let's get to the hard part," she says. "Do you understand that you'll need to express your feelings during the circle, even though it's difficult for you?" I wish Chela was on-screen so I could glare at her. Because how does this woman know it's difficult for me to talk about my feelings unless Che told her? Outside the closet, Fisk's voice rises even higher—is he straight-up yelling? I kick the door a little further.

"Where's your attention, VZ?" Ronnah asks.

"Right here!" I blink a few times, refocus.

"Good, because I'm guessing you have some feelings about what Bruce Walendorf said, is that right?"

"Who wouldn't?" I say.

"Fair," Ronnah says. "And since those feelings have to do with what happened to your friend Ed, you should spend some time thinking about them so you can talk about them at the circle."

"I have to talk about Ed at this thing?"

She raises a thick eyebrow so it comes up above the cat-eye glasses. "Unless you think it has nothing to do with why Chela slammed that door."

"It's got everything to do with it!" I respond.

"So . . . ," she prompts.

"Yeah, I get it," I say. Wishing like hell I could get out of this. I grab a peek through the door crack. Diamond and Fisk've got their heads together over one of their phones. Did I hear Jack's name . . . ?

"Here's something else," Ronnah says. "The harm Chela caused will be the focus of the circle. You'll have to express how you feel about what Bruce said, but this isn't going to be a Bruce Walendorf smackdown. That may be hard for you, too, so you need to understand."

I don't. But as I'm thinking about it, Fisk's voice comes from outside the closet and there's nothing chill about it. *Hell no! This is fucked-up. Fucked. Up. Fucked-up—*"

"VZ?"

I turn back to the phone, where Ronnah's intense black eyes aren't giving me an ounce of break.

"This is a lot," she says. "It can be too much. I'm sure Chela has other friends who can do it instead."

Even though I can't see her, I feel Chela like she's beside me. Waiting for my answer.

"But she wants *me*," I say. "So, I'm good, I got it. I need to talk about Ed." My stomach sinks as I say it, and I take a breath. "Do that, and don't bash Walendorf. Right?"

Ronnah lets it go. Starts talking about the rules we'll use in the circle, how you're only allowed to talk when it's your turn with the talking piece. Goes on about how we'll answer a series of questions. Finally, we get to hang up.

I jerk the closet door open. I'm disoriented, thinking how this circle sounds like a nightmare, and scared to find out what's up with Diamond and Fisk. They're still in the dining room, still too close together. Fisk looks up at the sound of the door, and I can tell something's changed since I left. There's no bullshit grin on his face. No pretending.

"You see this?" he asks, handing over his phone. I brace myself, taking it.

SINGER MURDER CASE: PERSON OF INTEREST IDENTIFIED

Brooklyn police have identified a person of interest in the death of 42-year-old Phillip Singer, found dead in a parking lot on April 3. According to an NYPD spokesperson, a

19-year-old male was brought in for questioning and later released. The person was not charged with the murder. Despite mounting pressure to bring charges in the case, the spokesperson said police are withholding the name of the person of interest due to the potential for a volatile response from the community. Still, he said, "It's only a matter of time before we make our arrest."

"It means Jack," Diamond says, finally looking at me.

"It doesn't have to," I say. "We don't know who else they mighta got hold of."

Fisk sighs. "It's probably him," he says. "You know that's how they do! They want to shake us all up, and hauling people in as a 'person of interest' does it, gets everybody doubting everybody else."

He's not wrong, though I hate agreeing with him. "If it is Jack, they're just using him," I say.

Diamond shoots me a look that says, *We don't know that.* I almost hate her right then.

"Still, though," Fisk says. "Jack needs to get back here so we can help him." All three of us turn, look at the stage, where Jack ought to be by now. My gut tells me he isn't coming, that we all know it, even Ms. Fox.

In my head, I hear Ronnah's voice, "This is a lot. It can be too much." She got that part right.

Jahvaris

"Let me get this straight," Chela says, as the car pulls off. "You and Diamond wanted to find Jack, right? So, you went to *Coney Island* instead of his apartment? What kind of dumbass move was that?"

We're in the musty back seat of an old black Corolla, heading to Jack's place. When Jack never showed for work, I called Chela, told her about the "person of interest" story. And she got a car from her ma's service to meet me after work.

"Don't worry about it," I say. "It made sense at the time." The last thing I want to do is go back over all the shit with Diamond. Anyhow, it's just ten days till JersiGame, and I want to figure out this Jack shit and get back to Ed's mutants. Chela's got on her soft yoga bottoms and some loose shirt that's basically pajamas. She's curled up in the corner of the seat. I'm by the other window, knee bouncing up and down on the taped-up leather seat. I usually like riding in cars, since I almost never get to. Tonight, it feels too closed in. I'd rather be walking, letting my thoughts have space to float in.

"There's this other thing," she says, "about the circle." She looks scared and sorry, and it makes me pay attention. "Walendorf's bringing a support person, too. Some friend of his named Guz. He's . . . a member of that student group Justice Team for Ed Hennessey—the ones that organize the pictures and speakouts every month." Something clicks in my brain. This is what she tried to message me about before I missed the meeting. Because she knows I can't stand that group.

"Those fools who didn't even know Ed, making like they're doing some big thing with their dumbass events? When none of them found a way to make Ed feel good *at* school, and now they're pretending to be all about him?" This is the last thing I want to be thinking about right now. I've hated that group since they did their first event back in January, an in-school memorial. Hated everything about it, down to their name. Justice Team for Ed Hennessey, using Ed's whole name, like they're putting him on a top twenty most-fucked-way-to-die list: Trayvon Martin, Michael Brown, Breonna Taylor, George Floyd, Ed Hennessey . . .

"That's why I'm asking. Are you gonna be able to handle that, Veeze?" Chela asks. "Being in the circle with him?"

How should I know? This whole circle thing's looking like hella more trouble than it's worth, but Chela seems so desperate I tell her it's fine. The driver rounds a corner, and we both look up.

"My GPS is getting screwed up here," the driver mutters. He's a white guy, our age. Robbie, the one Chela always calls when we

68

need cheap rides. Looks like he stepped out of an episode of *Jersey Shore*: wavy hair, checked button-down over his too-tight tee. I tell him where to turn, hoping Chela forgets what we were talking about. I just need Jack to be there, tell me everybody's getting stupid over nothing. Then everything else will be fine.

"Finally," Robbie-the-driver says. We pull up to Jack's building, three stories high, blue-painted brick with a gray steel door. When Jack first got the place, since sharing an apartment was cheaper than living on campus, I thought it was the coolest thing, him and his roommate having a place to themselves. Even though we were all a year apart—Jack, me, and Ed—Jack started school young and got to be two grades ahead of me, and Ed started older and ended up two years behind. Another way I was VZ in the middle—chugging along in the same-old-same-old lane. Anyhow, Jack's place doesn't seem cool tonight. Maybe it's my imagination that makes it look shady, but half the streetlights are busted. Only one car parked by the curb, a newish black sedan, and not a soul on the sidewalk. Chela and I head for the door, which is standing open. The dingy entryway's got metal mailboxes and round buzzer buttons on either side. No answer when I ring 3D.

"Come on," I say. Chela follows me through the inside door and up into the stairwell that smells like year-old grease. I take the stairs two at a time.

On the third floor, the walls are light green like in a hospital. There're four apartments, two on each side of the hall. I ring the buzzer—just like the one downstairs—at 3D. No answer. Chela and I look at each other, and she raises an eyebrow. Sniffs the air.

"What?" I ask.

"Check this." A second later she's on all fours, sniffing under the door. "That's fresh weed," she says. "Somebody's there."

She pounds like hell on the door. "Hullo! Hullo, I'm here in the hallway, locked out of the apartment!" She's actually doing a fake English accent, so it comes out *apaaaatment*. "Can't you hear me?" she calls. "Your roommate said I could kip at his place. He said he left an extra key with you."

Still no answer, so I follow her lead, pound too. If Jack's there, he needs to come the hell out. Finally, a voice comes through the door.

"You've got the wrong place! I don't have any key!"

We bang harder. The door opens, and I get a flood of relief. A guy who must be Jack's new roommate's standing in a haze of weed smoke. He's got heavy-hooded eyes and a long face, half covered by shoulder-length locs. His red tank top and cutoff sweats are the kind you wear to show off your muscles. Seeing him makes me remember stuff. Jack said he's a jackass, too cheap to share his weed. I remember his name, too. Jahvaris.

"You're trippin'," he says. "I don't have a roommate. Jack use'ta live here, but he's gone."

"It doesn't matter if he's not here." Chela tries to push past him, into the apartment. "He still said I could stay here."

Jahvaris isn't too stoned to throw an arm out to block her way. He glares at us, making it clear he's not letting us in. I try something different.

"Look, we're Jack's friends. We're worried, okay? He didn't show up for work tonight and he hasn't answered his phone since yesterday." I step back so I can see inside. The apartment's only two rooms, and the front one, what should have been the living room, was the one Jack used as a bedroom. All I can see's an old stuffed chair and a side table full of dirty dishes.

Jahvaris smirks. "If he's your friend, why don't you just text him?"

"He's not answering."

"Mm-hmm." He gives me the once-over, real knowing, like maybe Jack told him how it's been between us, since Ed. He steps back in order to close the door, and I catch a glimpse of a fish tank inside. The water's a bright acid green.

"Hold up!" I push on the door, half expecting to see orange zombie fish. "*When did you . . . Were the fish Jack's?*"

"*What? Fuck off!*" Jahvaris tries to slam the door, and I shove my shoulder in to stop him. For a second, I can see the whole room. It's like a different apartment, all Jack's stuff gone.

"Don't make me call the cops back here!" Jahvaris yells, shouldering the door back toward us. It takes me a minute to get it.

"What do you mean *back here*?" I ask.

"The cops were here?" Chela says, at the same time.

Jahvaris looks past irritated. "Pay attention, kids. What did I just say?"

I don't know what to ask about first, Jack's stuff being gone or the cops being here. Before I do either, a door opens behind him and a guy comes out of the other room. Tall with glasses. Nothing on but underwear.

"Never mind, Marcus, baby," Jahvaris tells the guy. Still not letting up on the door, he turns back to us. "Look, I'll tell you, same as I told the cops. Jack came back here after they let him go. He packed up some of his stuff, and I haven't seen him since."

I swallow. "You told the cops Jack packed his stuff and left?" I ask. "What'd they say?"

"They're cops, they don't talk much."

"Why would you tell them that, anyhow? It makes it look like Jack's on the run or something!"

Jahvaris sucks his lips in. "Maybe he is."

"Don't be an ass! Just tell me where he is!"

"He'll tell you," Jahvaris says. "If he wants you to know." The other guy—*Marcus, baby*—steps up to help Jahvaris with the door, and I stumble backward as it slams shut.

"Fuck you!" I yell.

"You don't think Marcus was trying?" Jahvaris shouts back. "Before your ass showed up!"

Chela falls back against the green wall. "Damn," she says. Then, eyeing my face, "*What?*"

"Jack's amp," I say. "And his bass and stand, his whole music setup. That's how he makes his money. It's all gone."

My stomach drops because I know I can't pretend anymore.

"Jahvaris's an ass," I say. "But he wasn't lying. Jack's not coming back."

The Chase

"What a weasel," Chela says, back in the car. "Talking to the cops, for God's sakes. He probably thought he had to, once he'd opened the door on a roomful of weed and God knows what else he's got in there. Weasel probably knows exactly where Jack is."

"Uh-uh," I say. "Jack never liked the guy—he wouldn't tell him where he was going."

I lean against the window, look out as Robbie-the-driver turns the car back onto Atlantic Ave. Jack wouldn't tell Jahvaris where he was going, but why wouldn't he tell me? Yeah, shit's strained now—but when it's this important, shouldn't we go back to the old ways? Since we were kids, we've told each other the important stuff. The day Ma found out about Pop and Caitlin, Jack was the one I told. 'Course he thought it was hilarious, Ma packing up Pop's record collection, donating it to a woman's shelter. Hilarious till they started yelling. I was hiding in the hall with Jack on the phone. They were angrier than I'd ever seen anybody. Jack kept telling me to be a man, get out there and protect my ma. But I remembered Ma telling her friend she'd get a butcher knife and cut a man's face if he even *looked* like he'd raise a hand to her. In the end, Jack brought me down, convinced me it wasn't gonna go like that.

All that was before girls, high school. College, for Jack. A lifetime before we lost Ed and weird, bitter air filled the space between us.

Up front, Robbie leans forward in his seat, showing the back of his checked button-down, the gold chain around his neck. He twists around to look over his shoulder, then at the road again.

"Maybe Jack's just scared," Chela says. "People get freaked out, right?"

"But they don't disappear," I say, distracted by the driver, who keeps on whipping his head back, ahead. Back, ahead. He catches our eyes in the rearview.

"*Excuse me?*" he says, loud, intense. "What the hell's going on?"

"Huh?" Chela says.

"How come there's cops following us?"

I twist around, see a car behind us. Looks like the black sedan that was parked by Jack's building. "It's just a regular car," I say.

"It's cops!" Robbie yells. "How the hell did you pick up a tail?"

A tail? I figure he's tripping, go back to stressing about Jack. Chela grabs my arm.

"Remember what Jack's roommate said? The cops have been

there, looking for Jack. They must've been watching the building, and they know we went to see him!"

Robbie curses.

My stomach rolls, but I play it off. "Even if they were watching, how would they know it was Jack we went to see?"

"Like they couldn't guess?" Chela says. "Or else . . . what if they followed us upstairs?"

I want to think it's stupid to believe the cops were staking out Jack's place, that they're following us right now. Except, I remember the cop at Yard, the way he stepped to Jack. Diamond, even Ms. Fox, acting like maybe Jack was guilty. Can all these people really think it's possible that Jack *killed somebody*? Just thinking of it makes me feel like that expression—shaken to my core. Like a tremor's buried deep in me, threatening to bust out.

Robbie lays on the steering wheel, takes a corner like he's driving a bumper car.

"Yo, Rob!" Chela shouts. "What's happening? Even if it is the cops, it's not like we did anything wrong. You gotta slow down and pull over!"

"My car's not . . . exactly legal," Robbie shouts. "Which is bad, *very very* bad, if you're driving for a service. I can't get stopped! And technically, they haven't got their sirens on, so I'm not outrunning them." We fly past a sign for the Brooklyn-Queens Expressway, speed up the on-ramp.

"You serious?" I yell, as we weave past an eighteen-wheeler.

There's tons of trucks, making what we're doing ten times more dangerous. A few cars back, the black sedan weaves through traffic just like us. And I realize something.

"Those could be the same cops we saw at Yard! They could recognize me."

Nobody answers. I wonder if I should duck if they can see me through the rear window.

Robbie cuts hard to the right, races down the off-ramp toward the red light at the bottom. Slams to a stop behind another truck, our headlights shining on its logo: *Goldie's Pest Control*, it says, with a picture of a giant water bug laying on its back, legs waving in the air. Reminds me of Ed's game.

"Come on come on come on come on," Robbie mutters, smacking the steering wheel. The light changes. The truck takes a right, and I get an idea.

"Follow the truck!" I yell, head swiveling back and forth to check that the black sedan's still out of sight. "If we can—"

"—get in front of it!" Robbie finishes the thought. "Okay, yeah, I just need to . . ." He swerves hard, goes into the oncoming lane, shaves by the truck, then cuts in front of it. Its headlights blaze into our car, like floodlights in an interrogation room.

"This is fucking insane!" Chela shouts.

"Sorry!" Robbie says. For a minute, there's no sound except our freaked-out breathing. Then Robbie mutters, "All right. I think this'll do us." He swerves the car over to the curb, and I realize the truck's stopped a few feet behind us. We're in front of some kind of warehouse. The truck lights go out. Robbie backs up a few feet, so we're right in front of it, hidden, at least for now. We crane our necks behind us, braced at the sound of a car coming around the truck. I'm holding my breath when a small white Prius goes by.

"It's cool," Robbie says. "I'm pretty sure we lost 'em." We wait another few minutes, Chela and I trading *What the fuck?* looks as our heart rates come down. Finally, Robbie pulls back into the street. For a while, we drive like normal people.

"How'd you know, anyhow," Chela asks, leaning over the seat. "How'd you know it was a cop car?"

"Please," Robbie says. "No letters on the license plates, just numbers. And the shiny hubcaps. Tinted windows. They think they're slick, but everybody knows."

Chela starts asking about the cops tracing Robbie's license plates, how it could come back on her ma's car service business. I get why she's worried, but I can't think about that. I grab my pack off the car floor, pull out the burner phone. The phone that was maybe Jack's. Whoever came up with the name for it got it right. The thing feels hot as hell in my hand.

Chela covers my hand with hers. "It's scary, how real this just got, huh?"

"Shut up," I say. Turn back to the window. Stay that way.

On the Stoop

Ed's open laptop rises and falls on my belly as I lay in bed.

The cops are for real on Jack's case.

How are the cops for real on Jack's case?

No answers, but it doesn't matter, 'cause when I feel this bad, I go back to stuck as fuck, shitty Ed-thoughts taking over. I was a crap friend, got everything wrong. Why was Ed even there that night . . . ?

Flashes of the worst memories cross my mind: the day it happened, the day of his funeral. I resist those, at least. Settle into an older one. Ed and me on a gray day on the sidewalk in front of school. Ed's first day of high school. He had his puzzle face on, lip between his teeth. Searching the crowd of laughing kids for somebody to fit with.

"Lemme walk you to your class," he said to me, when he didn't find anybody.

And I said, *"Just go in, you're good."*

Even though his face was lit with disappointment. He fiddled with the headphones around his neck but didn't put them on. When he walked away from me, he had his long neck bent, but his eyes looking up. Hopeful.

I hate that memory. He shouldn't've had to walk in there alone. If I was really so chill—really Easy VZ—I wouldn't mind keeping Chela waiting so I could help Ed get settled. I ache all over, thinking about it. And I feel the pull to uglier, harder memories.

My phone buzzes on the nightstand. Slowly, I turn my head. Pick it up. The message is from an unknown number:

Stoop. Now.

I don't move except for my brain, making its way from Ed to Jack. Because I'm sure it's Jack that's down on the stoop. Texting from an unknown number.

The relief is real, but I still get a powerful urge to turn my phone off. Ignore his ass like he's been ignoring mine. And it feels good, this fresh anger, not about Ed, at least not in the same way. I sit up, look at the message again. *Stoop. Now.* And I let the anger push me to my feet, across the dark apartment, heart racing. When I open the door at the top of the outside steps, there's Jack. Leaning on the railing, inside the front gate. The streetlights are on, the buildings dark. Jack looks regular—jeans, tee, his brown leather jacket. Hair tight. It pisses me off even more.

"I don't get you," I say in a tense whisper. "Nothing about you makes sense anymore."

"Me?" His eyebrows shoot up. "When you're the one showing up at my apartment, asking questions that aren't your business?"

I stare at him. Is he really trying to blame me? Across the street, somebody lets out a yell. It's just the old guys playing dominoes at the corner bodega. One of them's got both hands in the air, which means he just laid down the winning domino. Even the guys who lost are laughing, talking over each other, retelling every play.

"Boring-ass game," Jack mutters. A second later, we catch eyes. And I can't help grinning. Because Ed frickin' loved dominoes. It was that thing about him—if something struck his curiosity, he didn't care—or didn't notice—how stupid it looked to everybody else. He'd watched dominoes at fifteen the same way he'd walked around telling jokes from a joke book at six. The memory feels good. But it doesn't change what's right in front of me.

"Quit playing around," I say. "Tell me where you've been. Why you took off in the first place."

"That's what I'm trying to do," Jack says.

Now we're under the streetlamp, he's not looking so good, after all. His T-shirt, orange, with "Give a Damn" in black letters, is wrinkled as hell. Veins pop out on the sides of his neck.

"First thing," he says, "is those cops were full of shit that day at Yard. They had it in for me before they even got there. Already had me down as a suspect because they knew I'd done the demos and

I'd called Singer out for the piece of trash he was. They knew I had a record, too."

"What record?" I say. "The only thing you ever got in trouble for is weed!" I'm getting frustrated again. Jack's talking, but I'm realizing there's only one thing I need to hear. He didn't kill Singer. I need him to say it, plain and simple.

"Think they cared about that?" Jack asks. "They had their sights on me, and when I went off that day it gave them their chance to bring me in."

I shake my head. I know how cops can be, but this doesn't sound right. "Still," I say. "Why would you leave your apartment, take all your stuff?"

Jack shoots me an evil side-eye, like I got no business knowing what's in his apartment. When I don't flinch, he watches me. Shrugs.

"You wanna know so bad? It's because they gave me the speech." He puts on a deep thug-cop voice. "'Motive, opportunity, and means. You understand that's all we need, right?' That's what they told me. They have to prove motive, opportunity, and means, to take somebody down. And they've already got motive and opportunity on me. I hated Singer because of Ed—motive. And I worked at Yard—opportunity. If they find the means—the fucking murder weapon—they got me." His voice goes hoarse on the words *murder weapon*.

He's scaring me bad, and I don't like it. "Why would they tell you all that, Jackson? You sound like they're recruiting you for the police academy!" I swallow the hot muck that's rising in my throat and *will* his ass to *just tell me*. Across the street, the dominoes guys set up another game.

"That's how they do it!" Jack says, stepping closer so he can keep his voice down. "Lay their bullshit case out in front of you. Then, the next thing they'll do is offer the deal. They're desperate to make an arrest that'll stick, so they'll tell me that if I confess, they'll go easy, call it involuntary manslaughter, push for a lighter sentence. But if they get the last piece of evidence, then it's a slam dunk. I go down for life. And all they need is the weapon—the means—to make that shit happen."

A car drives by, headlights on. Jack turns from the light too late, and I see the fear in his eyes.

"Look," he says. "They're not telling me everything they've got; they just say they've got it."

"Got *what*?" It's all I can do not to shout. "I don't know what you're talking about!"

"Evidence! Jesus, Victor. Some kind of evidence against me."

"But if you didn't do anything . . ."

"If?"

"It's not just about you!" I say. Pissed because he called me out, and it feels like shit. I pull him back so he's inside the gate. Lean in closer and tell him what happened last night, the cops following us from his place. The story feels worse, saying it out loud on the dark street. I remember the part when we realized they must've followed us upstairs. The part when I thought they'd recognized me.

"They probably think following my friends'll lead them to me, so they can hound me some more," Jack says when I'm done. "Get me to say something they can use against me."

"You say that like it's not crazy!" I say. "Listen to me. Whatever's going on, you can't be hiding out like this. We gotta deal with it."

But Jack's not having it. "I've seen it before," he says. "They see what they expect to see, maybe even believe it, how should I know? But they build a whole case around what they think, find evidence to prove it. Make it good and scary. Then they roll up on you every chance they get. Intimidate you, make you nervous so you get freaked and take their deal."

I wait a beat, caught off guard. Because he's repeating the idea from Ed's game. The potato-banana thing. The cops think they see a connection because they *expect* to see a connection—angry Black kid with a record kills the guy he's pissed at, at the restaurant where he works. Easy. And once people get something like that in their heads, they can't see past it. I get it. But just because the cops're doing that, doesn't mean they're wrong, does it?

"Mm-mmmmm." Jack wags his head, neck bent. "I'm not about that life. I just came back here to set you straight."

I hold my breath, hoping he's just gonna say it—set me straight that he didn't kill Singer.

"Because you need to stay out of it," he says. "Keep away from Yard. This ain't the time to worry about your little wannabe girl-friend."

"*What?* You sound like my damn pop! And Diamond's got nothing to do with it!" I look away from him, out over the quiet street. Why can't he listen to me, when I'm the only one that's making sense?

"Lay *low!*" Jack says, mirroring my heavy breathing. For a second, we stare each other down. Hella years hang between us. The fun times, way back. The hard times, right before. The evil awful after. And the confusing, hurtful now.

I try to pull it together.

"Tell me how to get ahold of you," I say. "What if the cops turn up again? What am I supposed to say?"

Jack blows out air. Crosses his arms. "The cops'll turn up again," he says. "Bet on that. What you wanna do? What you wanna *believe*? That's on you. Just remember, shit ain't always what it looks like."

And before I can say anything—*do anything*—else, he hits me with the world's fastest man-hug. And he's gone.

Cheesy Revenge

Ma used to call us stairsteps, Ed, Jack, and me. It's what I remember when I'm back in the building, looking up from the bottom of the staircase. A year between each of us and, for a long time, a couple inches. Ed had just got taller than me, with his gawky self, when he died. We weren't stairsteps by then anyhow. Because Brienne had come along. And Jack had better things to do than hang with us.

I climb the stairs. Slow, like an old man. If I'm honest, Jack would've got the first girlfriend even if he wasn't oldest. Girls've liked him from the get-go. But there was nobody like Brienne. She was all over him. And Jack had no problem kissing and telling. *Obnoxious to the nth*, as Ed would say. Except he didn't say it, not about Jack. Ed looked up to Jack, no matter what.

On the second-floor landing, a door slams inside an apartment. The couple in 2B, arguing again. Something about a leather briefcase not paying the motherfucking rent. I keep climbing. The last time the three of us hung—Ed, Jack, and me—Jack had brought Brienne to one of Ma's Prospect Park barbecues. And he'd teased Ed in front of her. Called him his little pain-in-the-ass kid-buddy. Smart kid, he said. Just probably never get his hands off a computer keyboard and onto a girl. Ed turned red. I saw it, because I was standing close, at the food table. Ed turned red, but Jack kept talking, because Brienne was laughing. When Ed came over to me after, he just stood around, no jokes, no acting the fool. Didn't even eat. And he never said a word about it.

Maybe there were other times like that, because after Ed died, Jack said he hadn't been treating Ed right. Kicked Brienne to the curb, said he should've been at Yard the night we lost him, not with her. Because maybe things would've been different. I tried to be big about it, told him it wasn't his fault for not being on shift that night, shit happens the way it happens. All I wanted was for somebody to say that to me. It wasn't *my* fault for trying to get with Diamond that night when I should've been with Ed. Everybody—Ma, Bennett, Chela—they all said there was nothing to feel guilty about. Guilt's just a feeling that comes up when people die. You have to let it go. I tried. Never pulled it off. So, what if Jack couldn't, either? What if the guilt made him do something stupid?

I reach our floor. Before I unlock the apartment, I give the other what-if some mental space, too. What if the cops are doing the thing from Ed's game, making connections that lead the wrong way? What if there's another answer they're not seeing? The right answer. The Jack-didn't-do-it answer. Feeling like I've been on some faraway trip, I go inside.

Ma's long, steady snores cut through the quiet. In my room, I pull up Ed's game. Tired as I am, I'm not letting another day go by without playing. I'm on level two, "Cheesy Revenge." Know this backstory, too. Ed and I saw a video about these city rat-hunters who go out at night with terriers to hunt rats. The rats squealed like monster trucks grinding on their brakes. It was disgusting, even for Ed. And sad. So, now he's got the rats going for revenge.

Not sorry to have an excuse to contact her, I send Diamond a screenshot: Ed's mutant rats wearing combat boots and bomber jackets, their weirdly human hands holding leashes attached to feral goldfish.

Me: You up?

Diamond: Maybe

Me: I'm being attacked by amphibious mutant rats.

I send another screenshot of the instructions.

Kill minion-bugs to get a clue

of the kind of combat

where rats crush you

Diamond: Yeah, ok. Got it.

Me: ?

Diamond: Kill minion-bugs 2 get clues about the type of combat 2 fight rats

Me: Oh

Problem is, now I'm talking to her, I don't want to kill min-ion-bugs. I want to ask what's going on with Fisk since she told him we kissed. And, damn, I want to tell her about Jack showing up and how he wouldn't just say he didn't do it, but the potato-banana thing from Ed's game helped me see what Jack was saying. Then I could tell her how it's just like Ed to help me see Jack in a better way. And it feels good that him and his game are in this whole Jack mess with me. But Diamond hasn't been on Jack's side. I can see her thinking Ed's wrong this time, and the cops are right.

I find some minion-bugs to kill. Not easy, since I still haven't figured out how to unseal my avatar's mouth so I can get my deadly discharge back. After a few misses, I figure out that the silver sword from my inventory takes the minions out. I get rewarded with the next clue and send it to Diamond.

Me: You still there? Here's the clue:

> Brooklyn rats have a new gift
> That will help us if we need to shift
> The sticky stuff that won't come out
> of the thing that's at the end of a snout.

After I send, I read it again. The thing at the end of a snout is . . . a nose, right?

So . . . sticky stuff *in your nose is* . . .

Diamond: 2 sleepy. Ask me 2morrow

Me: It's boogers! The rats've got to pick their noses. Hands are their "new gift," now they're mutants.

Diamond: Prolly not hands. Thumbs.

Me: ?

Diamond: U were looking 4 a type of combat. Thumbs pick noses. So, thumb wrestle.

Me: Right . . .

I try it, click my mutant-guy's thumb, then the rat's. Both thumbs grow bigger, face off, vibrate as they come together. And then . . . my mutant's thumb goes *down*! A speech bubble pops up:

> Na na na boo boo boo
> Who's squealing now? Not us, but you!

Me: Wait. I fkn lost!

Diamond: U have 2 keep going—don't have everything you need yet.

I don't answer because I don't know what she's talking about.

Diamond: Something 2 make u stronger. Like spinach or Red Bull.

Me: How come you didn't tell me that before?

I look at what I wrote. Erase it.

Me: We make a good team.

It's a minute before she answers.

Diamond: Guess so. Sleep tight, VZ.

I'm grinning as I put the phone down. Start searching the screen for spinach and Red Bull. Still. Wish I could've told her about Jack.

Solid Evidence

Cops are on top of Jack and me. We're underwater, surrounded in acid-green waves, and they're trying to force us into some kind of dungeon. I wonder why their caps don't float off. And then, Ed's there, too. It's all three of us and we're forcing the cops back, moving up toward the surface. Ed looks so scared; I can't breathe, and I don't know what to do. I push against the water, which is weirdly solid. Closing in on us. My fists close around it. And I wake up, clenching the sides of my mattress.

Feet finding the floor, I stumble out of my warm bed, into the still-dark hall, thinking about breakfast and Sammy and extra-sweet black coffee.

There're voices coming from the front of the apartment. And it hits me, they don't sound like Ma and Bennett. I stop moving as soon as I see the living room. Ma's there with her back to me,

90

standing at the open front door. Got on her housecoat, hair still in the clips and rollers she sleeps in. For a second, I think some crazy sleep-magic's happening, because the person on the other side of the door is wearing a blue uniform, like in my dream. I step back into the hall. Can't see anymore, but I already know it's real. It's the cop from Yard, the Black guy who arrested Jack.

My groggy-ass mind races. *Do they know Jack was here? Did the bodega guys tell?*

The cop's talking. I try to chill the drumming in my ears, so I can hear.

". . . don't think you understand how bad this looks for your son," the cop says. "He was seen in a speeding car that was actively avoiding detection."

My hand seals itself over my mouth. *Fuck. The crazy car chase.*

"A car that started out," the cop says, "at the home of a kid who's already been brought in on the Singer case."

"You're not making sense," Ma says, sounding irritated. And I get this hope that she won't believe him, that it'll never make sense to her.

"Your son was in a car that outran a police vehicle last night," the cop says.

"With due respect, Officer," Ma tells him, "I doubt that."

"Why don't we ask him?" the cop says. "Bring your son to the door, if he's here. It won't take long."

My body goes haywire, full-on sweats. I can't believe how fucked I could be.

"Thank you for your advice, Officer," Ma says. "That won't be happening without a warrant."

I breathe, but the cop's not done.

"*Mrs. Gleason*," he says, like it's urgent. "I want to help you. So, I'm going to tell you some things the public doesn't know, all right? Singer was armed the night he was killed. That means the person who killed him probably acted in self-defense to some degree. If they cooperate, we could help them get a lighter sentence, in spite of their initial motives. Here's the thing, though. If someone like your son is covering for them, that's obstruction of justice. Your son could face a whole separate world of trouble."

"I'll keep that in mind," Ma says, dry-voiced.

"Mrs. Gleason!" The cop sounds irritated now, but like he's finally being for real. "The kid we brought in, your son's buddy? There's solid evidence against him. Physical evidence, witnesses. Self-incriminating statements. I suggest you and your family think about that."

For a second, my head leaves my body. What did he say? Solid evidence . . . physical evidence . . . witnesses?

I imagine what's happening next, the two of them staring each other down. It goes on and on, neither of them saying anything. I pray Ma holds out.

Finally, the door closes.

There's a beat of dead silence. Then the door opens again, and Bennett's voice asks about the cops in the hall. Ma must shush him with a signal, because he quits talking. More silence, and I know Ma's listening for the cops to finish going downstairs. Then comes an ice-cold whisper-hiss.

"Victor! I know you're there."

It's so early, the living room's full of shadows when I walk in. Ma throws her hands around, paces. I can't stand being still, either. Walk into the kitchen, grab the box of Cheerios off the counter, and scoop a dry handful into my mouth. Ma's eyes follow me. Then she turns to Bennett, as if she can't stand looking at me.

"They said Victor was acting crazy in some car last night. They think it has to do with that Singer man getting killed."

"That true?" Bennett asks, looking at me. The Cheerios taste like dust in my mouth. I'm grateful as hell Ma got the cop out of here, but what am I supposed to say? The whole car-chase thing makes Jack look guilty. Guilti*er*. And I can't stand the thought of them thinking he did it—or even thinking that I think he might've.

"They probably just came 'cause I work at Yard," I say. "They're on all of us."

"Mm-hmm," Ma says. "Cops are showing up at *everybody's* door talking about car chases?"

"Don't believe me if you don't want to," I say.

"You see any handcuffs on my belt?" Ma snaps. "I'm not the one who has to believe you!" She takes a breath, looking right at me now. "I'm not blind, Victor. I know how the police can be. But they didn't show up here for nothing. You going to tell us the real story?"

I make a big deal of chewing, search my brain for a way out. *Okay, see, this friend of Chela's is some shady-ass fool who had us racing the cops down the BQE. Oh, and they were following us in the first place 'cause they were staked out at Jack's apartment building . . .* I can't do that to Jack.

"There's nothing to tell, Ma," I say. "That cop was just wilding."

Ma wraps her arms all the way around herself. "I'm sorry, Victor," she says. "For once, your father's right. School's almost done. It just makes sense for you to go on and stay with him awhile."

It's a straight-up sucker punch. We don't even talk about Pop unless she's making one of her backhanded jokes. And I let her, take her side. *Now* she wants to pawn me off on him, 'cause of some bullshit that happened in that Robbie idiot's car? It cuts deep. I've been trying with her. Keeping it chill when she and Bennett say stupid shit about keeping my grades up or finding new friends. I haven't gone off once. And this is what I get—sent away from everything that might help—hanging with Chela, getting with Diamond. Helping Jack.

"Really, Ma?" I say. "You just gonna say that to me?" The dig comes out of me without my knowing I'm thinking it. "After I been having your back and you've been no help at all?"

I brace myself for her to go off. Instead, she looks away from me. "You think I don't know I couldn't help you?" she says. "You think somebody wants to see their child sink, day after day? Eyes going blank after two minutes of talk? Never coming out of your room, unless it's to go to Chela's?"

She wipes tears off her face, but I'm too mad to care.

"It was better than here," I say.

"Don't be disrespectful," Ma says, too quiet, not yelling like she should.

"Then don't be stupid!" I say. The minute I hear it, I know I shouldn't've said it.

Bennett jumps up, puts himself between me and Ma. "Watch yourself now," he says, like he's protecting Ma. *From me.*

"Don't you!" The sound of my voice is low and raw. "Don't you *dare.*"

My jaw and neck are so tight it hurts. All I know is I can't do this, can't feel this right now. My eyes dart to the door, the hall behind me, back to the door. Searching for my way out. Pants. Wallet. Ed's computer. That's all I need.

I turn, pound down the hall. In a heartbeat, I'm in my room. Pulling on yesterday's pants, shoving Ed's computer in my pack. And then I'm out the door, making sure it slams behind me.

Hot Apple

I walk like a madman, pass the gated-up bodega and laundromat, the open coffee truck. Never been so close to smacking Bennett, not once since I met him. Never thought of him as anything but a dad-joke stepdad. Now, though? I don't even know what just happened. Don't know where I'm walking, either, till I come up on the subway. Remember Chela's circle thing is *before* first period. Not a bad thing, though, having a place to go.

On the train, a woman lays across a bunch of seats, head on a trash bag, eating an apple. She nods at me when I get on, like I just came into her living room. I take a seat across from her. "Thank God for Uncle Ace's," she says. Got one of those hoarse, scratchy voices, like she swallowed broken glass. "Am I right?"

"Sorry?" I say.

"That's what we call the A, C, E line." She points to the

giant-sized letter *C* in the window. "Longest line, so it's best for sleeping. But now it's time to finish my breakfast." She sits up, then gets to her feet, holding her bags to her chest as the train pulls into the station. Waves her apple as she disappears behind the closing doors. I notice how nasty my mouth tastes from not getting to brush. And there's a sauce stain on my pants. I wonder if she told me all that 'cause she thinks I'm homeless.

The rest of the ride, my brain loops on the cop, especially what he was saying to Ma about Singer having a gun. *I'm going to tell you some things the public doesn't know, all right. Singer was armed the night he was killed. . . .* Bullshit. I already knew Singer was armed the night he got killed. I read it somewhere or heard it . . . from Jack.

I heard it from Jack. I stare at the homeless woman as the scene plays back in my head, Jack standing over Ms. Fox, going off on the two cops. *That Singer fool came at somebody with his piece? Everybody knows what he can do with that thing . . .*

But if the public doesn't know Singer had a gun that night, how could Jack know? Is that what the cop meant, just now with Ma? That they had solid evidence against Jack?

Potato-banana. I hold on to the idea like a life preserver. Whatever those cops think is evidence has nothing to do with Jack—they're seeing connections they expect to see and it's getting them to the wrong answer. Right? Right.

When I get to school, I go in a bathroom to clean myself up, then hit the cafeteria for some breakfast. By the time I get to Ronnah's room, I'm late, and still chowing the dry-ass cafeteria muffin.

Seven people are sitting in a circle in the middle of the room, all of them looking at me.

"We were just organizing the search party," Ronnah's voice rings out. "Please take a seat, VZ. No eating or drinking in the circle."

Fuck. I can tell from Chela's face, she's stressed. If the world was halfway right, Chela and I'd be at the diner across the street right now drinking light sweet coffee while I told her everything that went down last night and this morning. Jack, Ma, Bennett. Especially the cop at the door. I take the empty chair, between Chela and Ronnah. There're two people I don't really know in the circle. A teacher, who's sitting next to Ms. Doyle, and a kid sitting by Bruce Walendorf. He's got a big smug smile on his face, making me sure he's the one from the Justice Team for Ed group. He's an Indian kid I've seen around, named Guz. Got dark brown skin and a wiry build. He looks small next to Walendorf, who's got some height, and he sits forward, hands on his knees like the whole thing is fascinating.

Ronnah holds up a gold metal apple, tells us it's the talking piece Ms. Doyle picked because it was her first-ever teacher-gift. Ronnah goes over the rules, including how we can only talk when we've got the apple and the apple always goes in order. For some reason, the Guz kid keeps trying to catch my eye. I ignore him. Chela shoots me a *Don't fuck this up* look, and I sit straighter, try to focus. Ronnah gets us to introduce ourselves, then tell what we think happened with Chela, Walendorf, and Doyle the day it all went down. Goes well enough until Walendorf gets the apple.

"I can tell you exactly what happened," he says. "I made a comment on this flyer I passed. I was just saying my opinion on encouraging violence. And Chela made it a big race thing and got crazy mad. . . ."

Beside me, Chela goes rigid. I can feel her holding her breath.

"So when we got to class, she whaled on the door." He gestures with his hand. "And Ms. Doyle got a black eye."

Chela lets out a tortured sound, like a pissed-off cat. The apple goes to Guz, who I deliberately don't listen to, then to Ms. Doyle. The room gets even quieter as Ms. Doyle says how she was leaning against the wall by the door, rethinking the activity she'd planned for class. She was just heading for her desk when her face exploded in pain. Says she never thought something like that would happen at our school. Chela stays dead still. I drop my hand across the back of her chair, to remind her she's not alone.

Doyle's support, the other teacher, Ms. Enright, doesn't have much to add. And then it's Chela's turn. Her eyelids drop as she takes the apple. Stay down when she starts talking.

"What happened from my perspective," she says, like a little kid giving the title of her presentation. "Here it is. Bruce and I were walking to class—not together, just at the same time. He saw the flyer with the picture of Ed and he said, 'The person who wrote "at least Singer paid" ought to be expelled.' That is the same as saying they should be *punished* for *protesting racism*. Because what Singer did to Ed was *racist*—not rocket science." She looks at Bruce, who deadpans, making it clear he's not feeling her.

"After that," Chela says, "I *did* . . . slam . . . the door open, because I . . . was *mad* and I—I wanted Bruce to see how mad I was, how you can't go around saying shit—sorry—stuff like that."

She shoots a quick side-glance at Ms. Doyle. "I didn't know Ms. Doyle was there, though. But she was."

The room's dead quiet. Chela's eyes settle a little longer on Ms. Doyle's face. Then she sucks in her bottom lip, shifts her gaze to Ronnah. "Can I say something else, about something that was said this round?"

Ronnah nods that it's okay.

"Good," Chela says. "Because it's important. Bruce said I *made* what he said about race, which is crap. It *just is* about race. *Obviously*."

Bruce does an even bigger eye roll.

Chela grunts, shoves the apple at me. "Here! You try."

"What she said," I say. Ronnah glares at me, though, and I know I'm supposed to say more. "'Course it's about race," I say. "That's the whole reason Ed ended up—like he did. Chela had a right to be mad. And the rest was an accident, so . . ." I glance at Ms. Doyle, who's sitting there with her faded shiner, tugging at her sweater like she can't get warm. "So, that's it."

When the apple makes its way back to Walendorf, he goes for Chela again.

"All I *meant*," he says, "was that people shouldn't act like it's okay to kill a guy! *Any* guy. No matter what he did. But that doesn't matter, because whatever I say she's gonna call me a racist."

"Oooh, original," Chela mutters. "Think of that all by yourself?"

Ronnah calls her out for talking out of turn. Walendorf, who was about to hand the apple to Guz, pulls it back.

"I'm going to say this one more time," he says. "I never said Singer wasn't a racist. I'm pretty sure he was. But I don't think Singer should've got killed for revenge, no matter how bullshit— I mean, how pissed-off, or *triggered*, or whatever—the guy who did it is. And I think writing on a poster that killing for revenge was a good idea *is a bad idea*."

He eyeballs each of us, except for Chela. "*Why is that so wrong?*" he asks.

His words twist in my gut. It takes a minute to realize he's practically describing Jack as Singer's killer: *I don't think Singer should've got killed for revenge . . . no matter how bullshit or triggered the guy was . . .*

Guz gets the apple. And the first thing out of his mouth is my name.

"About what VZ said. It's not *about* who's *right or wrong*. It's about *justice*. It's about figuring out how to get to justice, you know, for everybody."

I want to throw up. He reminds me of Jack, both of them smug as fuck. On him, it shows up in a little half smile, the way he raises his tent-shaped eyebrows.

"And that's exactly what we're trying to do, man," he says. "At the Justice Team for Ed Hennessey! We're finding justice for Ed, keeping his memory alive. Making his name stand for something!"

And here I thought I'd slogged through enough shit today. Now this kid thinks he's got balls because he started some stupid school committee? When he was no help to Ed when he was alive, trying to make friends at this school? My knee's bouncing again, and I don't bother trying to stop it. Too hard to stay still in this room.

Ms. Doyle's got the apple. Puffs herself up, like what she's about to say is gonna cost her. "It's good, very good, you kids are keeping Ed's memory alive. True. But I don't want you being angry about what happened to be an excuse for misbehavior or . . . or violence. Because it isn't. It's no excuse."

Chela goes tight again. When the apple gets back to her, her eyes move between Ms. Doyle and Ronnah. "I'm not saying what Bruce said gives me a right to slam a door open and—hurt Ms. Doyle. I know I need to make up for that. *And* if we're gonna do right by Ed, then like Guz said, we have to tell the whole truth about what happened to him. About how it *was* about racism and there hasn't been any justice."

Like Guz said? What kind of shit is that? Chela hands me the apple. "No, not like Guz said," I say. "None of this is doing right by Ed! Ed was too busy doing Ed to worry about shit like the stupid Justice Team. Ed had games to make, jokes to tell. He had a *life*— and then he didn't." I look up at the clock. "We've been here almost an hour, and what's the point? Ms. Doyle's still got a black eye. Ed's still dead. How's all this frickin' talk helping them?" I hand off the apple like it's on fire. Pull my shirt away from my sweaty throat, already hating what I said. *Ed's still dead.* Feels like I just made him deader.

For once, I want Walendorf to talk awhile so the apple doesn't get to Guz again. But Walendorf hands it right over. And Guz jumps on my shit.

"What's up your butt about the Justice Team, huh? We do great stuff." He thrusts his pointy chin forward. "At the funeral, Ed's mom said she wanted his name kept alive. And I think that counts, too—what she wants. I think it's good the team's doing stuff that helps her."

Did he say *at the funeral*? This joker was *there*? At the funeral I didn't go to? Chela puts a hand on my bouncing leg. I know she's remembering how crazy it made me, the thought of seeing Ed in the open casket.

"At least the team's doing something real," Guz finishes.

"Fuck you," I mouth. But I should've shut up, because he's still got the apple.

He shakes it at me, starts up again. "This school's never even had a game design club," he says. "Now we'll have one with Ed's name and his logo."

I've got no clue what he's talking about, and it must show on my face, because Guz's lights up.

"Ha! You don't know about Edge Camp?" he asks. "It's our game design club. *E, D, G*—for Ed and Guz. And Camp stands for coding, art, mechanics, and play. Me and Ed wrote it all up to get permission to start it, and now the club's on our third action step. What are you doing for Ed that's cooler than that?"

I give him my best stone face. While I wonder the same thing. Maybe getting Ed's game to the contest isn't shit compared to a game design club. And why didn't Ed tell me about EDG Camp, anyhow? Was I that tuned out, he didn't even bother?

The apple goes around, and I try to get ready, but it comes back too quick. Guz's got his brows up, ready for my comeback. Chela's turned in her chair, watching me along with everybody else. And I got nothing. I twist the apple between my hands. And then—the bell rings. First piece of luck in forever! Ronnah asks if I'd like to speak before we close. I try not to look too relieved when I tell her I'm good. We end till Monday, same time, same place.

On the way out, Guz catches up to me. "What the fuck are you doing again?" he asks.

Apology Weed

All I want after school is to get to Chela's. Instead, I'm outside Yard's screen door, watching Ms. Fox give the beatdown to a mound of dough. I don't like lurking out here. But Ms. Fox isn't the person to talk to when you're up to something shady. So I listen to her sing to Jesus and wait for her to leave the kitchen.

All day, I've been thinking about Chela's circle. First, pain-in-the-ass Guz. A whole club Ed never told me about? Two reasons why play out in my mind. One, he was thinking of it as some big surprise that he'd unveil—ta-da!—when it was done, hoping to blow everybody away. And two—he didn't think I'd give a shit. I hate two. Don't know what to do with two, except have it sit in my belly making acid until I think of something else.

Except the something else doesn't help. Because then I think how people in that circle'd bought into the potato-banana mindset—acting like Jack, or somebody hella like him, killed Singer because that's what they expected in the first place. Walendorf straight-up said he thinks whoever killed Singer was pissed-off and triggered—like Jack would've been. Which tells me that if the cops arrest Jack—any day now, according to the cop who came to our door—nobody's even gonna question it.

I turn my back to Ms. Fox's kitchen door, look out at the miserable parking lot, my hand closing around the burner phone in my pocket. If everybody's potato-banana'ing like Walendorf—and not a soul in the circle disagreed with him—then there's no way the cops are letting up on Jack. And as long as the cops are on Jack, they'll be on me. What if they come for me on the street next time, instead of home? What if they make me empty my pockets and I've got this frickin' phone? What if Sammy's with me when they do? After the cops came to the house, even Chela said I should get rid of it. I didn't tell her I plan on putting it back at Yard instead of chucking it off the Brooklyn Bridge or something. But I know I can't do that. 'Cause I can't forget the cop that day in Yard's dining room. Twisting my arm, pulling me against him. *You gonna be next?*

Nope. Never gonna be next. Which means no destroying evidence. I wonder if it's ever gonna end, this feeling that I'm getting it wrong, letting people down, the way I let Ed down.

Inside, Ms. Fox switches to humming. Shapes a hunk of dough into a giant loaf of bread and pats it into an oversized pan. The smell's telling me there's already bread in the oven. My stomach may or may not growl.

"Victor?" Ms. Fox is leaning over, looking out the screen.

"Left my keys," I say, ready with the story I borrowed from Jack. Ms. Fox doesn't give it a thought. Opens the door and draws me into the warm kitchen. I know from the long pans and sweet smell that it's hard dough bread she's making.

"It musta radar you have," she says. "With this timing. The first batch is just done." She opens the oven door, pulls out four gigantic loaves. A minute later, she's slathering honey butter on a thick slice, handing it to me. I damn near forget why I'm there, except for Ms. Fox is watching me with so much sadness that the hot buttered bread sticks in my throat. I swallow it down. Find the guts to ask what I've been wanting to know.

"What do you think, Ms. Fox? *You* think Jack could've done something stupider than stupid?"

She takes a cloth from the counter, covers the bread loaves. "The ancestors tell us that madness is the brother of anger. You understand?" She pats my cheek. "You children must learn to listen to the dead."

I don't understand, but instead of explaining, she turns away, says she's got to take care of things in the dining room. When the door swings shut behind her, I know I can't waste time. I shove the rest of the bread in my mouth and head to the old wooden desk, pull the handle on the lost and found drawer. It sticks. I wrench it open, check to make sure Ms. Fox isn't coming back, and drop the burner phone inside. Then I haul ass to the door, calling to Ms. Fox that I gotta go. My hand stops halfway to the doorknob. Feeling like a turd, I go back, pull the drawer out again. And wipe the fingerprints off the phone with the bottom of my T-shirt.

* * *

At Chela's, we don't waste time. Head from the door straight to her bedroom and climb out the window. Chela shuts the window behind her and settles across from me on the cold iron floor of her fire escape. A late-day breeze carries away the noise of the city, so it feels like we're all alone in the world. In a good way. Especially after a day of crazy.

"Talk," Chela says. "Is cheap. But weed ain't."

"What's that supposed to mean?" I ask.

She pulls a baggie of weed out of her pocket and tosses it to me. I'm grateful as hell to catch it, sniff the sweet earthy buds. Chela's mom's rule is that we smoke out here, window shut. That's it. Perks of having a white mom who's not stressed about cops. It works perfect. Four floors up, so no one can tell what we're doing from the street anyhow. I rest my head against the black iron railings. The sky's still more blue than pink, which seems impossible since I've been up about a hundred hours.

"It means," Chela says, "the weed's from Robbie. I told him about the cops coming to your place, and the whole Singer story. He felt bad. Weird bad, to tell you the truth, like he'd really fucked us over."

"'Cause he did," I say. "But—what? He gave you apology weed?" There's something jacked-up about that—doing shady shit and apologizing with weed. After everything that happened, I'd almost forgot the whole cop-at-my-door thing was all his fault.

"Fuck Robbie," I say. "Bet no cops showed up at his door."

"He gave us *good* apology weed," Chela says. "Believe me, I read him. But forget that. You had cops at your door before you even got to the circle this morning? *And* Jack, last night! And Bennett! I mean, was Bennett really that much of a dick?"

She hands me the little pack of papers, and I roll the joint. "First time I ever even yelled at him," I say. "He deserved it, but still. Bennett's been cool, mostly."

"I always thought so," she says.

"I just got so mad. He was acting like . . ." I trail off, remembering the feeling of him getting between Ma and me.

Chela lights the joint, and I take a first good pull.

"He was showing off. Acting like he's the boss when it's not even his business."

"Like he was your dad?" Chela asks.

"Nah," I say, "I don't care about that. It's more like—it's been me and Ma for too long. Feels like forever. And here comes Bald Bennett, acting like it's all about *him* and Ma." The anger rolls through me again. I remember Bennett's balled-up fists. Ma's face all twisted.

"It's okay to crash here tonight?" I ask.

Chela shrugs, 'cause it's always okay. "What about Jack and the cops?" she asks.

I take another pull.

"Jack was scared," I say, "kept telling me the cops had it in for him. They had him on motive and opportunity, all they needed was the means."

My throat closes, not from the smoke. Jack being scared gets to me more than the things he said. If he's scared, there's something real going on. "Just 'cause he's scared doesn't mean he did it," I say.

"No, 'course not," Chela says.

We smoke awhile, and I get the slow goodness of my muscles unknotting. Only seems to happen here these days. Chela opens the plastic grocery bag she brought outside, tosses me a baggie of homemade chocolate-covered potato chips. A few crunches later, I let my head fall back on the rail. Forget.

"You know what I'm scared of, though?" Chela asks, stretching her long legs over mine. "Jack was at every protest I went to, after Ed. There's probably video all over the internet of him saying shit about Singer. It looks bad."

So much for forgetting. "Not just the protests," I say. "There's Jack's YouTube channel. Fool put his rants about Singer to music!" I take another hit.

"You ever think," Chela says. "What if it got even more real? What if we had to hide Jack, like get him out of town or whatever?"

"What? Why would you say that?"

"You know, hypothetically," she says. "Would you help him, knowing how it could come back on you?"

I think about the phone laying in the lost and found drawer at Yard. Was putting it back there my answer? Am I the guy who throws his friend under a speeding bus?

"Jack didn't do it, all right?" I say, too aggressive. "And he's not gonna go down for it."

She checks me out, clenched fists, bouncing leg. Reaches up and grabs a hunk of my hair. "Twist," she says. Then squashes the lit end of the joint against an iron bar, picks up her phone.

"I know you don't like to read this stuff," she says. "But I want you to see because it might help. At least there are people watching, trying to make sure it plays out fair."

She hands me the phone, on a *#SingerInvestigationWatch* Twitter search. There's a list of posts below:

> @nypd, stop fucking us over because a killer got got.
> #stayfocused #PoliceAccountabilityNow

> Singer investigation is full of hate. #PoliceAccountabilityNow.
> Check out Singer's rap sheet @nypd. #SingerHadHistory.
> #RacistMedia

> I saw it happen, but @nypd won't listen . . .

I scroll down. It's good, but if they're the same groups that did the protests to get Singer to trial—we all know how that turned out. I click on the article linked to *Check out Singer's rap sheet.* It's some advocacy group saying Singer had a criminal history but nobody's in it the way they get up in Black kids' histories when they're victims—making like they got got 'cause they did bad stuff in the past. Not news. If Singer was treated like a Black guy, the cops'd be looking into his rap sheet all day long.

"Hey! Where's your head?" Chela asks, wiggling her bare toes on my leg.

I hold up the phone. "Turns out Singer had a rap sheet," I say, "but the cops could give a fuck." Feels like another nail in Jack's coffin, the cops ignoring Singer's rap sheet while they keep after Jack. "And it's not even just the cops. People at your circle were acting like Jack did it—or somebody just like him. But it's like in Ed's game. Sometimes, the more obvious something seems, the less it's actually what it looks like. You just have to look closer."

Chela relights the joint and hands it over. I close my eyes, take a pull. I'm starting to get the on-the-tip-of-my-tongue, almost-there feeling, like when I'm missing something in Ed's game that's right in front of my face. Maybe *I* have to look closer.

In my mind, I break it down. It looks like Jack had motive and opportunity because he hated Singer and worked at Yard. Okay, but lots of people hated Singer. As for opportunity . . . I close my eyes, get into my game head. A grin spreads across my face.

"If you look closer," I say out loud, "*then it doesn't make sense*! How would Jack get Singer to come to Yard when the restaurant wasn't even open? And since Yard was closed—had been closed for *hours* when Singer got killed—the staff was long gone! But that gate doesn't have a lock, anybody could've walked in. So, working there didn't give Jack any special opportunity! Whoever killed Singer just as likely came there *with* him that night. Then, maybe they had a fight with him or something, and it got out of hand, and they ran off."

Impressed with my skills, I pull up a search: *motives for murder*, and scroll down the page. "Revenge doesn't even make the top two motives," I say. "It's always domestic disputes or money."

"Yeah," Chela says, listening now. "That's true. It's what you always hear, anyhow."

"I learned how to do that from Ed's game," I tell her, my pulse picking up. "There's all these tricks for figuring stuff out." I wave away the joint, let my mind stay in game mode. Move through all the tricks I learned. The potato-banana thing; the one where the answer can be in the question, and the one about clues being visual when you don't expect it. I stop at that one. Think about the giant dead water bug on the truck that saved us that night in Robbie's car. Talk about a visual clue. And there was the fish tank at Jahvaris's that had the bright green water. It helped me see more of the apartment, realize Jack had moved out, so I knew how deep in he was.

Weird as what I'm thinking is, my weed-soaked brain gets more excited. *Ed's game's not just helping me see how the cops might be wrong about Jack. It's giving me straight-up clues to figure all this out. And—the idea pops up behind my eyes like a lit-up bodega on a dark winter night—if it's been doing that since jump, it can keep doing it. It can help me figure out who killed Singer.*

"Might be I'm more fucked-up than I thought," I say, but Chela doesn't hear me. Instead, Ms. Fox's voice comes in my head. *You children must learn to listen to the dead.* I glance up, like you do when you're looking for somebody who's passed. Don't see anything except the cloudy Brooklyn sky. But I imagine Ed up there. Grinning.

Gotta Go

My alarm could give a shit about my weed hangover. I moan, squeeze my eyes shut for one more second, then hit dismiss instead of snooze. It's my day to drop Sammy at preschool. Last night on the fire escape comes back to me, the wild idea of Ed's game helping me figure out who killed Singer. I keep my eyes closed, go back over everything that seemed so right. Somehow, it still does.

I keep it together, make the train on time, thinking that at least Sammy doesn't change. Doesn't have anything to do with investigations or evidence or motives for murder. I pound up to our stoop at seven thirty, pumped to see her. And then there's Bennett, who should be asleep upstairs, walking up the sidewalk. He catches sight of me, and I know right off that he took Sammy to school. There's a shit-eating look on his face, like he's sorry and kind of glad, all at once.

"Just getting back from dropping her," he says. "Didn't know if you'd make it."

"When haven't I?" I ask. Stone-faced.

He looks me over, registering that I'm in day-old clothes, didn't have time to wash or mess with my locs. He looks disgusted, doesn't even try to hide it. Works my last nerve.

"True, true," he says. "Well, this will give you more time for your shower. Come on, let's go in."

"Mmm," I say. "Think I'll just get to school early."

Bennett's face decides what it wants to do. Settles into straight-up pissed.

"What happened yesterday," he says. "That can't be happening in our house. Not ever again."

"Right," I say, hearing the sarcasm in my voice. It's not like I go off on him every day. And he's the one who started it.

"Mmm-hmmm," he says. "So you know, no middle-of-the-night meetings, either." He throws up his eyebrows, letting me know he knows who I met in the middle of the night. Damn. Did the bodega guys tell? Or maybe they only saw me and Bennett's bluffing, just guessing it was Jack. I take the gamble.

"I don't know what you're talking about," I say. "I gotta go."

He gives me a loooong wise-old-Black-man look. Then he says, real slow, "You gotta go, huh? Mm-hmm. That might be truer than you think."

I nod, out of habit, even though he just threatened me. Then I pound past him, which isn't the direction I need to be going but seems better than turning around. I walk blind to the end of the block, take the corner. I miss Sammy, miss how the world gets Sammy-sized when I'm with her. I should be riding her on my shoulders right now, feeling her little fingers in my locs. But I gotta let it go. I stop at a bench outside a laundromat. Screw Bennett and screw school. What I need is to figure out what was going on last night—test it out in the cold weed-free morning.

The question settles on my shoulders as I sit down on the bench. Am *I* for real, right now? Thinking there's clues to finding Singer's killer in a game that was made before Singer even died? Still, though, it feels right. Better than right. *Good.* Like one of those Saturdays when there was nothing to do and Ed turned up and I wasn't lonely anymore.

I glance around, as if anybody on the street cares. Then I take out the red laptop and pull up the game. I'm on the next part of level two, Cheesy Revenge. A bright white maze covers the screen. Edric's gotta eat rat pellets all through the maze, and for every pellet, I answer a rat-trivia question. Get it right and the pellet's cheese, Edric goes forward. Wrong and it's poison. Edric goes back. I scrunch up my eyes as I read the question.

> They say we are the rattiest.
> But their brains are just the battiest.
> What city's heights must they explore,
> So they will learn that ain't the score? ·

For once, the answer's easy. Ed didn't like when people called New York the dirtiest, or nastiest, or whatever. So the answer's

116

gotta be New York. But is there a clue there, to Singer's murder? I study the words and a sound comes out of me, a deep humming. *Hmhmhmhmhmhmhmhmh.*

What city's heights must they explore? I have to explore NYC. Sure, except it's kinda big. I go over the whole thing again. This time my eyes stick on the word *heights*. I read somewhere Singer lived in Dyker Heights, Brooklyn. I have to explore Singer's neighborhood?

I sit still, because I'm on to something and I need to organize it in my head.

The info I found last night said most people get killed 'cause of domestic disputes, by somebody in their family or house. Singer's house would be in his neighborhood, which is Dyker Heights. So, the game's telling me to go to Dyker Heights to find his killer? Something in my weed-free brain pushes back. Am I really about to try to catch Singer's killer? And even if I did, so what? Not like the cops'd believe me.

I stay where I am, completely still. And realize Ed's game's got the answer again. I don't have to catch Singer's killer. I just have to get enough ammo to give the cops another lead—a *different* potato-banana connection. If I can get something solid, I can give it to one of those groups I saw online, get them to flood social media. The cops'd have to pay attention. And, boom! Jack's not the only easy suspect anymore. I check the calendar on my phone. Still got seven days till JersiGame. A second later, I'm off the bench, messaging Chela as I go.

Me: I'm going to find Singer's house.

Chela: ?

Me: Remember? Domestic disputes are the top motive for murder. I want to see where he lived. Could get a lead . . .

Chela: A lead?

I think a minute. Doesn't feel right to tell her that Ed's game's helping me figure shit out. At least not yet.

Me: Worth a try.

As usual, Chela surprises me.

Chela: K. School?

Me: This is more important.

I hit up Maps, head off toward the subway that'll get me to Dyker Heights, thinking about Guz. Because this is something I'm doing for Ed and, weird as it is, with him. It's probably the only way to help Jack. And who's gonna do it if not me?

It takes two subways and a long walk to get to Singer's neighborhood. According to my internet search, his apartment's in the middle of the block, the second floor in a three-story brick. I stop in front of the building next door, the only person on the empty sidewalk. And I wonder how I didn't get that it would feel like crap to be here. It's like I can reach out and touch his murdering ass. Except worse, because he's not in there. Never will be. Turns out, hating a dead guy's like being constipated. There's no place for the shit to go, so it piles up inside you. Just underneath your pissed-off, racing heart.

I hate every house on the block. All identical, black doors, white trim. Picture windows in front. I imagine a pair of eyes staring out every one of them—a whole neighborhood of Singerites, planning to come for the random Black kid who doesn't belong here. I do a

360, as much on the down-low as I can. See if I can see somebody watching. It's way quieter than my neighborhood at nine o'clock in the morning.

What the hell am I doing here? I try to get back the *rightness* feeling from this morning, but it's gone. A sound behind me makes me turn. At the end of the block, crossing the street, I see a tall Black guy. Cap pulled low, familiar leather jacket. What looks like leather high-tops. Jack.

Jack?

I can't call his name, not here. But . . . *is that fool following me?* Even worse, is he doing what I'm doing? Checking out stuff about Singer? Could he be stupid enough to call himself laying low and show up here at the same time? Fuck. *He could.* I whip out my phone.

Me: Did I just see your dumb ass?

Me: Quit playing! Where are you right now?

Me: Tell me where the fuck you are!

I'm breathing like a fool, pissed he's ignoring me, aware as hell I'm standing on Singer's block. Decide, *Screw it, I'm going after him.* Except, I hear a door close. I'm turned away from it, looking where I thought I'd seen Jack. But I know for sure which door it is. I turn, as chill as I can. A woman in a red jacket's just stepped out of Singer's apartment. She locks the door behind her, drops the key ring in her bag. As she looks up, heads down the walk, her eyes land dead on me. But then, thank the universe, she turns in the opposite direction.

If I thought my heart was racing before, it was nothing. The internet told me Singer had a girlfriend, Norma something-or-other, who co-owned the apartment. This woman looks the right age. And who else would be coming out of his house? I suck my lips in. The *nailed it* feeling spreads through me again, reminding me I'm here for a reason. I follow her. Keep a decent distance between us. When I'm level with Singer's building, I get another idea, snap a picture with my phone. Keep going. The woman hits a main street, full of stores and restaurants. There's a fruit stand a few doors in, where the fruit's all laid out in bins on the sidewalk. I turn my back to the street, like I'm choosing something from the bins. Take a breath and check for Jack. No sign of him. I keep following the woman.

She's tall, wearing shiny red shoes that leave her heels sticking out, and a red-and-white dress under the red puffy jacket that's made of something shiny, too. Don't know why, exactly, but she *looks* like she'd be Singer's girlfriend.

A few blocks down, she turns into a shop. Greets somebody in a high-pitched, hard-edged voice, "Hey now, sweetums!"

I walk past, see it's a nail shop. I know from waiting on Ma that she could be in there for hours.

Now what?

A few feet away, there's a sidewalk newspaper stand with neighborhood papers. To buy a minute, I grab one, look down at it. The middle-aged white guy staring back at me sends a chill across my back. Smiling, friendly, like a guy you'd talk to in the grocery line. The headline over his picture says, *A Memorial Service for Our Fallen Son. Join Us to Commemorate the Life of Phillip Singer.*

The rightness feeling floods through me, before I even realize why. I know about funerals because my grandma loves them, always calls Ma afterwards spreading trash talk she got from the service. And now I know where Singer's people will be talking their trash on Tuesday. I stuff the paper in my jacket pocket. Ed's game led me here and this is what I find? It's gotta be right.

Brienne

Why do Saturdays feel so different? Not just 'cause no school and
you sleep late. The air feels different, the floor under your feet.
I'm standing in the hallway, about to text Chela to ask her, when I
remember she's got some yoga thing today. No one else I can send
that to, so I go on in the kitchen, pop in toast, and pour a bowl of
Special K. Ignoring the pounding on the ceiling from the little kids
upstairs, I pull up Ed's game, study it long enough to get confused,
and then get lucky 'cause Diamond messages me. And she definitely gets my attention.

Diamond: The image you are about to see may be disturbing
to some viewers

I put the bowl down and wait. Up pops a picture of—black golf
balls in a muffin tin?

Me: Ooh

Diamond: I tried to make Ms. Fox breakfast. But we got to talking upstairs.

Me: Didn't know her oven could burn stuff

Diamond: True. She told me something. She hired somebody to do music, since Jack's not around.

Me: Not permanently?

Diamond: She didn't say

Me: Oh

Diamond: I know

I'm about to ask if I can see her later, so we can talk more. But she says she's gotta go, Ms. Fox is calling. I don't even get to ask about the game.

Pushing the laptop to the side, I pull over my plate of toast. The plan was to work on the game all morning, while Bennett's out on shift. See if I can't chill things out with Ma. But now I'm thinking about Jack. Is Ms. Fox really giving up on him?

"Oh!" I hear Ma's surprise before I see her, standing at the end of the hallway in her gown and slippers. "You're here."

"Got up early," I say, pretending she's surprised about what time it is instead of that I'm here at all, not at Chela's. "Want me to put toast in for you?"

She shoots me a tired smile. I go around to the kitchen side of the counter and pop two slices in the toaster. I don't know what to say to her, so I go back to my stool, stuff toast in my mouth. Ma fills the silence getting down a plate and glass, pouring herself some of the iced chai she's addicted to.

I remind myself I'm ready for her. I'm sticking to my story about why the cop came here, but this time I'm not gonna lose it. Easy VZ for real. The toaster dings. Ma grabs her toast.

"I heard from Carole," she says.

"Who?" I ask. "You mean Jack's ma?" My stomach drops, because this isn't what I was ready for. And I'm realizing, too, there's something cagey about Ma this morning—like she knows something she's not saying. She curls her hand around the butter knife, sucks in her lips, and looks at me.

"She's worried out of her mind," she says. "She wants to know if you've seen Jack."

"Not since that day I told you," I lie. "At Yard."

"Carole hasn't seen him, either."

"Okay . . ."

Ma just stands there, making me wait for it. Finally she says, "Carole's got a friend on the force. They told her Jack's gonna get picked up any day now."

My brain races. A cop who knows Jack's ma said they were coming for him? Were they just trying to get intel, like when they came here? Or is it true?

"Victor." Ma steps up against the other side of the counter, puts her hand over mine. "All this staying away from home. You want to pretend all these horrible things aren't happening. You *want* to be the same sensible kid you've always been. But, you and Jack, you're not the same kids anymore. And if Jack's done something crazy—"

I yank my hand away. "Leave it alone, Ma! I'm fine. Jack's fine."

Ma gets that raw look I haven't seen since the divorce days. Like somebody opened a door behind her face to all the stuff that's locked away. And I don't want to know what's back there. I keep it together as I walk around her, put my plate in the sink. Grab Ed's laptop and disappear into my room. I decide to hit the streets, worry about where to go when I'm out of here. But when I'm back in the living room, packed to go, I stop with my hand on the knob. Ma's still standing where I left her, in front of her unbuttered toast.

"Jack's ma," I say. "Did the cop tell her anything else?"

"Like what?"

Like what kind of evidence they've got on him. "I don't know," I say. "Anything."

"Not that she mentioned," Ma says. "But I know one thing. If they told his mother all that, they've got eyes on him. They're not worried she'll be able to hide him away somewhere."

Another surprise. Didn't know Ma thought that way. "Yeah, okay," I say. Tell her I'll see her later, to give Sammy a kiss.

"Can you just slow down, Victor? Please?" she asks. The answer is a hard no, with everything she just told me. But I lie one more time, this time for her as much as me.

"Yeah, Ma. I will."

On the other side of the closed door, I stop, take a breath. Now what? I look down the hall, to the left—the opposite direction of the stairs, where I usually go. Maybe it's 'cause of what Ma said, but all of a sudden, it doesn't feel like just any Saturday. Feels like one of those Saturdays, way back, when Jack came over and the three of us'd hit the landing and just go—never bothered planning ahead. Jack even came by a bunch of Saturdays after Ed. Guess he quit doing it when he got too pissed at me.

For the first time in forever, I go toward Ed's.

The door's identical to mine except for the bronze 3B. How many Saturdays did the three of us spend up and down this hall while our mas worked their way through a box of Entenmann's? Once we got older, Ed was the reason we still hung some Saturdays. He'd get us to meet at the diner or the park, catch a movie—end up watching him watch dominoes. Jack got restless most of those days. Just did it because Ed asked. I wonder if he'd've kept hanging with us even if Brienne hadn't come along.

And it hits me—*Brienne.* If Jack's ma doesn't know where he is, then he's not with any of his family. And he's not at his place, or with me. Which means he's probably with a girl—and the last real girlfriend he had was Brienne.

I remember what Ma said about the cops having eyes on Jack. It means they'll have eyes on me if I find him. But I'm doing it anyway. Jack probably doesn't know what the cops told his ma, since he's not answering her calls. I can warn him. And I can find out why in hell he's following me.

Out on the street, I head to the subway that'll take me to Canarsie. I don't have a number for Brienne, but I know where she lives. Jack took any excuse to see her back in the day, and when his ma'd rented a car this one time, he took Ed and me by. Trouble is, I'm not sure of the subway stop. She lived on a side street, and it was close to Shirley Chisholm State Park. I remember seeing the sign and thinking the park looked kind of pitiful. Maps tells me the stop for the park.

The subway's chill, since it's Saturday morning. The ride goes fast, and I get off at a station that's unfamiliar. I can smell the ocean, which is nice. But I don't think I smelled it at Brienne's place, so I head away from it, start making my way into the tangle of streets, searching for anything familiar. It's easier than I expected, because Canarsie people like to decorate. I remember a bright yellow railing, a bodega with rosebushes out front, and a house with a Jamaican flag next to a nativity scene—still there, all these months past Christmas. And then, there it is. A place I'm pretty sure is Brienne's.

It's a brick two-family house that her parents live in. She's got the basement to herself, with its own side door. I walk past it, checking for the black sedan or any other cars that look like cops. Don't see any, so I walk back—and stand there. Not as easy as I thought, walking up to a girl's door out of nowhere. But if Jack's in there, I'm not leaving without talking to him. After too damn long, I suck in my gut and walk up to the door. Which opens before I even knock.

Brienne fills the doorway. I'd forgot that she's taller than me, just as big, and all about the curves. Got a round face and a long weave, parted in the middle. She frowns, surprised. "VZ, right? I remember you."

"Yeah? Thanks," I say, sounding as stupid as I feel. "It's been a minute."

Her face softens. "What are you doing here?"

"I want to see Jack," I say. "Is he here?"

She doesn't answer right away. Studies me. And I remember that's her way. Slow, kind of thoughtful. "He was," she says. "But he's gone. He won't be back."

He was. Even though she's saying he's not here now, I'm excited. I got it right, almost found him. Instinctively, I look back at the street behind me. "Are you sure he won't be back?" I ask. Brienne cocks her head to one side, eyes wide. Telling me, *Of course I'm sure.* She's about to close the door, so I say, "Can I talk to you anyhow? Just for a few?" I don't know what I want to say, but if Jack was here, she must know something. She pulls her phone out of her pocket.

"I can give you ten," she says. She looks inside for a minute, before stepping back to let me in. The door snaps shut behind me, and I feel like I landed on another planet. It's dark, with only a couple of high-up basement windows and a dim floor lamp turned on in the corner by the fridge. Mostly what I see is her bed, purple sheets and blankets all rumpled up. A pillow on the floor. The sound of running water makes me turn to some kind of fountain on the bedside table. It's all way too private. Brienne points to a little purple couch. When we sit, she's close enough to touch.

"I don't think I ever told you," she says. "How sorry I am about what happened to your friend."

"Oh," I say, completely off guard.

"I didn't see you at the funeral, right?" she asks. "Or any of the protests."

I can't actually believe we're talking about the funeral and the protests, but I don't know how to bring the conversation where I need it, either.

Brienne shrugs. "Protests definitely aren't everybody's thing. Sometimes they help me get out some anger, but those ones didn't. Not when I knew somebody who was as tore up as Jack by what happened." She twists her lips—purple like the couch—up under her nose. "If I'm being a hundred, I went to those protests 'cause Jack organized them. I had a hard time letting go back then."

I like that she's being honest like that. Feel myself relax.

"Jack thought the protests were everything," I say. "Like there was no other way to do right by Ed."

"Yeah?" she asks, studying me. "It was more like, no other way to keep busy, I thought. You know, keep from having to deal."

I'm still thinking about that when she says, "I always knew Jack ended us because of Ed. It was all part of how he coped, not being with me, because I made him happy. Putting everything he had into the protests. He thought he had to fix it, the way he always fixed things that went wrong for Ed. And I get that. I've got a little sister." She gestures toward the ceiling, and I get that her sister lives upstairs with their parents.

There're so many things I want to ask about. Jack using the protests to keep busy. Him leaving her because she made him happy, which seems different than because he felt guilty. I go with "You thought Ed was like a brother to Jack?"

"He called him that all the time. You, too. He called you both his little brothers." She grins, getting that the *little* part will rub me wrong. Which it does.

"Well," she adds. "Okay, not last night. Last night he was mad with you. He said you were running around trying to figure out if he killed Phillip Singer."

Last night? All I can do not to look at the rumpled bed, wonder if Jack was just in it. Then I get to what Jack said, accusing me of trying to find out if he killed Singer. Which is not what I'm doing. Mostly. Brienne looks at me with these steady eyes, like she can hear it, one way or another, whatever it is.

"That's not it," is all I can think to say.

"Okay," she says. "I told him he was probably being dumb."

"Something else new?" I ask. The rush of relief that she took my side relaxes me some more.

Brienne laughs. Waits.

"Okay," I say. "What I'm doing is trying to help him. As usual. And I just found out some shit he needs to know."

Brienne's still listening, but something's keeping me from telling Jack's used-to-be-girl his business. Then I think about him following me, and decide, *Fuck it*. I tell her what his ma said about the cops having eyes on him and them getting ready to pick him up for good. And I tell her what I'm up to.

"Jack said the cops won't look for other suspects since they've got it in their heads that he's the one who did it. And for once, he could be right. So, I'm out here trying to find something else, another lead to put in their heads—"

"Wait," Brienne says. "You're—?"

"Yes!" I say. "Looking for leads. And I'm actually getting somewhere. I'm doing it! And if he's trying to do the same thing, he's gonna fuck it up." I know I sound defensive, but I can't have her saying it's a dumb idea.

"Wow," Brienne says. "Jack said you—"

"*I what?*"

"—you backed off after what happened to Ed," she says. "He

130

said you didn't want to talk about it, even to him. You wouldn't hang out, or answer his calls. And I thought, well, that's probably just the way he grieves. But now it sounds like you're past all that. And good for you."

I want to full-on lose it. Jack put *his* disappearing act on me? But I shut up because I'm surprised and not surprised. I mean, did I know that? That he blamed me for backing off?

"Anyhow," Brienne says. "He really isn't coming back, so I don't see how I can help you."

"Right," I say. Bring my head back to the problem in front of me. I don't want to act like she's wrong about Jack coming back here, but he's a bigger fool than I thought if he lets her go for good. My ideas come out in a rush. "He could call you from some other number," I say, thinking of his burner. "And if he does, and you pick up, will you tell him I'm trying to *help* his ass? And he needs to trust people. And tell him his ma's a wreck and he should call her. And find out what she knows."

A little smile comes on Brienne's purple lips. "I made him call his mom before he left, so that's done, at least."

"She told him what the cops said?" I ask.

"Yeah," Brienne says. "Everything you just said." She presses her lips together, like she's not sure about letting her next thought out. "He told me all that, and then he said something I didn't understand. He said there was something he had to do, and if the cops were about to be on him, he'd better do it quick. And that's when he went booking out of here."

"Aw, fuck," I say. *Something he had to do, quick? What's this fool up to now?* "You ask him about it?"

She sighs. "He's a mess. He should have let me help him back then, when I wanted to."

"So you didn't ask," I say.

"I told him to be careful," she says. "Watch his back." A sad look pulls at her round face, but she shakes it off, flips her hair back. "I'm only telling you now because it sounds like you're both into some stuff. Anyhow—" She takes out her phone, letting me know my time's up. We get up and walk to the door. When she opens it, daylight shocks the hell out of me—like I forgot it existed. She tells me to take care of myself.

"You don't have a clue what he was talking about?" I ask, stepping outside. "This big thing he had to do?"

"No point in guessing if I don't want to know," she says. Steps back and closes the door. I don't waste time getting out of there. All I want is to walk fast and think about what just happened.

Ripples

"Can you not look so out of it?" Chela asks. "Doyle hates me. This is gonna be a total shit show. And where the fuck is Walendorf?"

It's early Monday and we're in the back of Ronnah's room waiting for circle, the sequel, to start. On the other side of the ring of chairs, Doyle, who Chela thinks is out to get her 'cause she iced her out in class Friday, is talking with Enright and Ronnah. Guz is by the door, and I'm glad he hasn't come harassing me about his game-design club. Chela's not wrong about me being out of it. Everything Brienne said about Jack's still rattling around my head. Then there's the five days till JersiGame and Singer's memorial *tomorrow*. After a Sunday of taking care of Sammy, I need time to think about my own shit. Right after I help Chela out.

"Doyle doesn't hate you," I tell her. "She's what my ma calls a flush-when-it-drops kind of person."

"A what?" She shoots me a curious squint in spite of her rotten mood.

"Somebody who flushes the toilet"—I do air quotes—"each time it drops."

"I don't think your mom said that," she says. Gives me half a grin, though.

"Uh . . . excuse me." Guz's voice interrupts us. He's in the middle of the room now, turning his skinny self on the spot, like he's got some big announcement. "Just heard from Bruce!" he says. "He's— uh. He's not coming. He's not sick or anything, he's just . . . not coming."

"What?" Chela takes a step toward Guz, eyes hot enough to melt metal. She turns to Ronnah. "He can't be serious. Walendorf can't just bail, right?"

Ronnah's thick brows slide over her cat-eye glasses. "Anyone can bail before agreements are final," she says. "As long as you and Ms. Doyle are here, the circle goes on. Unless you want to stop it?"

"No, but . . ." Chela goes red-faced at her crush calling her out.

"Then let's get to our seats," Ronnah tells us. She pulls one of the empty chairs out of the circle, and Guz jumps in to move the others closer together. I tell Chela it's gonna be all right, which I'm starting to think is a lie. When Doyle takes her seat, she leans forward, loafers flat on the floor, looking colder than I've ever seen her. The circle feels too small now. Across from me, Guz is close enough to touch if we both stick our hands out. He pulls off his jacket, and I do a double take. He's got on an acid-green T-shirt with a giant decal of SirBugUs, Ed's boss bad guy, on the front. The body and all three heads are glossy black. Six creepy eyes shine. Six legs go every which way. Across the bottom, it says: "EDG Camp. In honor of the brilliant gamesmanship of Ed Hennessey."

Guz notices me. "Sweet, huh?" he says, smug grin lighting up his whole face. "Got them made for the club. Brought in twenty new members already."

I'm not surprised, because fuck if the shirt isn't perfect. I don't answer Guz, though. And, anyway, Ronnah's starting the circle and Chela's already gone stiff in her seat. After the intros, Ronnah puts out the first question:

"What's come up for you since last circle—including Bruce not coming today, if that affects you?"

Guz gets to go first, now Walendorf's gone. He's into it, like before. Eyes wide, tent-shaped brows high on his forehead.

"I told Bruce he should come," he says, righteous as ever. "I told him, 'People are gonna be mad at you. You think they treated you bad before, but they'll be super pissed-off now. And it'll be, like, like these ripples'"—he props the apple between his knees, uses his hands to do ripple-motions—"'these really bad ripples that spread further and further out, with what happened to Ed in the middle. You know, where the stone fell.'"

Chela scooches her chair closer to mine. "Did he just say we treated Walendorf bad?" she hisses in my ear. *"Unbelievable."*

Doyle takes the apple. "It doesn't affect me, whether or not Bruce is here," Doyle says. "But I've given this process a lot of thought since last time. We can't have students knowing a teacher got a black eye and the school didn't respond." She points to her eye even though the shiner's gone now. "I'd like us to recommend a policy to make sure something like this doesn't happen again."

A groan only I can hear comes out of Chela. Enright agrees with Doyle, as usual, and the apple goes to Chela, who steals a glance at Ronnah, before talking.

"I'm not dodging responsibility," she says. "But I hate that Walendorf's not here. The day this went down, he was in my face, saying something ugly about something really painful. And that's why what happened happened." There's a shake in her voice but she keeps on. "It's not like I walked up to Ms. Doyle and just hit her! And now Walendorf gets to erase himself out of it, and I'm here, alone, to take all the blame . . ." Her voice trails off.

The room feels extra quiet as Chela hands me the apple. Before I take it, Doyle jumps in.

"I'm sorry," she says. "But this is not what I came here for. That sounded like a lot of deflection and excuses, and—"

Ronnah throws a hand up, cuts her off since she doesn't have the apple. Doyle doesn't look sorry.

Chela swallows. "It's not what I came for, either," she says. "Walendorf was supposed to be here."

"That doesn't change your responsibility!" Doyle says. She's in full-on teacher mode, not caring that it's not her turn to talk. But Chela's not giving up.

"It changes *something*!" she insists.

"Not to me!" Doyle shoots back.

"*That's enough, please!*" Ronnah holds her hand out for the apple. When she gets it, she takes off her glasses, sits back in her chair. "High emotions," she says, "are absolutely welcome here. We just need to listen to each other. So. When your turn comes, please tell us whatever it is that you need to say right then. When it's not your turn, your job is to listen."

Chela takes in a slow, steady breath. I don't like how this is going. Chela's miserable, and Ronnah's acting like we're all supposed to have some big important thing to say, which I don't.

When he gets the apple, Guz comes out of left field. "I'm the one that got Bruce to come to this in the first place," he says. "I don't know, maybe it's worse with him quitting halfway than if he never came at all. I just thought it'd be a chance to talk about what happened to Ed, and all the ripples from it." He shrugs, and the bug on his shirt moves with him. "Isn't it always worse if you don't talk about it?"

He reminds me of Jack. For the umpteenth time since I left Brienne's, I think about what Jack told her. . . . *He said you didn't want to talk about it, even to him. You wouldn't hang out, or answer his calls.* Okay. On one hand, there's something real there. It's on me that I quit answering his texts. Because before that, Jack wasn't nasty when he tried to get me to go to the demos. But he got nasty, later. And weird. And he quit showing up for me, like on those Saturdays. . . .

"Here's what I have to say." Doyle's voice, high-pitched and intense, brings me back to the circle. She undoes her scarf, pivots in her chair. Laser-focuses on Chela. I shift in my seat, too, give my attention back to what's in front of me.

"You still don't understand what you did," Doyle says. "I was doing my job, I was planning my lesson, which is hard enough as a new teacher. And out of nowhere, my face exploded in pain, in front of my whole class. I was confused and hurt and—and then some of them were *laughing*. And I had to *deal* with all of that." She holds her face hard and steady. "It doesn't matter if you knew I was behind that door. Because *I was* behind it. And using that kind of force in a school is not something that should go unaddressed!"

Everybody's heads turn from Doyle to Chela. I know Enright's gonna pass, so I whisper a quick "You got this" in Chela's ear.

"*How?*" she whispers back.

For a long time, it's all she says, even after she gets the apple. I'm about to ask if she's okay, when she says, "I'm just gonna say it. I hear Ms. Doyle. I get how bad it must've been for her. But I want her to understand how it was for me, too."

There's a beat of silence. When Chela talks again, her voice's stronger. "Every time I see those posters of Ed? I think of him and VZ. And my guy cousins who I worry about all the time. Then, that day, Walendorf sees that same poster, and he comes with some crap about how *the guy who killed Ed* shouldn't've got killed." Her voice gets louder with every sentence. "He didn't say how bad it was that *Ed* got killed. He went straight to Singer, like what happened to Ed wasn't part of something so much bigger, so old and huge and . . . ahhhh! How was I supposed to explain that? To *Walendorf.* When I knew he wouldn't get it!"

I don't bother trying to follow that. But I think about how Guz wasn't lying about the ripples. So much happened because of what Singer did to Ed. Chela in trouble for the first time ever. Doyle having a black eye and this new pissed attitude. Jack and me getting so we don't know how to be with each other.

Ronnah tells us we did good work, and she hopes we heard each other. Gives us a stretch break. Outside the window, kids are grouping up, waiting on the bell.

"You all right?" I ask Chela.

"Fuck if I know," she says.

When Ronnah brings us back, she's got a question that's just for Doyle.

"And it might be tough," she says. "You said what happened to you shouldn't go unaddressed. I'd like to know if you actually meant un*punished*. I have to ask because these circles deal in accountability—people taking responsibility for harmful behavior and then doing something about it. If you're more interested in punishment, this process may not be right for you."

Everybody turns to Doyle, who picks at the knees of her pants before she talks. Chela takes a breath, holds it.

"In this particular case," Doyle says. "Accountability is fine. *But*. It's a slippery slope. I want a policy that links this to more deliberate acts of violence. We have to be clear in advance that we won't tolerate them."

"Would your policy include stuff like what Walendorf said?" Chela asks when her turn comes. "Because that hurts, too, and people should be accountable for it, right? Just because something isn't physical, doesn't mean it isn't violent."

She looks at me, brown eyes so full of understanding that it startles me. Then I remember, she came over back when I was stuck as fuck. Did I tell her about the red-hot body aches, or the shitty Ed-thoughts pinning me like a hundred dumbbells?

I don't appreciate the attention she's sending my way, right now, but I take the apple. Say, "All right, yeah. Violence doesn't just come at you physically."

Voices and the sound of moving feet come from the hallway. I shove the apple at Ronnah.

"Good work," she says. "Lots of interesting ideas between us. So, now it's time to turn them into action, to actually make things better for Ms. Doyle and our community." She leans in closer, eyeing each of us. "At Ed's funeral, his mom said that we have to find a better way than violence. When we're angry or scared, we have to find a new way. And she also said, we *all* have to be accountable when we hurt each other. In that spirit, I'm proposing, for our first agreement, that we make a statement to the school that says those things. But we don't limit it to physical violence, as Chela suggested. Ms. Doyle will get a school-wide response, but it won't just be about physical acts."

She asks us to agree, disagree, or amend. Before she hands off to Guz, Chela signals for us to fast-track the apple to her.

"Okay," she says. "I think I know how to say it this time. I shouldn't have rammed into that door. I shouldn't have, because I was at school, and I didn't know who could have been behind it. And because people matter, and Ms. Doyle's had to deal with a lot because of what I did." She licks her lips, looks straight at Doyle. "So, yes. I agree to the statement. And I hope Ms. Doyle will, too." She's wearing a relieved grin as she hands me the apple. I know it's big for her, saying what she needed to, getting the words right.

"I'm in," I say.

Guz gives a thumbs-up.

When Doyle takes the apple, she's twisting the scarf between her fingers. Again, talks right to Chela.

"My heart bled for Ed's mother at that service," she says. "Her wound was deeper than even just losing him. I know that's what you meant about the thing being huge and horrible. And I appreciate what you said just now. So, yes. I can live with that agreement."

"*Thank fuck*," Chela whispers, as Enright agrees with Doyle.

After that, we all suggest agreements. End up doing the statement, plus Chela has to write about violence and anger, turn it in to Enright, and, once it's approved, teach it to kids during lunch-and-learns. I agree to help her and Guz does, too, though nobody asked him. On top of all that, Chela has to help Ms. Doyle after school for a month.

Ronnah makes us wait after the bell to sign the agreements, which include what happens if people don't come through. Chela signs, looking so happy, she's like a different person from the one who started the day.

"You did good," I tell her, as I sign. I'm glad she got what she needed. Doyle, too. But a bad feeling's starting to settle over me. That was a lot of Ed-talk, and I can't see how it does me any good.

"Got you a present," Guz says. Tosses me something big and acid green. The "SirBugUs" T-shirt in XL. "On the house. Ed would want you to know what he could do."

He takes off, and his shit-eating grin seems to hang in the air like the damn Cheshire cat. Chela takes the shirt and holds it up, the back facing us. On that side, it says, "Join Us!" Then there's an orange letter *U*, a red letter *E*, and a black *Y-E-T*.

Ed's riddle.

"I'm not saying he's not a prick," she says. "But the shirt's good."

I don't laugh. I don't need Guz to show me what Ed could do. Everybody thinks they're doing shit for Ed, but I'm the one who's got his masterpiece. His game. I glance at the shirt. *Aren't you ready yet?*

"Whatever," I say, snatching it back from Chela. "I'm making the game happen for Ed. And it'll be way better than a stupid T-shirt."

Yo! Sweetums!

"What could go wrong?" Chela asks. "We're just spying on a bunch of racist white folks at a memorial service, trying to frame them for murder." We're perched on milk crates outside an old bodega a block away from Singer's service. I toss the cup from my first mega iced coffee, stick the straw down in my second. I'm fired up. Got the laptop in my pack for later, because I'm not blowing off Ed's game anymore. Chela's back to normal after the circle, and we're actually going to the memorial, which is way better than being home worrying about it.

"Other way around," I tell Chela. "We're not framing *them*. We're trying to keep Jack from *getting* framed."

"Eh," she says. "Details. Let's go."

It's five o'clock, and the block's the busy commercial kind, bakeries and clothes shops. As we walk, I shake out my arms, straighten the cuffs on the button-down I've got over my T-shirt. The plan is to look like we're just hanging out, enjoying our iced coffees. Then, when people take breaks, like they do at stuff like this, we'll be right there, eavesdropping outside the church.

I don't actually believe Jack would be nuts enough to come here, but I can't help looking for him anyway. There's no sign of him, but as we get closer, I see something else I didn't expect. A group of Black people standing on the sidewalk. Holding what looks like a bedsheet between them. We stop.

"What's this about?" I ask.

We get the answer quick because they open the sheet. There's pictures on it. Row after row of pictures. Black people who got famous for getting killed by white people. Trayvon and Michael and Eric and Breonna and Ahmaud . . .

"Still wanna do this?" Chela asks.

"'Course," I say, way more chill than I feel. I scan the rows of pictures and find what I know'll be there. The blue-striped shirt. Light brown eyes. I suck down more coffee, remember I'm following the clue from Ed's game, which so far's been keeping me on track.

"That's powerful," Chela says as we reach the sheet holders.

"Hang around if you want," a guy tells her. He's thirty maybe. Short hair and a scar under his eye. "Believe it or not, that's Phillip Singer's memorial service in there." He chin-points to the church, which is just an ordinary building except it's got fresh paint and bright white doors. Standing in front of them are a bunch of white guys in military uniforms. All of them sporting white hair, big bellies, and old-man shoes.

"Vets," the sheet-holding guy says. "Protecting the good people who wanted to pay their respects to Phillip Singer. But there's nothing they can do to us. As long as we don't block the sidewalk, we're in our rights." Two of the women with him unfold another sheet. It's got the names of all the same victims written out. They're surrounding the entrance to the church with all the people who were killed like Ed. Names on one side, faces on the other.

"*Crap*," Chela whispers. "Good for them, but nobody's coming out for a break if they have to look at all of this."

"How long will y'all be here?" she asks the sheet guy, who's not bothering to hide that he's checking her out.

I walk a little way away. The thing about that picture of Ed is, it's not just sad 'cause of what happened. It's also a dumb picture. Ed's ma liked it 'cause it looks like Ed's having some kind of deep thought. But that's not what it is. We talked about it, Jack and me. How Ed had on his Eddie Murphy face—the one you see in the movies when Eddie's supposed to be paying attention to something, but really he's about to let one loose. And his face is saying, *I can't be stressed about what's going on right now 'cause I'm listening to my inner fart joke.*

"They're staying till the end," Chela says, coming over.

"Oh," I say. Take a last slurp of iced coffee, which is just ice now. Not bad, being pumped up on game clues, coffee, and fart jokes. "Okay. You don't need an invitation to a memorial service, right? We have to go in there, eavesdrop inside instead of out here."

Chela cocks an eyebrow, and I like being the one with the wack plan for a change. She shrugs. "Why not?" I feel the protesters' eyes on our backs as we walk to the church doors. The old guys see us coming, stick out their chests. Chela gestures that she wants the lead.

"How can we help you?" It's a round-faced old guy with wispy white hair.

"We're going to the service," Chela says, polite as damn Sunday school. "For Mr. Singer. We're friends of the family."

The old guys stare. Finally, the round-faced one says, "You were just talking with those kids down there. They're not here for the service."

"Just being polite," I jump in. I don't say it that polite, though. Because now I'm here, I really want in. The killer could be in there, hiding behind preachers and funeral clothes.

"Uh-huh," the old guy says. "Mm-hmm." He silent-chats with his buddies. "They might be praying. Can't let people in during prayers." The prayer thing surprises me. Before I can react, he slips inside. Another guy steps in front of the door.

"I don't think they're praying at all," Chela says, taking over. "*I* think *you* think we're here to cause trouble. But, honestly, we just want to pay respects." She inches closer to the door. But the round-faced guy's back. A white girl with pink hair sticks her head out behind him.

"No," she says. "I don't fucking know them!" Instead of going back inside, she pushes the door open, a pack of cigarettes already out of her dress pocket.

In a heartbeat, Chela slides through the wide-open door, me

right behind her. Now we're in an entry hall. Soft lights, organ music, the big wooden doors to the sanctuary open in front of us. The old vets are behind us, and I know they're stuck. No way to get us out without making a scene. Before they can decide, Chela and I walk inside the sanctuary. The air's heavy, alive. Rows and rows of pews full of people who came for Singer. The iced coffee in my stomach starts to turn. I know sitting down would make me feel trapped in here. I pull Chela to the back wall. We stand next to a table with Bibles on it.

Slowly, I look around the room. The ceilings are high. Gold shines up there. At the altar, a big white Jesus hangs on a cross. I think of Ed's ma's little sidewalk church, how the crucifix painting freaked him out when he was little. The place is less than half-full, people spread out in the pews, backs straight. I look from one to the next. None of the white necks are tattooed with *I killed Singer*.

Up front, the preacher's got a dull, sad tone. Says something about losing "our fallen son."

A shadow falls across the doorway. The girl with the pink hair's back. She stands a sec, showing much leg in her short dress. Then takes a seat in the back row. I still don't see Singer's girlfriend, the woman in red.

"Whoa," Chela whispers. "Veeze . . ." She leans closer. "It's . . . that's Robbie. That's Robbie there, next to Pink Hair." I look back at the girl who'd gone for the smoke. Next to her's a kid in a black suit. Looks familiar, but . . .

"I'm sure," Chela says. Pressing her lips together, she looks around. Walks up behind him, bends to whisper in his ear. When he turns, it's Robbie-the-driver looking shocked as hell to see her here—which is pretty much how I feel about seeing him. A second later, Robbie gets up, steps to the aisle. Chela and I are right behind him. Going out the front door feels like breaking free of an airless hole. Soon as we're out Chela grabs Robbie's arm, pulls him to the sidewalk.

"Why in God's name were you in there?"

"Uh . . . ," Robbie says. He looks like a whole other guy with his hair slicked back, white shirt under his suit jacket. "It's not what you think—"

"Rob, what the hell?" the pink-haired girl yells. She's storming out of the church, looking pissed. "Who's she?"

The protesters perk up, start paying attention. I'm still by the church doors with the old guys. Watching. Because there's something familiar about the pink-haired girl.

"She's a friend of mine," Robbie says to the pink-haired girl.

Chela's got serious saucer-eyes. "Holy shit," she says. "This is why we got apology weed? It wasn't guilt about the car thing! It's because you *knew* that creep!"

"Whatever." The pink-haired girl gives a massive yank on Robbie's arm. "Rob, let's get outta here. I'm done!"

"Jeez!" Robbie says, trying to shake her off.

"Just answer me!" Chela says. But the pink-haired girl's not having it.

"Yo! Sweetums!" she yells at Robbie. "I need the fuck outta here. Now!"

My caffeine-laced adrenaline pumps up another notch and I

move toward them. *Sweetums?* I know where I heard that before. Whoever the pink-haired girl is, I'm betting my ass she knows Singer's girlfriend. I jog the short way to the sidewalk.

"Who's your friend?" I ask Robbie.

"Not you, too!" he says. "Look . . . let's not—"

"Jesus, who the hell *are these people?*" the girl asks. Chela catches my eye, gets that I know something—or hopes I do. She shuts up. All three of us are waiting now for Robbie to say something. He wags his head, defeated.

"This is Junie," he says. "She's . . ." His tongue rolls over his bottom lip, slides back in. "She's why I'm here. She's Phil Singer's kid."

The Devil's Daughter

I must've known it was coming. I'd heard Singer's probably-girl-friend say "sweetums." But still. *Singer's kid? Right in front of me?*

"We, uh, went to school together," Robbie says. "Way back, like middle school."

"Yeah, well, great to meet you," the girl says, dripping sarcasm. She's so white she looks almost see-through. "Can we get out of here, Rob? I don't care where we go, just get me the fuck outta here."

Robbie tries to pull us to the side, but the girl's right behind him. "Look," Robbie says. "I know this is weird. . . ."

Singer's kid, I think. *The kid of the guy who killed Ed.* She's young. Cute. Couldn't look less like Singer. But my body doesn't know that. Something sharp and acidy boils in my gut. And at the same time, I'm thinking—she must know stuff. Has to. If somebody

150

close to Singer killed him, his kid's a hell of an intel source.

"Like she said," I say. "Yeah. Let's get out of here."

"All of us?" Robbie looks like I've lost my mind.

"All of us, Rob," Chela says. "You got that great car of yours. Let's go get some chow."

"Whatever," the girl says, like she's been in the conversation all along. "Let's just go. I vote for pizza."

She takes the front seat, a slice of pink neck showing under her pink hair. I stare at it. The car feels the size of a coffin. Robbie gets in, twists around in his seat, asks if I'm sure. I nod. And he drives off.

"What a shit show," the girl says to Robbie, ignoring Chela and me. "I don't know how long you were in there, but those assholes actually—"

"Junie!" Robbie cuts her off. "Look, I needa concentrate on driving, okay. We're gonna—I guess we're gonna go for pizza, all right?"

"Whatever," the girl says. But a minute later she's pointing out the windshield. "Pizza Beach, right? How come you're going this way?"

"Just gimme a minute!" Robbie snaps. He takes a few more turns, and I know he's buying time till he can think what to do. I wonder if the girl can feel me staring at her. If Robbie's right and I lost my mind. All I know is, I'm feeling big hot anger, and there's zero reason to try and shut it down.

Robbie slows the car. "All right, there it is," he says, pulling into a parking space. A "Pizza Beach" sign's at the end of the block. There's something final in the sound of our shutting the doors, *thwup, thwup, thwup.* Then we're walking up the sidewalk. My eyes stuck to the girl, hers on Robbie, who's marching straight ahead, not looking at any of us. Inside, it's tiny, two rows of booths with a skinny aisle between. Not too crowded, and not all white people, I notice. The smell of baking crust hangs in the air as the girl slides into an empty booth, her pink hair clashing with the red plastic seat cushions. I sit across from her, feel the hardness of my face. Grip the table. There's nothing between me and Singer's kid but a strip of wood with a red checked tablecloth. I ignore the part of me that's shouting to get the hell out of here.

Robbie starts spouting random mouth-diarrhea. "Like I said, Junie here, we grew up in the neighborhood together. And she's, uh, you know, Phil Singer's kid. But we—"

"Stepkid!" the girl cuts in, loud, sharp. "Not his kid, his step-kid. Not even that, since he never married Ma." She's got a serious Brooklyn accent. I know her type, tough-girl cute.

"You ordering?" a guy behind the counter yells. Robbie looks relieved.

"Italian sausage and red pepper," he shouts back.

"Trust me, all right?" he says to us.

"Singer's *stepkid*?" Chela asks the girl, too loud. "So your mom's with that creep?"

The noise level in the place drops. The guys at the next table, all Black guys, zone in on Singer's kid. Robbie makes a show of standing up, telling the pizza guy he forgot to ask for double cheese and why not make it two small pies instead of one large. I catch Chela's eye, have a whole conversation without talking. Even though we

152

rode here together, we didn't want to say too much in the back of Robbie's car. Now we're here, though, we have to deal. Find a way to get useful information out of Singer's stepkid.

"And you lived with him?" I ask, thinking about the second-story apartment with the driveway.

"So? Who cares if I lived with him?" She lets out an irritated sigh. "Why don't we just get it over with?" she says, looking from me to Chela. "I'll even get you started. Phillip Singer was a racist asshole, and any kid of his—or any stepkid—must be an asshole, too. So I should get my racist white ass out of your face, right? Trust me, I've heard it all before."

She's trying to stare me down, and I like it. I want her to be a jerk, like Singer.

"Shy type?" she taunts, like we're little kids. "Cat got your tongue?"

"*They knew him!*" Robbie says, in a tight whisper.

"Knew who?" the girl asks.

My stomach rolls with hate.

Then, she gets it. "Oh," she says. "Ed Hennessey. Of course. Like I said, I've heard it all. People who went to school with him, his teachers. He was a saint, right? Saint Ed Hennessey."

She's a piece of work, I think. The fake smile on my face feels creepy. I hope it looks that way to her.

"Like the memorial wasn't bad enough," she mutters. "Half of them there to turn it into a shit show, the other half acting like it wasn't one. His buddies trying to give me *flowas*, for God's sakes. And now, fucking this."

I want her to keep talking, but the pizza guy comes over, a pie on each palm. Smelling so good that for a second, it's all I think about. But instead of putting the food down, the guy just stands there, till we look up at him. Wiry, white. Long hair tied with a bandanna. "Everything okay here, Junie?" he asks.

"Leave it, Mike," the girl says. "Okay? I can't take any more today." She pulls out her glittery pink iPhone, fiddles with it like she can't be bothered with the rest of us. The pizza guy glances around the table, giving us some kind of warning. I hold his gaze, let him know I don't give a shit what he thinks. Finally, he puts the pies down. Robbie starts playing host again, serving up slices.

And I remember that I'm here to get intel from Singer's kid. Pick up on the first scrap that comes to mind. "Why's it bad?" I ask.

"Huh?"

"You said Singer's buddies wanted to give you flowers like it was a bad thing."

She narrows her eyes, suspicious. "Some of 'em are assholes," she says. Plays with the garlic shaker. "The whole thing was stupid, Phil's brothers, Ma's family. Those kids from the hospital."

"Hospital?" Chela and I both ask. Pink-haired Junie looks at us like we're way too deep in her business.

"What's with you?" she asks. "This some freaky shit 'cause you knew Ed Hennessey?"

Hearing his name come out of her mouth doesn't help me calm down. I look at Chela, see if she has a clue how to get what we want from this girl. She tries.

"No, no! It, uh . . . it looked like an okay service to me," she says.

Bad call. Junie narrows her eyes even more.

"Jesus, I forgot. You were the two who were trying to get in. What was that about?"

Damn.

"Nothing!" Chela says. "We were curious. We weren't gonna make a scene or anything. We just . . . wanted to see."

"Because who doesn't love being a circus act?" Junie says. Chela shuts up, 'cause she knows she blew it.

"I get that," Robbie says, surprising me. "When somebody dies, like their friend, you wanna know everything you can know, right?"

We go quiet. Even though it's not why we went to Singer's service, what he said's still true. I guess we all know it. Chela lost her dad in a lousy accident. I lost Ed. And this Junie girl lost Singer.

"Whatever," Junie says. With less heat, though. "You couldn'ta made it any worse. Ma's family, assholes from her job. Guys from Phil's job, and his"—she shoots a look at Robbie—"his *other* job . . ."

My eyes move between the two of them. If their look means what I think it means, there's shady shit about Singer's *other job*— maybe the "job" that got him the rap sheet. I'm so ready to hear it, to get to my next clue. But Singer's kid quits talking, turns toward the aisle. Two guys, the Black kids from the next table, are coming up to us. One steps right to the edge of our table, the other one behind him. The guy in front's got glasses, a skimpy beard. Got his hands in the pockets of his black hoodie. There's something off about his face.

"What's up?" I ask.

He doesn't answer for a couple of beats too long. Then he raises the pocket of his sweatshirt. Points it at us. *Like there's a gun in there.* My body functions slow way down. Heartbeat, breathing. The guy's looking straight at Singer's kid.

"Gimme your phone," he says. I laser-focus on the hand with the gun. The red-brown color of the wristbone sticking out of the sweatshirt pocket, the Adidas symbol on the cuff. I do the math: four against two. Four at the table, two standing. Another thought pops in the back of my mind. Four Black people, two Singerites . . .

The pocket moves. "Give me your phone!" Louder this time. The sweatshirt pocket's right in Singer's kid's face. I could grab it, but that'd be stupid. No sudden moves, right? A quick look tells me the guys behind the counter haven't caught on.

"Give it to him," I say to Singer's kid. Which she should know. Somebody pulls a gun, you do what they say! The guy with the gun turns to me. Our eyes lock, and I wonder if he's coming for me now. His hand moves. Instinctively, my hand shoots out, pushes his back and down. It's too easy. I'm on my feet, figuring my next move. But the guy's—laughing. He steps back. Pulls out his sweatshirt pockets to show they're empty.

"Oh, hilarious," Singer's kid says. "Splitting my gut, it's so funny." She turns to Robbie. "Did I tell you? Did I tell you, I can't fucking go anywhere without bullshit like this?"

I'm watching the jerk with the fake gun, not believing anybody'd be that dumb. He quits laughing, pushes his glasses up his nose. I get what's going on with his face, now. He's got old-man eyes, like he's seen too much and it all sucked. There's so much going on in his eyes that Singer's kid quits babbling. She watches him like the rest of us, waiting.

"You're right," he says to her. "Not funny. You know how many kids do time for stupid shit like that? *Robbery with what appears to be a weapon.* Hundreds, probably thousands. Not your pops, though. He shot a kid *dead* and didn't do a single day. That sound fair to you?"

"How's that supposed to be my fault!" Singer's kid says. "Do I look like a cop to you? Or a district fucking attorney?"

"I'm just telling the truth," the kid says. He makes like he's going back to his seat, but Singer's kid stands up.

"It wasn't up to me that he didn't go to jail!" she says. "But I'm not sorry! You wanna know what would've happened if Phil had done time? I'd be in a shelter right now, because Ma can't pay the mortgage from doing nails and Phil wasn't a life insurance kind of guy."

Doing nails. Sounds like Singer's girlfriend was going to work when I saw her that morning, not getting her nails done. I wonder if there's a clue in that.

"Aw, that's rough," the backup guy says, all sarcastic.

"Oh, yeah?" A fierce look comes on the girl's pale face. "Okay, I'll tell you something else. The only reason we're not going to a shelter *now* is 'cause there's plenty of people who think what Phil did was a good thing. They're sending my ma money. And she's taking it. Enough to pay the whole back mortgage." Angry-looking tears stand in her eyes. She shoves at Robbie to make him get up. "So, there you go," she says. "That should keep you talking all fucking month."

She pushes past Robbie and busts out the door. But I don't want to lose her yet—not when things were just getting good. I kick Chela under the table, nod to the door, asking her to follow, which'll go over a helluva lot easier than me doing it. Chela rolls her eyes but goes.

"Damn." It's the kid who's been playing backup to the fake-gun fool. We all nod, watch the door close behind Junie and Chela. *Damn* pretty much covers it. Robbie and I stay where we are when the other guys go back to their table. My phone buzzes. It's Diamond.

Diamond: It's getting weirder. Can you come?

Diamond Roller Coaster

I hang on to the subway pole, eyes closed. Only for Diamond would I be on this train tonight, instead of playing Ed's game. But I won't sleep before I play, no matter what. And after today, I could use a hit of Diamond.

The scene plays like a TikTok in my head. The pocket going up in Junie's face. The slo-mo feeling. Me thinking *four Black people and two white Singerites*. Not like I wanted him to shoot her. Maybe I even knew he wouldn't.

More important, though, is what happened before we got interrupted. Singer's kid'd been telling us who was at the service. *Ma's family, assholes from her job. Guys from Phil's job, and his—his other job.* When she said it, she'd shot a look at Robbie, like there was something about the other work she wasn't gonna say in front of us.

It's not much, but it could have something to do with whatever got Singer a rap sheet. I text Chela.

> **ME:** If you're still talking to her, see if you can get intel about Singer's "other job."

At my stop, I take my time walking to the restaurant, my caffeine high draining away. It's clear out, the moon pale white in the dark starless sky. I stop under the green neon sign, check the cars in the lot, making sure none of them are police. There're two blue ones that make my heart stop before I realize they're just regular cars. Now I'm here, my body's on alert, focused on Diamond's message. *It's getting weirder. Can you come?*

The dining room's quiet, no staff in sight. In the kitchen, my stomach roars at the smell of roasting fish, reminding me I never got any pizza. Ms. Fox is chopping at the sideboard.

"Ah," she says, like the sight of me explains something. "Diamond called for you, eh? No surprise, with the two of them shouting to wake the dead." She reaches for the pan on the cooling rack, sticks a sweet potato fry in my mouth. I look around, see Fisk's blue scooter leaned against the back wall.

"Diamond and Fisk?" I ask, after chewing. Try to keep my voice chill. "They're fighting?"

Ms. Fox shoots me a smirk, like she knows all my business. "She's out back," she says. "Nursing her wounds. And he's down in the cellar." I grab a handful of fries and hurry out through the kitchen door, feeling like this shit of a day might actually end okay, if Diamond and Fisk are in a fight and she's calling me. Diamond's huddled in her jean jacket, sitting on the bench by the back door.

160

It's next to the dumpster, but I only smell Diamond. Fresh and flowery, like a field I want to lay down in. Enough light comes through the kitchen window to take the edge off the darkness.

"Thanks for coming," Diamond says, smiling through tears. "I didn't know who else to call."

I'm too tired to front. "Because you had a fight with Fisk?" I ask.

"Ms. Fox told you?" she asks. "Yeah, we had a fight. We fight all the time, these days, it's not even just that I told him about our kiss." Damn if I don't feel the words *our kiss* in all the right places.

"But that wasn't all," she says, sliding over on the bench so I can sit next to her. "Something happened right after the fight. Fisk stomped out and I was in the kitchen alone, feeling awful. And the burner rang in the lost and found drawer."

"The burner phone?" Whatever I expected to hear, it wasn't that.

"I didn't want to answer it," Diamond says. "But I had to know. You know, like when there's a crazy person on the subway and you know if you look at them they might come at you, but you look anyhow because you have to know what they're up to? My hands were shaking when I picked the thing up."

"So, what happened?" I ask, needing her to get to the point.

"Whoever it was stayed on a long time. They kind of breathed heavy. And they said . . . something about disappearing, like, 'Might want to make this phone disappear,' something like that."

"What kind of voice?" I ask.

"I don't know. Maybe they were drunk or something."

That makes me feel better. Could've been a random wrong number. Some drunk fool not making sense. Diamond closes her

161

eyes like she's fighting bad memories, and I drink her in while she can't see me. We stay that way long enough that I know she knows I'm watching. Then she opens her eyes, gives me another sad smile. But there's more in it this time. Something just for me. She slips her hand in mine.

"Maybe it wasn't just the phone," she says. "I was thinking about us, too, when I called you."

"Yeah?" I sound hoarse as shit. The whole day: the memorial, the pizza place. It all feels like it's laying itself out in front of Diamond, for her to make it better. I don't care about the burner phone, Singer's kid. Pocket pistols. I just want to be with her, let her look at me like this.

"You and me," she says. "We never talked about what happened at Coney Island."

"I wanted to," I tell her. "It's just . . . you pretended it didn't happen. I didn't know what you wanted."

Here we go, I think. We're finally back to where we were on the beach. I'm about to be kissing Diamond again.

"It's confusing, with Fisk," she says. "But the truth is, you and me, we've been so close since . . . that night." She means the night Ed died. I go stiff, hating her making it about that.

"That's got nothing to do with it," I say.

"It *does*, VZ," she says. "What happened to Ed is part of everything for us. We can't help it or change it. It just is." She twists around at the sound of voices from the kitchen.

"Can we talk . . . later?" she asks. "Fisk left when he got so mad with me. I thought he wasn't coming back, and you could fill in for him. But he did come back, so . . ." She squeezes my hand. "I don't have to work tomorrow night. Maybe you could come over then and we can talk . . . ?"

I squeeze her hand back. I'm not turning this down, not letting that last part ruin what she said before. We stand up, and she wipes away the last of her tears. The smell of fresh roti mixes with the fish as we walk back into the kitchen. Ms. Fox flips it over in the pan as the door to the dining room swings open. Fisk comes in. He and Diamond look at each other, but only for a second. She pushes past, goes into the dining room.

"I thought you weren't working tonight," Fisk says to me, pretend casual. The kitchen's small enough that we're close. I straighten my back.

"Just came for a visit," I tell him.

"Cool," he says. Doesn't do a bad job of faking like he means it. Then he turns up the bullshit grin. "Better get back out there. There's a table of dudes all over Diamond. Gotta show 'em who's boss."

I don't answer. Hope my face says who might be showing who, soon enough. Ms. Fox eyes me, like she knows something went down outside. When Fisk goes back to the dining room, she says, "Who would tink me restaurant would be a stage for teenage children and them love troubles?"

I laugh, grab another handful of fries. Watch her sauté a pan of spices till they let off a new delicious smell. My muscles relax for the first time since who knows when. By the time I head outside, I actually feel decent. The homeless guy's turned up. I watch a minute while he pokes through the trash. I feel him tonight. Because now that I'm out here, I realize I don't want to go home.

"Lemme ask you something," I say. "Where are you going when you leave here? Like, to sleep?"

He just looks at me. Got on a sweatshirt over his suit jacket, long johns and socks. He looks cold and pissed off. I go in my wallet, take out two bucks, hold it out.

"I got choices," he barks, snatching the money. "Might be the twenty-four-hour Dunkin' downtown, or the platform over on the R train where they got a bench up in the tunnel. Might not do either one. Might settle right here, after I eat what Ms. Fox got for me. I ain't scared. Don't care how many people got shot here."

"Got you," I say. Tell him good night, feeling glad I have my bed tonight, even with all the drama. It's some crap, having to sleep on a bench all night. At the gate, I remember something from that cop, the one who came to our door. *Your son's buddy, there's solid evidence against him . . . witnesses . . .*

I turn back. "The police talked to you, huh?" I ask. "After Singer got killed."

He holds up the money I gave him. "Fuckers paid for it, too. You think I can pass up a chance for cash when I'm eating out the trash?" He squints, getting a better look at me. "I didn't say nothing about you, if that's what they're saying."

"Nah, it's not that," I say. I watch him a minute. Can tell he's feeling guilty, which means I can guess the answer to my next question. But I ask it anyway, to know for sure. "You told them you saw Jack that night, didn't you? The tall skinny one who works here."

I hold my breath, waiting on the answer.

"Nice kid," he says, "that one. Friendlier than you. Me seeing him that night, it doesn't mean nothing. I didn't see nobody kill nobody, I told them that, too." He sucks his teeth, like I pissed him off. "I didn't tell 'em everything I know, anyhow," he says. "How 'bout that?"

"What the hell does that mean?" I ask. But he turns his back, walks off, waving a hand behind him. I'm alone in the parking lot, realizing how much the temperature's dropped since I got here. Up in the sky, the moon's disappeared. And I wonder if I'm losing it, out here trying to prove something's not true when it keeps on seeming truer.

The Mom Card

Three years later and the memory still stabs me in the gut. Jack and me in Midtown, Christmas lights blinking on all the stores. And jokers in the middle of the sidewalk, running a shell game, which I knew was a con because Ma'd already warned me about it. But would Jack listen?

"You gotta trust me," he says. "I got this. You could buy your ma a real nice present and have cash left in your pocket after I win this." And what does fourteen-year-old VZ do? Hand over the last forty bucks of his saved-up Christmas cash so Jack can play. And lose.

I pedal faster on Bennett's stationary bike. Nothing in this crappy basement gym but the bike, an old armchair, and a set of weights. Best place for tonight, though. Close to my bed without risking running into the parents before they're asleep. Since it's almost midnight, might as well call it Wednesday. Just three days till JersiGame. But before I play, I need to get off some energy. Figure out why I keep trusting Jack when he keeps fucking up.

My phone lights up on the handlebars. Chela's face fills the screen, hair pulled back, a green silky bathrobe covering her shoulders. Nice sight, down in basement hell.

"I thought you should know," she says. "I'm a shitty hu— *Wait*." Her eyes scrunch up. "Where are you? Why are you *wet*?"

"Bennett's man cave," I tell her. Hold the phone so she can see, then slow my legs and spill the whole story about the homeless guy seeing Jack the night Singer died. By the time I'm done, I'm out of the seat, bike tension turned up high.

"It was bad enough," I say, "Jack showing up over by Singer's place. But *this*? Why wouldn't he tell me he was lying to the damn cops? If he won't talk, I don't see why we're busting our asses all over Brooklyn, trying to help him."

I wipe my face with my T-shirt, turn the tension down.

Chela looks irritated but doesn't say anything.

"What?" I ask.

"Be in your feelings if you have to, Veeze," she says. "But if we're really doing this, Jack pissing you off can't be in it."

I pedal harder, not used to Chela saying stuff that cuts. "Why? We're doing this for him, aren't we?"

"It's not a *favor*," Chela says. "We're doing it so he doesn't go down for a murder he didn't do. It's not like we're buying him a muffin." She takes a minute, watches me pedal. "I know you hate when he doesn't do things with you, but that's not gonna happen this time."

"You think I need him to do this with me?" I ask, more pissed than I wanna be.

"No. But . . . maybe you think that?" She must catch a look on my face, 'cause she adds, "Sorry! It's just, you were so mad at him when he wasn't around, after Ed. Remember? You said he wasn't about Ed anymore. And you didn't even tell him when Ed's dad brought over that box of stuff from when you were kids."

I did *not* remember that. I turn up the tension, think about what Brienne said, about Jack blaming me for not being around, after Ed. Pedal harder, not wanting to feel what's there. "Anyhow," Chela says. "You want to know why I'm a shitty human?"

Don't know what she's talking about, but I'm past ready to change the subject. "Okay, yeah."

"So I didn't have any luck with Singer's kid when I followed her out of the pizza place," she says. "But I gave her my number, tried to get her to call me. *And she did.* I just got off the phone with her."

My legs grind to a stop. "*What?*"

She grins at my expression. "The shitty part was, I played the mom card to get her to call."

I get off the bike, confused as hell. Try to shake off *my feelings* about what she said before, so I can get to what she's saying now. Grab a swig from my water bottle. "What does that mean, you played the mom card?" I ask. "Her mom's a piece of work, isn't she? And your mom's the shit."

"Not the cool mom card," Chela says. "The *white* mom card."

I raise my brows, and she keeps going. "I told her I felt bad about those kids getting in her face at the pizza place. You know, because I've had to deal with shit like that for having a white mom."

It's the first she's talked about taking shit 'cause of her ma, but now's not the time to ask. I put one foot on the pedal, spin it around. "Okay. So . . . what'd she say?"

"Her mom's got a major temper, Veeze. She goes off on Junie a lot. And she's taking mad crap right now for what Singer did. Junie said she threw a bunch of glasses at the wall one night, had broken glass all over their kitchen. You see where I'm going with this?"

"Hell yeah," I say. "If Singer pissed her off, she might've gone at him. She could be the one who killed him!" Can't help getting excited in spite of everything. I'm thinking of Ed's game. Did I miss a clue about Singer's girlfriend?

"I kind of felt bad for Junie, though," Chela says.

"Huh?" My brain's going down a different track, following the sweet *rightness* feeling that's finally coming back. I *did* miss a clue, and I think I know what it is. "Do you remember her name? The mom, Singer's girlfriend?"

"Norma," she says. "Why?" Her eyes move back and forth, studying me.

"And their last name's Camron, right? I saw it when I looked up where he lived."

"Junie didn't say," Chela says. "Are you working on your next hunch?"

"Sure am."

"I guess that means we're not giving up," she says. "Which, for the record, I knew we weren't."

When we hang up, I open a Word doc on Ed's laptop, plunk down on the musty armchair, and check my theory. I type *Norma Camron*. Yup. It's a palindrome, the exact same backward and forward. A total Edism. Satisfied, I pull up the game.

I'm at the end of level two, the last of the rat trivia. There's a rat in shades holding one of those clapper things movie directors use. The clue says:

> You scream when we're in your cookie jars.
> Steady there, mate, we're movie stars!

So . . . rat movie stars. *Ratatouille*, right? Or whatever the rat's name from that movie was. I rack my brain, come up with Remy, which I'm pretty sure is right. But there's spaces for three answers. Feels like a thousand years ago I had those mega coffees this morning, but something must still be kicking in, because I close my eyes and my brain takes me back to the movie, which I haven't even seen since I was little. And I remember Remy had a brother . . . whose name was Emile! Two out of three.

Now, I'm thinking of a song. A song from another movie, an old one that people still talk about because Michael Jackson was in it. And it was his song, about a kid who had a rat friend. This time I use the internet, look up MJ rat movie. And it's there! The rat's name was Ben.

I type it all in, and Edric the Great gets delivered, via rat litter, to the end of the level. I'm feeling good, but I don't move on. Something about that puzzle's still pulling at me.

> You scream when we're in your cookie jars.
> Steady there, mate, we're movie stars!

Steady there, mate. Does it mean stay steady, keep on with what I'm doing to help Jack? The sweet feeling starts up, and the low hum breaks out of me. If I'm staying the course, I should go back to Singer's neighborhood. I think of Robbie, who grew up with Singer's kid, must've known Singer at least a little. I message him, even though it's late. Tell him I need a ride after school tomorrow. And I'm paying full price. No idea what I'll say when I see him, but at least I'm making a move.

I close my eyes, lean back in the chair.

The day we played the shell game, the Black guy running it made like he wanted us to win—nice young boys and all that. Let us watch a couple times as he mixed the jar lids around, lightning-quick, with the quarter underneath one of them. Find the quarter and you win two hundred bucks. Jack got it right on all three practices. Truth is, I knew it was a scam. But it was easier to let Jack do his thing. It's what I did, how Easy VZ played it back then.

So, maybe VZ's not so easy anymore.

I'm finding leads on Singer's killer. Doing it *for* Jack but not with him. Because it's time Jack and I got out of the mess we're in. And this time, I'm taking the lead. Plus, on top of it all, I'm finishing Ed's game for him.

On to level three.

Side Hustle

"Right or wrong?" I ask Robbie, as I get in his car. He's double-parked in front of the school building, surrounded by kids weaving their way through the traffic. Rain patters on the windshield, but the car's warm, even smells like a bakery. I ignore it, keep my eyes on Robbie. I'd thought about it all day, decided to go on offense with him. "Right or wrong, what Singer did to Ed? You knew the guy, went to his service. That mean you're okay with what he did to my friend?"

"Jesus," Robbie says, looking blindsided, which was the point. "No, I'm not okay with it!"

"And the cops, how they handled it? Letting Singer off?"

He sighs. "I know they didn't give a rat's ass about convicting him, and yeah, that was wrong, too. But it's got nothing to do with me going to the service, okay?"

"Good," I say. Let out some breath, relieved my gamble paid off. "Because I got a way you can do something about it." He doesn't say anything, so I play my trump card. "Chela—you know, Chela, who didn't turn you in to her ma for driving an illegal car for her service? *Chela* thinks the cops aren't really investigating who killed Singer unless it's a Black kid. We know Singer had a criminal history they aren't looking at. So we thought—Chela and me—maybe you know some stuff that'll help *make* the cops look. Stuff that leads to other motives." I don't say I saw the look on his face when Junie brought up Singer's *other* job.

Robbie reaches for a box on the dashboard. Doughnuts. He takes out a powdered, offers me the box, but I shake my head.

"I don't see what I can do," he says, taking a bite.

"You know Singer's neighborhood," I say. "People he knew. I just want us to go there. Look around, talk. I'm still paying," I add. Try to look righteous and intimidating at the same time.

"I never thought what Singer did was right," Robbie mutters. "Where d'you wanna go?"

I do a happy dance inside. "Head to the neighborhood," I say. "We'll figure it out by the time we get there."

Robbie pulls away from the curb, rain tap-dancing on the windshield. It's lighter than it was before, though. Even the weather's cooperating.

"You know why Singer left your neighborhood?" I ask.

"Nah, it was a long time ago. Junie still goes to school by me, though. Technically. She never was big on going to class. Got some kind of traveling nail polish business, where she goes to people's houses. Following in her mom's footsteps, I guess."

"What else?" I say. "Know anything about this criminal-history thing?"

He rolls his eyes. "It's not what you think. Just a side hustle. He got picked up a couple of times on some kind of larceny charges. I think he got a conviction once, but just a misdemeanor. Didn't do time or anything."

Of course he didn't. "The cops should be all over that."

"Not really," Robbie says. "All Singer did was sell stolen shit outta his van. Low-key."

"How come you know about it?" I ask.

He shrugs. "He and his guys brought in a friend of mine once. They'd give the kids booster bags. You know, to block the electronic tags on the merchandise so they won't set off the alarm when they take the stuff out of the store. The kids took the bags in, used them to clear a few shelves of whatever it was—random shit, diapers one day, watches the next. And the old guys would resell it out of a van. Simple."

I am eating this up. Singer was a straight-up thief. And it sure as hell could've been what got him killed.

"Show me," I say to Robbie. "Show me where all this went down. Show me everything you know about Singer and his little side hustle."

Twenty minutes later, we turn onto a dead-end street. Nothing but warehouses and car lots.

"That's it," Robbie says, pointing to a beat-up metal sign bolted to the chain-link fence of a car lot:

BEN'S AUTO BODY
CERTIFIED AUTO REPAIR CENTER
COLLISION BODY SHOP

We park across the street. The chain-link fence around the lot's ten feet high with a gate at the front. It's stopped raining, but the place feels extra dismal in the gray day.

"Singer was in with these guys here," Robbie says, nodding toward the lot. "They run shit outta that van." He points to a dark blue van parked to one side of the lot.

"No way."

"Way. *Why?*"

I grab my phone so fast I drop it, have to fish it out from under the seat. There it is, the photo I took in front of Singer's house. I can even read the license plate on the dark blue van parked in the driveway. Yup, same one.

"What?!" Robbie asks again.

"Never mind." I shove the phone away, not giving him a chance to tell me it doesn't mean anything, that van being here and in Singer's driveway. I check out the rest of the scene in the car lot. There's a three-sided shed near the back, a couple of random cars spread around.

"You know we might not see any action," Robbie says. "For all I know, they mighta quit by now."

I don't say anything. Now I've seen the van, the rightness is throbbing in me.

"Fine," Robbie says. "If we're hanging out, I'm eating." He grabs the chocolate-glazed doughnut, tilts the box toward me. I shake my head.

The street's out of the way, you'd only come here for a reason. It's not hard to picture Singer, skulking around by the van.

Robbie chews, does stuff on his phone, while I stare out the window. After a while, a girl walks up. Goes through the gate. I sit up straighter, smack Robbie. Lean closer to the window. It's a white girl, not much older than me. Got on jeans and Jordans, a fleece vest with no shirt underneath even though it's not warm today. And she's got a bag over her shoulder. The reusable kind to keep from wasting paper at the supermarket. For all I know, that's what "booster bags" look like. The girl walks straight up to the van, looks in the driver's-side window. I guess she sees nobody's there, so she puts her back to the van door, leans against it. Waits.

I'm breathing so heavy you'd think there was something happening besides a random girl standing in a parking lot. But this lot's a window into Singer's life, and I'm about to see something I wasn't supposed to see. Something dirty and wrong that's gonna feel satisfying as hell. Minutes pass. The girl just stands there. Robbie fidgets. Then, out of nowhere, a guy walks out from the back of the lot. Middle-aged white guy, half-bald. He nods to the girl. She opens her bag, takes out a smaller paper bag. My pulse goes nuts as she opens it . . . and . . . hands him a takeout cup.

"Coffee?" I say, feeling all kinds of letdown. "That's bullshit!"

"Hold your horses," Robbie says. He leans into the window, watching close. The guy and girl rest against the side of the truck as he takes a sip of his drink. A couple minutes later, the girl leaves. The guy disappears again, to the back of the lot.

"You think there's a building back there we can't see?" I ask.

"Nah," he says. "He's hanging in a car at the way back. So—did you see it?"

"See what?"

Robbie grins. "I'm pretty sure that was a handoff. They traded bags. She's probably doing little stuff, perfume or something small. She brings him a full bag, he gives her an empty. Happened when they were standing next to each other, up against the van."

This makes zero sense. I stare at the spot where they were. The girl had the bag on the shoulder I couldn't see when she was standing next to the guy, but . . .

"The guy didn't even have a bag," I say. "So how could they've traded?"

"His was an empty," Robbie says. "Probably had it folded up in his pocket."

"But he didn't have one when he walked away, either."

"Why you think the whole thing happened next to the van with the open window?" Robbie asks. "They just drop it right in there. That way, nobody's got anything on them if the cops come by—if there's any cops they're not paying off, that is. The van's probably registered to somebody dead or something."

"Shit," I say.

178

Robbie laughs. "That's the way of the world, my friend. You gotta be slick." He eyes me, brows up. "You seen enough?"

"Hell no." I take a doughnut, maple-glazed. It's damn good.

"What's it stand for, anyhow?" Robbie asks. "VZ?"

"Not your business."

"Then it would be NYB, wouldn't it?" He looks impressed with himself. Like I haven't heard that one before. In the end, though, I get less shit for not admitting to Victor Zemblist. Robbie polishes off his doughnut and right away opens his door, brushes out the crumbs. 'Cause his car's his job, I guess.

"So, what else?" I ask. Because what the hell. Here we are, in his car. "Like about Singer's kid. She ever say anything about the night Singer . . . did what he did to Ed?" It costs me to ask, so I keep talking to cover it. "Or anything about what happened after . . . ?"

Robbie shoots me a glance, like he's asking if I really want to know. I don't bother responding.

"All right, sure," Robbie says. "Junie called me last night to talk about what went down at Pizza Beach. Started telling me how it was after it happened, you know, from her end of things. She remembered how relieved he was that they didn't lock him up that same night it happened. Drank all night, when he got home. Wouldn't shut up."

"What'd he say?" I put the doughnut on the dashboard. Can't help holding my breath.

"Just kept saying how close he'd come," Robbie says. "How bad it coulda been. He was relieved as shit. And of course her mom was, too."

179

"You're telling me they went home and partied?" I don't want to hear that. Start to take a bite of the doughnut. But something catches my eye. Somebody else's walking up to the lot. A guy this time, Latino, maybe. And he's carrying a box. He goes right up under the shed, puts the box on a table. I drop the doughnut, starting to get excited. The same guy comes out from the back of the lot, goes under the shed, too. Stands on the opposite side of the table from the Latino kid.

I open my car door.

"Whoa!" Robbie shouts. "What are you doing?"

"I wanna hear what they're saying." I jump out before he can say anything. Halfway across the street, I scope out a tree, stroll over and put my back to it. It's damp from the rain, and I can't see the lot anymore. But I can hear the guys talking, 'cause they're not bothering to whisper.

"I want something more interesting next time," the kid says. "Something worth my while."

"We'll call those shots," the guy says. "But if you wanna *buy* something interesting, I'll give you a good deal."

The kid tells him, "I need electronics. Phones, tablets, that kinda thing."

There's a snort. "Get outta my face! This ain't wholesale. Buy from me so you can sell someplace else? Please."

The kid takes off, walks straight past me. I can't help looking at him. He looks irritated, but not like he just made some shady deal. Which I think he did. I look around the dead end, mind racing ahead. What next? What do I do with this new intel? Across the street, Robbie rolls down his window, flaps a hand for me to come back. Instead, I dig around in my mind, figuring out what it really means that Singer was out here doing dirt. If Singer went to Yard to sell stuff the night he was killed . . . maybe he had beef with somebody there and shit got out of hand.

Footsteps come up the block. I lean out from my tree. Another guy's walking up. Can't see him good, 'cause of his pulled-up hoodie, but the parking lot guy's at the gate, like he's waiting to meet him. I lean farther out, to see better, just as the parking lot guy turns to look up the street. And he spots me! His face is reddish, eyes bright blue. None of it friendly. I don't know why, but I don't look away. I hold his gaze. Long enough to know he looks like a guy who's up to some shit. I pull my eyes off him, pretend to do something on my phone. Feel hyperfocused, like when the wannabe gun was in my face. But this time, it's not bad. Something in me likes that this guy saw me, knows he's caught. I can feel Robbie freaking out across the street, but I don't look up.

"You need something?" the lot guy shouts, after a minute.

"Nah, I'm good," I say. Pulse gunning it, I shoot him a nod, then go back to my phone. Still, he doesn't back off. There's a beat of intense quiet, his eyes on me, mine on the phone. Then, Robbie shouts out the car window, "Yo, I'm right here! Can't you see? What're you texting me for?"

I wave at him. Cross the street thinking he's smarter than he looks. The parking lot guy follows me with his eyes the whole way.

"What the fuck was that?" Robbie asks when I get in.

I turn back to the lot, don't see the guy or his buddy, either. An engine revs to life, though. A second later the van backs toward the gate.

"Oh, shit!" I say. "We gotta follow 'em. Come on, let's go!"

"Are you for real?" Robbie says. "We're not doing that!"

"How're we supposed to know what they're up to?" I ask. "Come on! This could be it!"

"Honest to God!" Robbie shouts. "They call the cops 'cause we're tailing them, you think the cops're gonna search *their* car?"

"Then don't get caught!" I say. "Aren't you supposed to be good at shady driving?"

He holds up a hand to stop me.

"I didn't wanna say this," he says. "But you gotta get your head on right. There's no way Singer took his van to that place where he got killed. It's the hood out there. It's crawling with cops. You'd have to be nuts to leave this neighborhood to sell your shit out there."

"And Singer wasn't nuts?"

"Not that way. *And* . . ." Robbie raises his hand higher. "He wasn't even driving a van that night, remember? He just had his old car."

It's too late to follow the van now, so I shut up. Robbie's not wrong about cops in Ms. Fox's neighborhood. Or about what Singer drove that night. But it doesn't change how I feel. There's something going on with that van. And I know it matters.

Robbie looks relieved I quit telling him to chase the van. "I recognized that last guy," he says. "He used to hang with Junie's dad."

"For real?"

"Back in the day," he says, like it's no big deal. But it is.

"Huh," I say, and change the subject, since there's no point letting him know what I'm thinking. "You ever buy anything from those guys?" I ask.

"Nah," he says. "Their stuff's crap."

The Spot

I get Robbie to drop me at Yard with an hour to spare before time to meet Diamond. Less than three days till JersiGame. I set myself up on the bench behind the restaurant and hope nobody bothers me.

I'm on level three, The Mu'Maid's Kiss. All about mutant mermaids that are fish on the bottom but have human naked-to-the-nipples boobs and human heads—most of them bald. Which, if I'm honest, isn't *not* hot. What gets me is, I never heard a thing about mutant mermaids from Ed. Never saw the drawings for this level, like I did the rest of the game. Maybe he showed them to his good buddy Guz.

In the game, the mu'maids are the resistance, trying to take down SirBugUs and his minion-bugs. If I get enough puzzles right, the mu'maids'll give Edric a kiss, which is supposed to help him beat the boss bug in the end. I click on an especially busty mermaid. And choke back a laugh. Ed did tell me this joke.

Why did the mermaid wear seashells?

I type in the answer. *Because she outgrew her B-shells.*

Pathetic, but at least I knew it. After a few more mermaid jokes (*Why did the mermaid fail her math test? Because her algebra was off*), the level gets harder. I push through until I'm checking the time so often, I might as well just get up and go. When I snap the laptop shut, I feel decent about it. I'm getting faster. A level and a half in two and a half days shouldn't be too bad.

To get to Diamond's, I walk back to the street, take the long way around to her house. I think about Ed's game helping me figure out about the blue van, Singer's *other job.* And his girlfriend, who pops off when she's pissed. I decide not to tell Diamond. We've got plenty in common. Don't have to talk about everything to be a couple. Anyhow, I'm hoping tonight we have better things to talk about.

Halfway down the block, I spot her, sitting on her stoop, arms wrapped around her knees. "Finally!" she says, like I'm half an hour late instead of five minutes early.

"You okay?" I ask. There's something sad about how she's sitting alone in the dark.

"Huh-uh," she says, soft-voiced. "I wouldn't say I'm okay. I don't know what I am." She stands and pulls out her keys. "Come on."

I follow her inside, wondering what's going on. But not for long, because Diamond shuts the door behind us and I know, right off, that we're alone in the house. We're in a high-ceilinged hall with rooms leading off it, a staircase straight ahead. It's big, dark, empty-feeling.

"Up here," Diamond says.

It gets darker as we climb the steps. Diamond's hips swing side to side, her hand runs along the banister. At the top, she goes through a doorway. She flips on a light, and we're in her bedroom. A double bed with a soft blue-and-white quilt. Blowups of photos on the walls, candids mostly. A headshot of a pretty woman I'm guessing's her mom. In the corner across from her bed, she's got her game setup. All of it sitting on a blue-and-white carpet that my feet sink into. Being in here makes me feel all kinds of ways.

Diamond nods toward a trunk under the window for us to sit on. On the way, she pulls the burner phone out of her pocket and hands it to me. I could truly care less, right now.

"I didn't want to be a baby about it," she says. "And call you again. But they called back. See how there's two different calls from different numbers?"

"Wait," I say, getting my mind out of her bed. "They called again? When?"

"Last night. The phone was back in the lost and found drawer. I was alone in the kitchen, putting away the stuff from the dishwasher. It scared me bad, but I couldn't resist. I picked it up."

"Shit. What'd they say?"

"At first, nothing. Just this awful breathing. Then they said . . . they said, 'You're not as smart as you think you are. Lose this and get over it.'"

She grips my shoulder to show how scared she is. I know it's real for her. But that doesn't mean her Jack-dropped-the-burner idea isn't over the top.

"You don't think it's some kind of prank?" I ask, keeping my voice chill.

"I knew you'd say that!" she says. "But how is that funny, 'Lose this and get over it'? It doesn't even mean anything if you don't know what the person's talking about." She rocks side to side while traffic sounds drift up from the street. "VZ . . . I really think it was Jack."

I sure as hell don't want to fight with her tonight, so I try to stay with her. "It sounded like him?" I ask.

"No, I told you, it didn't sound like anybody, the voice was disguised. But what they said, 'You're not as smart as you think you are.' You have to admit that sounds like Jack. He's always saying how I'm a—"

"Know-it-all?" I finish for her, hoping to lighten things up.

"Yes!" she says, not smiling. "It just shows it's probably him."

I play for time, look over at her gaming corner. She's got a bunch of old-school relics, a Wii, a PlayStation. An old leather gaming chair that looks as soft and warm as a good jacket. But then, a brand-new Alienware laptop, too.

"VZ." She puts a hand on my leg. "I know it sounds bad, but can't you see it in your head? Singer showing up at Yard just to be a dick, and Jack seeing him and losing it. You know how he can be." Her eyes beg for me to see it her way.

The problem is, I do. The message did sound like Jack. And it takes zero imagination to picture him losing it with Singer. Plus,

Diamond doesn't even have all the intel I've got, like Jack knowing about the gun when nobody else did. And the homeless guy seeing him that night.

"Look. Even if it was Jack . . ." I feel the wrench in my gut for being a disloyal piece of shit. "Even *if*, Diamond. What're we supposed to do about it?"

"Exactly!" she says, her eyes shiny with relief. And for one fantastic second, I think she actually knows what to do. "If Jack gets in touch with you, you tell me right away. And I can tell Daddy. He's good at stuff like this, finding ways to help kids when they're in trouble."

Her dad? The hope explodes in my chest like the sack of gas it was. Diamond's gotta be the only person in Brooklyn who actually trusts her dad. And it tells me I can't trust her. Can't tell her what's going on with Singer and his van, because she'll think it's stupid. Definitely can't tell her if Jack gets in touch. I can't even tell her about my doubts, the part of me that thinks she's right. Because telling somebody who believes it is way worse than telling somebody who doesn't. I can't do Jack like that.

Diamond lets out a sigh of relief, like we settled something. "Honestly?" she says, coming back over to sit. "I really needed to tell you. I didn't want to tell Fisk, because Jack's your friend and, I don't know, it felt weird talking to him about it. But I feel better now." She smiles at me, almost like her old self. And I try to let go of the Jack stuff, at least for now. I'm in her *bedroom*. And it's not like she's gonna do anything with her theory about Jack.

"There's one more thing," she says, before I can shift moods.

Like she's warning me not to feel better just yet. "It's something I want to show you . . . in Daddy's room." She sounds scared, which freaks me out even more. But I follow her down the still-dark hall. The house smells the opposite of Chela's. Too clean. Like nobody ever cooks, gets funky, hangs out with a mangy cat in here. Diamond turns into a room, reaches down, switches on a lamp. Her dad's room's big with dark wood furniture, even an easy chair. Its own bathroom. Diamond takes my hand, walks me to the window. And I feel wild, because even though I don't know what's coming, I know for sure I won't like it.

"See?" she says, pointing out the window.

I see the last thing I expected. The window looks down on the spot. *The spot.* Where we were standing when we saw Ed on the stretcher. I hadn't realized her building was *that* close to Yard. It's worse than that, even. The way the light falls from Ms. Fox's apartment above the restaurant, it's like a stage light. Darkness all around, and a patch of pale gold showing that spot. And I'm back there. Feeling the excitement of my little errand with Diamond, getting the Christmas decorations Ms. Fox stored in her garage. Smelling burnt meat as we came back along the cut-through between the house and the restaurant, because Ms. Fox was burning residue off the grill.

"Why are you showing me this?"

"I see it every day," she says. "And I need to talk about it, VZ. I been looking at it all this time, remembering. All by myself."

I don't say anything because there's something fair about what she said. She shouldn't have to see it alone. I know what she wants now. She's hinted at it before, but I've ignored her.

"You wanna go down there?" I ask. I don't like seeing it from her house, knowing it's always gonna be there, outside her window. Waiting for us. Like it's telling me there's no choice but to deal with it.

Diamond squeezes my hand. We're at the top of the stairs when she says, "Jackets." She starts to pull away to get them, but I keep hold of her. We go back to her room together. Rejoin our hands when our coats are on. Now I'm feeling her and feeling sick about the thing we're doing, all at the same time.

It's warm enough to smell the dumpster as we walk toward the restaurant. That's different, because the night it happened, we smelled the grill. Tasted the cold December air. I wonder if Diamond walks the path all the time, notices those differences. If she thinks about why Ed was here in the first place that night. That if I didn't work here, didn't blow him off at home, he wouldn't've come to eat at Yard. *Facts.* He wanted to hang while I worked, go home together after. He wouldn't've been here at all, if not for me.

My feet quit walking. We're there. The spot where I stood that night. And the whole night is playing out in my head. How I stopped in my tracks, the red lights swirling in front of me. And slow, real slow, realized the siren I'd been hearing all along wasn't coming from the street. It was coming from here. Yard's parking lot. And my eyes focused for real. The ambulance. The stretcher. Ed.

"You know what?" I say. "Bad call. We shouldn't be here." I want to go back to her house, with all its dark bedrooms. But she's

190

gripping my shoulders, turning me the wrong way. Toward the spot. So I'm standing at the exact angle I was standing that night. She steps behind me.

"It was like this, remember?" she whispers. "You had your arms full of Christmas stuff, and I was behind you with the rest. And when you stopped, I told you to hurry up."

Part of me goes somewhere else. High up over the buildings, in the wind. *Not* trying to hear this. But the rest of me's here. Remembering dark red blood on Ed's bright white T-shirt. How he wasn't moving and I was begging him to move.

"You'd already seen it, right?" Diamond says. "I remember thinking there was something strange about how you were standing. Real still. And then I looked past you. And I saw, too. And I dropped my boxes and ran over to him."

I'm shaking my head. "This isn't helping." I'm pissed at myself for agreeing to it. Diamond steps away from me, hugs herself.

"I know what you think," she says. "You think I did better than you. You think you should've gone over to the stretcher, too."

Now she's just torturing me. We both know she went to him while I stayed right here. Frozen like a little kid, stuck as fuck, as if *willing* him to be alive would work. And when I finally moved, the EMT held me back so they could put Ed in the ambulance. *He's gone, but we gotta take him in anyhow.* That's what she said. We both heard her. But Diamond was the one who asked if it was okay to close his eyes. When the EMT said, *No, don't touch him,* Diamond bent over him anyhow. Whispered something in his ear.

"You think I was brave," Diamond says now. "But it's not how

191

you think it was. I'm pretty sure the EMT was right. He was already dead when I got there."

I clear my throat. "You said he blinked," I say, voice raspy anyhow. "*You told me he blinked when you bent over him.*" Feels like dredging the words up from somewhere deep inside me. They leave an acid trail behind.

"I looked it up," Diamond blurts, like it's a secret she's been holding. "People can blink after they die. It's just a muscle reflex. I was in the waiting room with his mom when the doctor came in. The doctor, she said he died right away when he was shot."

This is news. I look up at her. "How come you never told me that?"

"Because we don't talk about it!" she says. I guess that's true. But all this time, I'd thought Ed was alive, that I could have talked to him one more time, been with him when he went. And now it sounds like that couldn't've happened. For a split second, I feel relief. Then it drains out of me like the blood from Ed's body. If he was already gone, it just means I should have been there even sooner. Before Singer ever got to him.

"Come on." Diamond puts a hand on the middle of my back. "Maybe we better go back."

In the Blue Room

"Did I mess up?" Diamond asks. "Making you go out there?" We're back in her room. Feels like a hundred years since I walked in here, thinking tonight was the night. Diamond turns to face me. I look in her eyes, which are wide open, looking just at me. I can feel her willing the sadness to go away, to make it okay that she got me to go out there.

"It's all good," I say. Don't want to get into everything I'm feeling, anyhow.

She hangs our coats in her closet. Inside, there's a little thin nightgown hanging on the hook. White but see-through. Fuzzy slippers, too. I think what it means, her hanging my coat up in there, like I'm staying a while. Feeling better, I drop down on the padded chest, like before. Look around for something to say that'll keep the mood chill.

"Didn't know you gamed like *that*," I say, pointing to her top-of-the-line Alienware laptop.

"Guys never think girls game like that," she says, grinning. "Fisk's the one who gets me the fancy stuff. It's nice, but the classics never get old. They were better at good, solid design back in the day."

I smile because, even though she brought up Fisk, she sounds so much like Ed I can't help it. Things get even better when she sits down next to me, rests her head on my shoulder. I can tell she's not thinking about gaming anymore. All the parts where her body touches mine melt, like butter sizzling in a hot pan.

"VZ?"

"Hmm?" I shoot up a prayer that she can't hear my heart hammering.

"Is it okay if you stay here tonight and we just snuggle?" she asks. "I don't like staying alone, especially not now."

"Stay?" I say. "All night?"

"If it's all right," she says. "You should know, I told Fisk I liked the guy I kissed. But it's complicated with him. We're not doing good, but we didn't break up yet. So I can't"—she turns her head so her lips touch my shoulder—"you know."

For an answer, I pull her closer. Because I'm not letting Fisk wreck this. Diamond squeezes my hand. Says she'll be right back.

When she's gone, I pace. Try to calm my body down. Then I remember about home, how pissed Ma is at me. How the last time I saw her, I slammed out of the house. I've got no problem letting her sweat, but I can't have her calling the cops, so I text. Tell her I'm

194

staying at Chela's. Then shut my phone down.

Diamond comes back in. Got on nightclothes, soft pajamas in pink and green. She doesn't look away when my eyes eat her up.

"Bathroom's down the hall, if you want," she says. I get up, move toward the door, but stop.

"About your pop . . . ?"

"He's not coming home tonight, he already texted."

I nod, head down the hall. *Is this about to be it?* I know she said nothing would happen, but maybe she wants me to make the first move. I can do that. I move fast when I get to the bathroom. Strip off my shirt, sniff under my arms, wash even though it doesn't smell bad. Stuff the washcloth down my pants and wash there, too. When I'm dressed again, I look in the mirror. Twist the hair that's looking crazy. Grab the toothpaste, impressed with myself because I remembered to put a toothbrush in my pocket. Then I realize I brought a toothbrush but not a damn condom. I feel stupid. Think about her maybe having one and feel worse. But it's Diamond, I tell myself. We're meant to be, and it's gonna be fine. Whatever happens. I rinse my mouth, splash my face, and get the hell out of there before I freak myself out.

Diamond's still sitting on the padded bench. "I meant what I said before, okay?" she says.

"I know!" I say. Too fast. Grin.

She gets up, goes over to her bed. I feel like I'll turn it into one of those vibrating beds like they've got in gadget stores. She gets in, looks up at me. *Damn. Damn, damn.* It's a good thing getting in bed's something I've done for seventeen years, because I go autopilot, feel myself get on the mattress, pull up the sheets. Diamond holds her body like she's waiting to lay on me. I stretch out and hold out my arm for her. She puts her head on my chest and my arms close around her. Like I've been waiting to do it my whole life.

"That's nice," she says.

She's soft, warm. Curving places pushing against me.

"Mm-hmm," I say. She starts talking, something about her pop's girlfriend. I'm feeling her. Hoping she doesn't move too much and feel how much I'm feeling her. Hoping she does.

Diamond goes quiet and we lay for a long time. I slow my breathing. It's past nice, laying with her in my arms. And I want her to know I can chill, before I make my move. After a while, she asks, "What helps you, VZ? With Ed and everything. What makes it better?"

Not the question I want right now. But the answer comes easy. "His game," I say.

"Because it reminds you of him?"

"Because he wanted so bad for people to play it, see his animation. Laugh at his stupid Ed-jokes." I've got a hand on the back of her head, the other one around her back. I can feel her relaxed, listening. So I tell her more. The dumb ass puzzles that keep on tripping me up, but how I keep pushing anyhow.

"He wanted it so bad," I say. "So he should still have it, even if he won't know. Because I owe him." God help me, my lip starts shaking. I shut up, try to swallow back the clump of crap pushing its way from my throat to my eyes.

Diamond presses closer. "It's okay," she whispers. "I promise it is."

Fuck. The sound of her whisper cuts something loose in me. My willpower breaks, the clump of crap in my throat bursts open. Tears pour out of me, so hard I'm sobbing like my little sister, like Ed's ma. Like nothing will ever feel okay till everything that wants to come out of me is out.

Sweet Gordy

Sunlight's coming through Diamond's thin curtains. I'm in her bed, our legs touching.

No surprise there's morning wood. I lay as still as I can, try to think about unsexy things. The sound of footsteps helps.

"Shit. Diamond!" I whisper, shake her. "Diamond, I think your dad's home. What should we do?" I'm picturing all the movies where the dad whales on the guy he finds in his daughter's bedroom. Takes care of the wood. Diamond blinks herself awake.

"Oh," she says, still out of it. "Okay."

"No. Not okay!"

She props herself up on her elbow. "He doesn't come in without knocking. I'll just tell him I'm getting changed." The way she says it, I get the feeling she's been here before. With Fisk. Who probably didn't cry and talk about games all night.

"*I don't like it,*" I tell her. "What if he waits for you to get done changing?"

Diamond sits up. "Okay, I'll go talk to him. But Daddy's not like that. He doesn't really have time to wait around for stuff." She gets out of bed, closes the door behind her. I wonder if her dad's really that out of it, that he's got no idea who's in his house half the time. *And he's the one she wants Jack to spill his business to?*

I get up, rub my eyes, sore neck. Look back at her rumpled bed. Last night wasn't what I wished, but there was still something good. Diamond liked being close like that, I could tell. So fuck Fisk. Whatever happened before, she's damn near done with him now. I pull on my pants. Go to the door to listen, just as Diamond comes back in.

"Daddy won't be here long," she says. "He just has to shower and change, then he's going to work."

"Which means I'm leaving when we hear the water running?" I say, getting it.

"I'll go with you," Diamond says.

I put my arms around her. She presses to me. Feels what she feels. "You didn't think . . . ?" she says.

"No!" I lie. She giggles.

"I never lied about me and Fisk," she says. "Or about you and me."

"I know."

"And it's not like it can't happen with us, someday . . ."

I hold her, rest my head on top of hers. Until we hear the whoosh of the shower.

We get dressed in a flash, make a run for the front door. Walking outside feels good, me and Diamond starting our day together. It's nice out again, the air easy, chill. We walk the long way to her bus stop, and I hug her before she gets on. When the bus pulls off, I check my phone, realize it's been off all night. It dings like a fire alarm when it powers back up.

Ma: This is ridiculous. COME HOME.

Pop: Your mother says you're not coming home. CALL ME.

Ma: Chela's mother said she didn't see you last night. Ms. Fox says you weren't on shift that other night. I don't care what's going on. CALL ME.

Robbie: Just checking in. ALL GOOD?

Ma: Are you even going to SCHOOL?

Ma: WHAT IF SAMMY WERE MISSING LIKE THIS? HOW WOULD YOU FEEL?

I know it's not right, making Ma worry. Skipping school, like I'm about to do again. But Ed's game is due day after tomorrow, and I have to be ready. Without giving up on helping Jack. Ten minutes later, I'm in an Uber with a turkey club from the bodega by Diamond's. We'll park at the blue van lot. I've already got proof that the van's the same one I saw in Singer's driveway. And I found plenty of news stories about petty-thief-guys getting in fights over deals. So, all I have to do is hang out at the blue van long enough for something to go down. Take pictures and, boom! Proof that Singer's scam led to violence. Add the fact that Singer's got a record, throw in how his girl, Junie's ma, pops off on a dime, and it'll be enough for the advocacy groups to blast on social media, showing that the cops should be investigating more than just Jack.

And, in the time it takes to get to the van, I play the game.

I'm on level three, still. The mu'maids have gotten wilder-looking with blazing purple lips—*nothing* like Brienne's—and spikes on their tails. The biggest one challenges Edric to a tail fight. I go through the junk heaps, find superglue and nails to stick to Edric's tail, so he can keep up with the spiked mu'maid. I remember another one of Diamond's lessons—make sure I'm strong enough for the fight. I click on protein powder and a bottle of bone broth.

The driver blasts his horn . . . outside, we're under an overpass, cars jammed in on all sides. Like the beeping isn't enough, the usual idiots try to yell over the horns.

BEEEEP!

"Shaaaaadup!"

BEEEEP! "You shaaaaaadup!"

It's damn near impossible to concentrate. I stay glued to the screen anyhow. Win the fight on the fourth try. The driver whips the wheel left and right, forcing other cars to let him through. My eyes hit on something on the screen—a can of "magic mud" sticking out of the junkpile. Ed was into women's mud wrestling, so I'm guessing his mu'maids are about to get into it. I look around the screen, trying to find a way to use the mud. In the door at the end of the level, there's a keyhole shaped exactly like one of the mu'maids.

"Kinda sexist, buddy," I mutter, clicking on the right-shaped mermaid, greasing her up with magic mud, and sliding her through the keyhole.

The door swings open. It seems way too easy. Still, it looks like I'm about to meet the big boss bug on the final level of the game. I hit pause, wait for the noise outside to die down.

The driver grunts, swerves hard, and we break out into a side street. I hit play. And damn if it isn't the next level.

On-screen writing says:

Level Four:
Game Over, Rover!

Tonight, SirBugUs will claim his most precious prize.
It's time to destroy the Brooklyn Bridge. Once it's down,
Brooklyn will crumble into the river and be his!

There's a cut-scene. We see SirBugUs on his throne, three crowns on his three gross heads and a million minions at his back. Up around the ceiling, the air's full of blue-white pixels, like an icy mist. SirBugUs gets up, marches to a staircase in the middle of the room, and puts two of his six booted feet on the first step. The red door at the top of the stairs bursts open. Edric's mutant hand reaches through. It grasps the banister at the top of the staircase.

The cut-scene ends.

On the next play screen, I'm at the top of the stairs that lead down to the throne room. I try to move down the stairs, but the blue-white mist attacks me, seals itself around the leathery mutant hand. A speech bubble pops up from one of the minions:

> Please! You think you're nearly there?
> You have no chance of survival!
> You'll be forever frozen here
> 'Less you blaze a trail to your fearsome rival.

I click the hand, the steps, the banister. Start going through every item in my inventory, but nothing works to fight the frozen mist. No matter what I do.

"This is it," the driver announces.

"What? Oh, right." We're at the lot. The blue van's where it was before, its back end to the street. I get him to park across the street, a little further down from where Robbie parked the other day. "We're just gonna wait a while," I say. "A dollar a minute to wait, right?"

He grunts again, turns on his radio to soft rock. I make myself put the game down, which is hard when my guy's so stuck, but it's gotta be eyes on the van for as long as Ma's emergencies-only credit card holds out. I check my phone camera to make sure everything's set. Remind myself I just need one little video of Singer's dirty deals. Then bust out my sandwich and chew while I wait.

A sound pops off, close. I jump, stare around. The driver's snoring like a rhinoceros. Knocked out, mouth hanging open. I settle back. An old song, the one about getting watched with "every step you take" is playing, so familiar it feels like it's playing inside me.

It's good, being here. Doing something, not just letting shit happen. Sun pours in through my window, because there's parking lots on either side, instead of buildings. The heater's on, too. Warm, but not too hot . . .

I jolt awake. A noise? A car door slamming? The driver's still down, radio going. The blue van's still there, and my sandwich is open on my lap. I blink and yawn like an idiot. Stuff the sandwich back in its bag and get out of the car, hoping the fresh air'll wake me up. On the sidewalk, I stretch my back. Just as I'm straightening up, there's a sound from across the street, and the van door opens. But I don't get it, because I thought it was empty. A guy gets out, the parking lot guy from yesterday. He's got a dog with him, on a leash. I wake up so fast I feel dizzy, because they're walking toward me. This guy and his dog. Recognition shows on the guy's red face.

"What can I do for you?" he asks. The dog's a pit bull. Mud brown with cold black eyes. It lets out a low growl.

"I'm good," I say. Give him what I hope's a friendly grin. "Just waiting to meet somebody."

"Yesterday too, right?" The guy isn't pretending shit. His face is cold and hard, just like his dog. "You were waiting to meet this somebody yesterday, too?"

"Mm-hmm." I'm right by the car door, but I don't get in. This is what I wanted. Proof these fools are dangerous.

"Gordon here," the guy says, nodding to the dog. "Gordon's waiting for a friend, too. Maybe I leave him here to wait with you." He unwinds a coil of the leash, so the dog comes closer. The growling turns up. I can't step back now without being a punk.

"You wanna tell me what you're up to?" the guy says. The dog crouches low. Right by my shin. I don't want to be scared . . . but this is Singer's territory. Singer's people, coming at me for standing on the goddamn street.

"Since when's it a crime?" I ask. "Minding my business on a public sidewalk?" The dog's two inches from my leg. And my camera isn't even on. I need this Uber driver to wake up, get out of his car.

"Gordy's just standing on the sidewalk, too," the guy says. "Gordy! Wanna *greet* this guy?"

It must be a command to the dog, because it goes ape, snarling, pulling at the leash. One more coil from the leash and it's all over me.

The van guy laughs. "You know how dog bites work in Brooklyn? There's a one-bite rule, and Gordy's record's clean. Worst that can happen is I have to pay your medical bills, and I'm fine with that. So. What do you have to tell me?"

I don't answer, don't back up. Only thing I'm clear about is this guy was Singer's friend. I'm not backing down from him.

He shrugs, his fist moves, the leash uncoils. The dog's teeth sink into my leg. I stumble backward, but it doesn't let go. I think, *This is what shock is,* because it doesn't hurt. Feels unreal, like me and the dog's jaws are in some alternate universe. Somebody screams, and I hear it like through a tunnel, from the other world to mine.

"Jesus! Andy! Chill!" It's a girl's voice. Then another shout, from the parking lot guy.

"Enough!"

The dog lets go. And pain sets in, like waves of fire burning through my ankle. Blood seeps through the bottom of my jeans.

"What the fuck?" the girl's voice says. Closer. Familiar. And, of all people, Singer's kid's running up from the lot.

"Gimme a minute, Junie!" the van guy yells.

I blink, switching from the pain universe back to this one. Her being here is good. More proof that Singer was in this shit.

"I know this guy!" Singer's kid says, close to us now. The parking lot guy looks from me to her.

"What do you mean?" he asks.

"Jesus," she says. "I mean, *I know him*." She looks at my leg. "You okay?"

"Yeah," I lie. Thinking of rabies and what-the-hell-all else.

"Look, Uncle Andy," Junie says. "I don't know what's going on, but I'm gonna go, okay?" She bends, pets the dog. Calls him Sweet Gordy.

Uncle Andy and *Sweet* Gordy? My mind's reeling.

The parking lot guy shakes his head, like her going isn't an option. But Singer's kid points to the Uber, looks at me.

"This you?" she asks. And when I nod, she gets in.

I limp around to the other side, heart pounding off the charts. When I get in the car, the parking lot guy leans in the girl's window, asks her if she's sure. Somehow, she gets rid of him.

And then it's just her and me. All kinds of cozy in the back seat of the Uber.

Means

I lift the bottom of my bloodstained jeans. It's a bite like in the goddamn movies, teeth marks dug in my ankle. Which throbs like hell. I breathe in, press my hand against it, catch the scent of blood mixed with perfume from Singer's kid.

"Two stops," she says to the driver. Gives him a street name. But I shake my head.

"Nah, we need to talk," I tell her. Check that it's late enough for Chela to be home, tell the driver to go there instead. The girl looks at me like I've got nerve. Then she twists around to the back windshield, looks at where we just were. Sighs.

"Will this ever fucking end?" she mutters, pulling out her phone. "I'm calling Robbie. If we're talking, he better be there." She pulls up his number one-handed. With the other one, she rummages in her bag, pulls out a flowery scarf and shoves it at me, nodding toward my ankle.

"Thanks," I say. Lean down and tie the thing around my throbbing leg. And try to figure out what's next. What I know is, this girl turning up at the van means she knows some shit about Singer's dirty deals. I don't know how I'm going to get her to tell me, but once we're at Chela's, once I do something about this leg, Chela and I'll work on her together. It's gonna pay off, me going there. Getting myself bit.

Junie gets Robbie on the phone. While she talks, I text Chela, tell her we're coming. Then I close my eyes, hoping for a minute to chill.

"Gordy's had all his shots," Junie says, when she hangs up. "Uncle Andy treats him better than he treats his kids."

"Perfect," I tell her. "Now it's no problem, getting bitten by a fucking pit bull." I'm relieved, though. I don't open my eyes again till we get there.

Chela and her mom are waiting for us in the living room. It's late afternoon, when her mom's usually working, but Chela must've given her a heads-up, because she points to the couch, settles next to me with bandages, paper towels, and a bowl of soapy water. Her faded dress looks like it was made in 1910, but she's still got swag, with her bright eyes, serious cheekbones. I thank her for hooking up my leg. Robbie and Junie sit on the floor, on the other side of the coffee table. Awkward as hell.

"And your mother?" Chela's ma asks, unwrapping Junie's scarf and dabbing the wound while I wince. "I won't be getting another call from her?"

Right, I remember. "Sorry," I say. "I'll let Ma know about this, I promise." I'm careful not to say what "this" is, though. Or when I'll tell Ma. I can't think about it anyhow, because my leg is throbbing, the paper towels are red with my blood. Chela goes to the kitchen, comes back with a glass of water and some pills, which I take without asking what they are. Robbie and Junie sit on the floor, watching Chela's ma spread ointment that stings like hell on my leg. Finally, she pins up the bandage, disappears back to her office.

I know it's on me to get this thing going. But the room, this stupid assortment of people, it's all filtered through the pain in my leg, which is worse, somehow, now that it's wrapped. So, I start with a question, put the heat on somebody else.

"What were you doing at the lot?" I ask Singer's kid. "Did you just go to play with Fido, or are you taking over your dad's business?"

"Classic," she says, shooting a look at the ceiling. "You think you know something, right? You think Uncle Andy's lot's got something to do with Phil getting offed." She rolls her eyes when I look surprised. "I *told* you. People make sure I know shit like this. *Singer had a record. Why aren't the cops investigating his history?* They scream it at me, write it on my locker, put it all over social media."

"Can we not do this again?" I ask. But I'm thinking about her glass-hurling mom, wondering if she thinks of her as a suspect, too. What I say is, "Just answer the question."

"Whatever." She scooches back on the floor, further away from all of us. "I'm just saying, I know that's why you were there. Robbie

209

told me your friend's, like, a suspect."

Doesn't matter that she knows what we're trying to do, I tell myself. She could still have intel that'll help. "Does that mean you know something about the car lot?"

"No, that's not it." Junie reaches for a mini bagel from a plate on the table I didn't even notice. She puts it back again. "Look, fun as this is, I didn't come here for the kicks. I thought I should tell you something. It shouldn't be me that's telling you, but . . ." She trails off. Chela and Robbie look as confused as I am, which is confused enough to almost forget the pain. This Junie girl looks like she's about to drop a bomb.

"Just tell us!" Chela says, annoyed.

Junie licks her lips. "The cops came by last night to tell Ma. It's over. They know who killed Phil. It's why I went to the lot, to tell Uncle Andy."

My body gets it before my brain. It hurts. Then, slowly, I understand why.

"Who?" Chela's asking. "Who do they think it is?"

I don't know if it's the pain, the painkillers. Or knowing that hearing Jack's name right now's more than I could take. Because it's supposed to be Junie's mom, her uncle Andy. Anybody but Jack. What comes out of my mouth is, "Don't. I don't wanna hear that shit from you."

Junie waits a beat, watches me. "They didn't give a name, anyway. It's not official. They only told us 'cause Ma keeps begging for information."

"Okay," Chela says. "Okay."

"Jesus," Robbie mutters.

"They said they got the murder weapon," Junie goes on. "They found it in the guy's apartment. It's not official because they haven't tested for fingerprints or DNA yet. But—you know. What are the chances they won't be on there if they got it from his own apartment?"

"They found the murder weapon?" My voice cracks. I'm remembering what Jack said, *They've got motive and opportunity. All they need is means.* I hate asking, but I have to know. Because there's still a chance it's not Jack. Maybe the weapon's something crazy that couldn't have anything to do with him. Maybe we can still tell the cops what we know about Uncle Andy and Junie's ma. "Did they say what it was?" I ask. "The weapon?"

Junie looks scared when she answers. "A wrench," she says. "An ordinary fucking wrench."

What Happened

The word *wrench* throbs in my head, along with the pain. "Okay, where?" I ask. "Where was the apartment they got the wrench from?"

"I don't know," Junie says. "But they said it was a lead they'd been following."

"Whoa." Chela falls back, like she got smacked. Her eyes are on me as she asks, "They said that? Are you sure that's what they said?"

"I'm sure."

I run the video in my head, watch what she's saying play out: somebody rolling up in Ms. Fox's parking lot, bashing Singer with a wrench. "Wouldn't that mean whoever killed him had a car?" I ask. "Where else would you get a wrench from in a restaurant lot?"

Junie shrugs. "They didn't say. Only that they were testing it for fingerprints."

But that doesn't sound right, either.

"If they're looking for evidence on the wrench," I say, talking slow because the painkillers are starting to kick in. And they weren't Tylenol. "If this wrench is evidence . . . shouldn't it show that *Singer* touched the thing, because maybe he tried to fight the killer off or something? That'd be much better evidence considering where they found the thing." I look at Chela, the only person I trust in this group. "Right? Like she said, of course it's gonna have fingerprints from whoever's apartment it came out of."

"Makes sense to me," Chela says. "But honest to God . . . I don't even know what's happening right now." She looks around her living room at my bandaged leg, Robbie, Junie. Her cat, Walter, comes over, settles himself on Junie's lap.

"*You?*" Junie says. "One minute, I'm talking to my uncle, the next minute I'm calling a dog off this guy. What the fuck?" She scratches Walter's ears.

Chela and I move closer on the couch. It's like the stupid, sad ugliness of it all's sitting in the room with us, and we all feel it.

"We don't know anything for sure," Chela whispers. "Maybe tomorrow, but not now." I'm grateful as hell that she read my mind. That somebody's in it with me. She shoots me a side-eye, nods toward her bedroom. And I know what she's asking. *Should we smoke with them? Take the edge off this shit?*

I wonder how much further my edge can go, with the painkillers already in me. But I nod. And she leads the way out to the fire escape. The four of us fit okay, as long as we keep our legs in—me and Robbie, knees up and out to the side, Junie cross-legged, Chela twisted into one of her yoga positions. It's still nice out. Breezy, the sun gone, but not quite dark. We don't talk, watch Chela fill her pipe, get it lit. Junie looks hungry for the weed.

The pipe makes its way around. Robbie babbles about people he sees down on the street. Chela kicks him to shut him up. We smoke until we breathe slower. Till we can look at each other and not feel too weird. I look at other stuff, too. The blue-gray sky, lamplight coming through Chela's window, flakes of black paint coming off the railing. It's so much easier than anyplace else my mind might go.

Chela nudges my foot with hers. "What?" she asks.

For an answer, I take another pull. Pass the pipe and let my eyes settle on the next thing. Robbie. Always the same look, open button-down over a plain white tee. Shiny black hair, a little messy. I bet it works for him, with girls. Bet he's got it good, like Jack. An image slams in my head, the last one I want. Jack in an orange jumpsuit. Surrounded by nothing but guys.

"Jack better not get fucked over by this," I say out loud. Comes out in a growl, like Gordy the pit bull. Doesn't seem like anybody's listening, till Junie talks.

"If your friend killed Phil," she says, "he's fucked anyhow. That's how it was for Phil. Fucked from the minute he went to that restaurant last winter and did what he did."

There's a beat of silence. For the first time since we came out here, we're all tuning into the same thing.

"He didn't used to be so deep in the remarketing," Junie says. "That's what he called it, remarketing stolen shit. Anyhow, after he did what he did to . . . he couldn't keep a job anymore. *All* he did was remarketing. And he wasn't even careful. It's not like we were having heart-to-hearts, Phil and me, but he told me stuff when he was drunk. I think he needed to be—like—self-destructive. You know, because of what he did."

"Hold the hell up!" Chela says. "You're not trying to tell us Singer punished himself enough, or some shit—"

I shut her down with a look. *He told me stuff when he was drunk.* Could be the only person alive in the world who knows what happened that night *before* I saw Ed laying on that stretcher is sitting right in front of me. And I grab the pipe, take a hit. Then, close my eyes and ask.

"Did Singer ever say anything about the night he did it? Anything at all he remembered?" I'm grateful for how steady my voice sounds. Wind blows the leaves on the trees, below us. I take a breath, try to brace myself for the answer.

"Uh-huh," Junie says. "He did."

I want to know, more than anything. But she waits for the pipe. Looks down at her folded knees as she takes a pull. Finally talks again. "Phil said . . . he said, the kid kept coming at him, even when he shouted at him to stop walking, keep away. The reporters got that part right. Phil wanted to say more about it, but his lawyers wouldn't let him." I seal my lips against the words that want to burst out of me, about how ridiculous it is to say Ed was coming at somebody. But I'm scared she'll quit talking, and I can't have that.

"He was paranoid," she says. "Phil. He sold in Black neighborhoods a lot, and he'd had beef with people for being in their

215

territory. But then Ed, your friend, he was younger than Phil thought. And then when he said what he said—"

"He said something?" Somehow, I'm holding my breath and talking at the same time. "Ed talked to him? What'd he say?"

Junie looks straight at me. "He said, '*What happened?*' After Phil shot him and he fell and he was lying there. He said, '*What happened?*' like he didn't get it. I think it got to Phil, because that's when he saw he was really young and not what he thought he was."

"He said, '*What happened*'?" I ask. I know she's not lying because it makes complete, perfect Ed-sense.

"Yeah," Junie says. "That's it. That's all he said."

I stand up. Climb back inside Chela's window, which I'm sure would hurt like hell if not for the painkillers. I need to be alone, so I go in the bathroom, lock the door. Sit on the toilet with my pants still up. Hearing what Ed said doesn't hurt the way I thought it would. It aches. Sharp waves of something true, spreading out from my chest to my head, fingers, toes. Ed said something. Asked a question. Was himself till the very end.

Countdown

"School, pal. I know it's a foreign concept at this point, but we gotta do it." Chela's finger's poking my ribs. I'm laying on her bed wearing the shirt I had on last night and my boxers. Last thing I remember, we were in here talking after Junie and Robbie left. Sitting up feels like moving through mud.

"Wait," I say. "Ed's game. I was supposed to—"

"Finish it last night, yeah," Chela says. "Mom said those painkillers she gave you knock you out, so there was no getting you back." She holds up a hand to shut me up. "I've got it all figured out. You *cannot* skip Doyle's class again, after all we've been through with her. But you also can't finish the game without Diamond, right? You're stuck; you need her. So, go to school and get her to meet you after, because she won't be free till then anyhow. If you meet her at four thirty, you'll still have," she counts on her fingers, "seventeen and a half hours to finish and get to Jersey. Not bad, right?"

"Bad," I say. "Very bad." My head's pounding as much as my ankle, and everything that's happened is coming back. Gordy the pit bull. Junie's news, the wrench, the cops' plan. "No word on Jack?" I ask.

"That's another reason you might as well be in school," Chela says. "Keep your mind off it."

She's wrong, though. I go to school, mostly because I do need Diamond's help to finish the game. But I only pay attention in Doyle's class. Otherwise, I think about Jack and the wrench, which sounds like the title of some sick kids' book. Between classes, I work on the game and try to get news on the case, get nothing on either. My ankle kills. It's a huge relief to finally slide into the booth across from Diamond at the diner we picked.

It's dreary as hell, mustard-color booths and dingy white walls. But it's open all night, and Diamond agreed to stay as long as it takes. She squints at the screen forever and finally looks up.

"It's definitely a hard lock," she says.

"Okay. What's that mean?"

"A hard lock is when you can't solve a puzzle because you're missing an item you need. It's a mistake in the code, because the game shouldn't let you get off a level without all the items you'll need to beat it in the end." She flags the waitress, who pours us coffee from the pot she's carrying around.

"The problem probably started on the level before," Diamond starts again while I hook up the coffee with milk and sugar. "The one with the mermaids. You shouldn't've been able to get off that level without another inventory item, something you needed for the future."

"Okay, so . . ."

"So, we need to figure out what the missing item is. Remember when you're at the top of those stairs on the boss level and you get that minion's speech bubble? Look at it." She turns the screen toward me. The speech bubble isn't any more help than it was before.

> Please! You think you're nearly there?
> You have no chance of survival!
> You'll be forever frozen here
> 'Less you blaze a trail to your fearsome rival.

"If you don't blaze a trail . . . ," Diamond says, a serious *duh* tone in her voice.

I drink coffee. Try to read the answer off her face. When it doesn't work, I think about the mermaid level where I was supposed to pick up this mystery inventory item.

"Come on!" Diamond says. *"Blaze* a trail . . . think about the creepy ice-mist that keeps you from getting to the boss."

I let what she's saying sink in. "Fire," I say. "I was supposed to get fire to burn through the mist?"

"Exactly! You probably should've got it for a reward."

"The mermaid's kiss," I say, remembering the level. "I was supposed to do something to get a mermaid to kiss me after their lips had got all fiery and purple." I glance across at Diamond. "But it

219

never happened. I remember that level seemed way too easy."

Diamond nods. "I bet I know what happened. Sometimes you figure out the puzzles based on knowing Ed. But he didn't build the game for people who knew him that well. I bet you skipped over a step, and Ed wasn't a good enough coder to make it impossible for you to keep going without it."

"So now?" I ask.

"Now I fix it," she says, already biting her bottom lip, concentrating. "I change the code so you can go back and get your fire."

"You can do that?" I ask, checking my phone for the time.

She ignores me.

Four hours later, the glitch is fixed. The diner's empty, darkness pressing against the window. Nine hours and counting till JersiGame.

Diamond puts her head on the table, takes a break while I go back to the mermaid level. I solve a crossword where all the answers are seafood, get the mermaid to give me a kiss and a firebomb for my inventory, then use the bomb to burn through the mist so I can get down the stairs. That all goes okay. But it doesn't do me much good, because once I'm down there, SirBugUs keeps on killing me. I'm guessing I need Edric's superpower, the deadly discharge, to finish him off, but Edric's lips are still sealed. And I can't find another way to kill the damn thing.

Six hours left to finish and get myself to Jersey for the contest.

"Want me to take a turn?" Diamond asks. She's sitting up now, elbow on the table, her head resting on her closed fist. I don't want to tell her the truth. I'm guessing it's another glitch—I was probably supposed to find some way to get my deadly discharge back before I got here.

"Gimme a minute," I say, stalling. If it's another coding glitch, we won't have time to fix it anyhow. And if not, I want one last shot to figure it out. Diamond drops her head again like I hoped she would. Falls back asleep. Deep down, I know it's over. And I'd rather know it alone than know it with her, at least for as long as I can.

I stay awake. Go at Ed's boss bug with everything I can think of. And fail, time after time.

Gray light's drifting through the window next to us when someone knocks on it. Hard. Diamond wakes up as he presses his face up against it. I'm so mad I could smack the glass.

Fisk.

"Oh, yeah," Diamond says, blinking sleep out of her eyes. "I told him we were here when he texted last night. He must be on his way to make Ms. Fox's deliveries at the Buy-By Brooklyn." Fisk holds up a finger, disappears from the window. And, if the situation wasn't crap enough, Diamond smooths her hair, wipes a napkin under her eyes. A second later, Fisk slides up to the table on his scooter, Yard delivery bags hanging off the handle. Six in the morning and he's already wearing his bullshit grin. He sits down next to Diamond, grabs a piece of her muffin, and pops it in his mouth. I hope it irritates the hell out of her, him coming in here acting like he owns her.

"We can't really hang," Diamond says. "We've still got a long way to go."

"And we need to get back to it," I add.

Fisk tries to play it off. "It's good of y'all, what you're doing for Ed," he says. "But I didn't just show up for this muffin." He gives Diamond a deep eye-contact thing, then turns to me. "You mind giving us a minute?"

"Nobody's got time for that!" I tell him. "Diamond just told you. Or don't you listen to her?"

"Oh, I listen," he says. Leans over, kisses Diamond's cheek. "We can talk later, baby. I got a surprise you'll like."

"What kind of surprise?" Diamond asks. At least half-irritated, I'm glad to see.

"You gonna make me say 'I can't tell you or it wouldn't be a surprise'?" Fisk asks.

She laughs. I try not to barf. Fisk drops his voice, and the two of them talk another few minutes before he hops up, like he's nothing but energy. He wishes us luck, jumps on his scooter, and rides off. A few more people are in the diner now, but it feels dead quiet once he's gone. Diamond doesn't quite look at me.

"We got a deadline, right?" she says, pulling Ed's screen to her side of the table. I let out a breath. I don't want to play Fisk's let's-pretend-we're-not-fighting-over-Diamond game. Don't want to go back to not being real with her. But she's right. Ed's game's the thing to be thinking about now.

"I'm worried it's another glitch," I say. Feel even more like shit. "I been working on it all night, used up all my inventory. I can't see a way to get new stuff, and I can't see a way to beat him."

She doesn't answer.

"Look," I say. "I couldn't've got this far without you. You were amazing."

She still doesn't answer. Still doesn't look at me, but her face is going dark, like a shadow's settling over it.

"What?" I ask.

"You gave up," she says. She sounds angry, disgusted, even. And I don't get it.

"I don't know what you mean," I tell her.

"If it was a glitch, you should've given it back to me as soon as you thought that. But that's what you do. You give up, give in. Take the hit."

"Excuse me?"

"I mean it!" Diamond says. She grabs the muffin, tears off a hunk, and shoves it in her mouth. Chews hard. "You just give up on stuff. Like when Jack got arrested. I thought you'd try and go see him in lockup or something. You didn't even think of looking for him till I got you to go to Coney Island."

Where the hell is this coming from? I stare at her, wondering if not sleeping turns her into Godzilla or something.

"I haven't given up on Jack," I remind her. "*You're* the one who thinks he killed Singer, so . . ."

"I never said that! But you wouldn't even talk to me about him, would you? You just shut down, held it in. That's not the way you act with a girl you wanna be with."

I don't know what to say to that. She's right, about Jack. But not because I didn't trust her. Because she didn't trust Jack.

"You know," she says, and I want more than anything for her

223

to shut up, because I know nothing good's gonna come out. "After Ed, you're the person it's been easiest to be around, out of anybody in the world."

"You're saying you were with me because of what happened to Ed?" I say it deadpan. She's almost admitted it before, so I can't be that surprised.

"It's a bond between us, what we went through that night. Something nobody shares but us. And the more we were together, the easier it felt. Safe, almost. But I still had Fisk, and he took Ed's death hard, too. I didn't know how to get out of it, with him, even though it wasn't good anymore."

"So, you wanted me to break up with Fisk for you?" I ask. "Because I offered to do that!"

"No! I needed you to make me want to break up with him. Need to, even. I wanted you to be somebody I knew was right to go to. And not just because of Ed."

A shitstorm of pain spreads across my chest, bitter as all-night coffee. I wait a few beats. Let the anger get bigger than the pain. "Guess Chela was right about you," I say. "You just fuck with people."

"I guess Fisk was right about you," Diamond shoots back. "You don't have much of a spine."

I feel my face twist. Ugly, like the words in my throat. I know I shouldn't say them. But she's telling me I've got no balls.

"I try to be a nice guy," I say. "And nice guys don't call girls bitches. But what are we supposed to do when they act like one?"

She looks like I smacked her. I drop my eyes. *FUCK!* The

waitress comes over, makes a show of picking up all our dirty things, stacking them on her tray. Silence seems to swallow all three of us. When the waitress leaves, I grab Ed's computer. Snap it shut and shove it in my pack. Throw money on the table. Don't look at Diamond.

"Thanks for your help," I say, over my shoulder.

Finally

Huge black letters cross the front of a block-wide building: BUY-BY BROOKLYN MARKET. I've been walking the streets without a clue where I'm going. And now I'm here. Where Fisk makes his deliveries.

I shouldn't go in. That asshole's in there. I shouldn't go in.

I go in. Losing it on Fisk seems like the best idea I've had in a long time. The only right thing in a sea of shit choices.

Inside, it's an old warehouse—tunnel-like passages, twenty-foot ceilings. A zigzagging green arrow painted on the white cement walls shows the way to the market. People come in behind me, make me feel like there's no going back. The food hall, with all the stalls and restaurants, is at the end of three turns. Huge glass doors lead into it. And who's coming through the doors but Fisk? Pulling his scooter.

I wait for him to catch sight of me. Which he does, immediately putting on his bullshit grin. "Feeling like a double venti iced latte?" he says. "I had me a cinnamon mocha one. It was the shit."

My face must be telling some kind of story, because all of a sudden, I know he knows. He won. Maybe there wasn't even ever a game. His grin gets bigger, nastier. "She finally tell you what's up?" he asks. "Got tired of you sniffing behind her like a sick-ass puppy?"

A lie comes easy. "She just let me know you two were done," I say. "Then we made plans for tonight."

He doesn't fall for it. Smirks. I want to wipe that smirk away. Both fists ball up. Fisk looks down at them. Like he knows I won't smack his ass, no matter how much I want to.

I aim straight for his smirking mouth. He's quick. Blocks me, his other hand already hauling back. I duck, but he grabs me. Slams us both into the cement wall. Pain sears through my bit ankle. But every muscle in me comes awake. Knows it's time to fight. I barely feel the punch that lands on my shoulder. Aim for his face again, punch with everything I've got. He turns his head, but I catch the side of his neck. I follow up, use my weight to pin him against the wall. Smack him again. And again. And—

"What the hell?!" a guy's voice yells. "GODDAMN YOU. I'm calling the cops!"

I freeze. Fisk doesn't. He slams his fist in my gut so hard I double over. For a second, all I know's the pain spreading through me in waves, blacking everything out except Fisk's best-bullshit voice.

"You know I wasn't looking for trouble, right? I was just doing my job when this guy showed up."

"It's always something out here," the man's voice says. "I'm sicka this shit." I straighten up. See his black apron, round pink face, angry. Fisk's got his hands in the air like the guy's got a gun instead of a phone. I look him dead in the face, breathing hard. Let him know I'm ready to go again, soon as we get the chance.

He ignores me. Talks to the guy, real slow. "I'm'a just take my scooter and go, okay?" He turns his back to pick up his scooter off the floor. The thing looks wrong, all bright and shiny when we're in the middle of shit. Fisk steps onto it, puts his bag on the handle. I start to follow, but the market guy stops me.

"One at a time!" he shouts. "I'm not having you start up again out front."

Since Fisk's already on his scooter, I'm the one who has to wait. I nod, let it go.

It's all over anyhow. Everything. Diamond's with Fisk. The cops are going for Jack. And JersiGame's about to start without me.

Be the Gamer *and* the Game

All this time, Ed was only five subway stops away. I walk toward the graveyard, every word Diamond said on repeat in my head. I imagine the cops, too. Passing around the wrench in an evidence bag, like on TV. Making plans to get Jack. I even imagine Jersi-Game, where I should be right now. Diamond was right. I didn't mean to give up on Ed, but it happened. Didn't find a way to help Jack, either. Maybe I gave up on Diamond, too, who knows.

A text comes in. From Fisk. No words, just a picture of him and Diamond at the diner. Diamond's smiling over her laptop, and there's a fresh plate of pancakes in between them. The knife twists in my gut, like the gloating fool means it to. I check his face for damage, don't even see any.

The second I shove the phone in my pocket it buzzes again. I rip it out. Is he sending video? But it's not from Fisk. It's Chela.

Chela: Went to see Jahvaris. Asshole let the cops in. They took a toolbox. Also, other news. CALL ME

I read it twice. Three times. I thought I knew they were coming for Jack. But I know I didn't really believe it—until now. They took a *toolbox* from his apartment. . . .

The graveyard's empty. Cars fly by, but when I close the gates behind me, it still has a graveyard quiet. I don't know where he is. After the service, Ma just said it was "nice." Jack never said a word. Or Diamond, or Ms. Fox. I wonder if they thought I couldn't handle it. I pass a tiny headstone, like they do for a kid, and have a second of worrying Ed's ma let them do a small one for him. But then I see it, catty-corner from where I am. A wreath of fresh red flowers surrounds his name. Somebody's been to see him.

There's more writing than I expected on the stone. I read the top part first, his name, the dates. That his parents loved him. Then I read the bottom. "Be the Gamer *and* the Game."

I sit down in front of it, read it again and again. A brand-new Edism I never even heard before. Who came up with it? His ma? Jack, maybe? I look down at the grave, try to figure where his body is, exactly. They call them headstones, so his head must be under it. I lay the other way, belly down. Ed loved having his funky feet in somebody's face.

"Would it be different, if you were here?" I ask. "Would Jack still be going through all this?" Then I realize how stupid the question is. If Ed were still here, then Singer'd be nothing to us . . . the whole evil chain never would've started. But Singer did do what he did, and he got away with murder. And the evil chain got picked up again by whoever killed him. I flip over, look at the sky that's on the blue side of gray. Plenty of clouds, morphing shape to shape. Did Jack really do the thing that made the nightmare go on and on? Never let us get away from it? Did he put revenge over what it would do to the rest of us? His friends. His ma.

Laying by Ed, blinking at the clouds, the answer comes. Feels comfortable and whole, like a perfect piece of music. Jack wouldn't do that to us. He wouldn't. He didn't.

Knowing it fills me up, pushes all the stupid doubts away. Jack wouldn't do that to us.

I flip over again on the cold ground, rest my head on my arms. Bad thoughts try chasing the peacefulness away. *Does it even matter that Jack didn't do it? Is he about to go down for it anyway?* I shove the thoughts out of my head. Take a minute just to be here with Ed.

People walk by, reading headstones. I look over at Ed's. "Be the gamer *and* the game," I say, out loud, to Ed.

Feels good to talk, so I keep doing it. "We almost finished glitch-proofing," I tell him. "Diamond and me. But I messed it up and we had a fight, and I didn't finish. I'm sorry, buddy." I wait for the shit to hit, the guilt of not finishing. But it doesn't come.

Every once in a while with Ed, I'd get a turn to run my mouth like this. No interruptions. He was too young when my parents got divorced. But when Bald Bennett came along, I spent more time at Ed's house, and he did more of the listening. He's the one I told how good it felt to not worry about Ma so much. By the time I got a girlfriend, Ed was old enough to be in it with me. I got to answer his dumb questions about girls. *How do you even walk around after kissing them? It must be the coolest thing. . . . How do you know you're allowed to touch their boobs? You can't just do it 'cause you want to, right?*

"I guess that's the thing," I tell him. "I wanted so bad to win that contest for you. Thought it'd make up for all the times I was a shit friend. But I was an okay friend, too, huh?"

It's good, laying there, remembering. I think about our talks. The serious ones, about his ma, her church. How real bad dreams could be. And the stupid ones, about whether farts could get in your food. I remember Ed's jokebook, the one he took everywhere when he was a pesky little kid. I remember exactly how it looked, with its dusty purple cover . . .

I jackknife upright. Pull out the laptop, right there on the ground. Hold my breath as the screen comes to life. There I am, on the boss level, surrounded by the piles of river crap. I ignore my buzzing phone, sort through the piles till I find it. A dusty purple book, next to a magnifying glass. My mouth goes dry. Heart pounding like I'm about to scratch the last winning number on a lottery ticket, I position the cursor so I can do two clicks right in a row: glass, then book.

And . . .

Bam!

The book grows, and I can read the title: *101 Fun and Funky Riddles*. It's Ed's jokebook. Clicking the book to read it is the obvious move, so I try it. And the book opens:

> Sometimes I am born in silence,
> Other times, no.
> I am unseen,
> But I make my presence known.
> In time, I fade without a trace.
> I harm no one,
> but everyone's on my case.
> What am I?

My face burns before I even smile. I'm embarrassed that my buddy's this goofy. That it took me so long to figure out. That I'm freezing my ass off in a graveyard right now, reading fart jokes.

The answer to the riddle is *a fart.*

The answer to the *game* is a fart. I don't need to unseal the mutant's lips, so he can spit his deadly discharge through his mouth. I need to make him *fart deadly discharge gas*! And, hell yeah, I know what to do. My eyes smack right onto the can of beans I'd sorted in one of the junk piles. Mad fast, I click the can, then the mutant. And . . .

RRRRRRUUUP! A fart graphic rips across the screen, sound and all. The mist clears. The bug staggers and falls on its ass, legs jerking all over the place. The camera pulls back, and we suddenly see the full mutant in all his glory, nose to toes to gassy tail. The screen changes. The mutant stands in the middle of the Brooklyn Bridge again, fist-pumping his triumph. Victory music plays.

I fall back, flat against the grave. Cooked. Relieved. Maybe even happy. Feels like Ed's happy, too. Like we can both get some rest now.

"Can't wait to tell Jack this one," I tell Ed. My phone buzzes. I hold it upside down, over my face.

Chela: Fine—don't call me. Here you go.

There's a picture. It's my parents. Sitting side by side, which they haven't done for years. Where would Chela get an old picture of my parents? I'm about to sit up, call her, when something else registers. There's a cat in the picture. Chela's cat, Walter. And it hits me. My parents are there. Now. At Chela's house.

Pop came to Brooklyn. He and Ma have joined forces against me.

JersiGame

"The Bloody Bishop welcomes you," says a massive Black guy in orange tights. Got on a red tunic. Fake muscles bulging on top of his real ones. Behind him's a roomful of costumed people pounding on laptops, throwing dice, dealing cards. I close the door behind me, knowing I made the right call, coming to JersiGame. Put some distance between me and the parent posse. I'm doing everything I can for Ed's game to get its chance.

"Here's the thing," I tell the big guy in the tights. "I forgot to submit my game online. But I still wanna—"

"You brought your eight-minute demo?" he interrupts in a fake ultra-deep voice.

"Uh . . ."

He sighs. "Alas, you are not alone. Here is how it works." He starts rattling off rules like the voice-over in a car commercial. Behind him, the place is almost all guys. A few girls stick out like something green growing out of the sidewalk, in full armor and headgear, or skimpy tops and thigh-high boots. One of them actually *is* green, head to toe, in a snake-woman bodysuit.

"Since you did not submit *and* have no demo," the Bishop guy's saying, "you can set up eight minutes of play per player. You will have to reset the challenges for each new player, which will slow you down and reduce the number of people who can play and therefore vote for you. Please remember, that is your own fault. After the con, the committee plays through the whole game and awards additional points based on the full gaming experience. Results will arrive in your email."

"That'll work," I say. All I got for sure is I can still enter Ed's game, which is good enough. He leads the way to a long table that cuts through the middle of the room. The whole place stinks like a locker room. At the table, there's a Wakanda warrior on one side of me, a kid in a stormtrooper suit on the other. This much I get: contestants like me are sitting on this side of the table with their laptops in front of them, facing away. On the other side of the table, people line up to play the game and vote. All the other contestants have lines already. I pull out the laptop and set it up as quick as I can. I don't even feel tired anymore. The room's got that feeling of intense anticipation, like the last minute of a tied basketball game.

A kid walks up. White kid with ears that stick out, wearing fake-leather boots, suspenders, vest. A dagger pops out of his belt.

"What's here?" he asks.

"Classic point-and-click adventure," I say, sounding like Ed. "Kick-ass puzzles. Surprises on every level. You get to be this mutant kid, and you have to beat a three-headed bug that's taking over Brooklyn." I had practiced my pitch on the way over, put as much Ed in it as I could. I can tell it worked because the kid sits down, rolls up his sleeves.

"These graphics are insane," he says. "You drew all these?"

"Nah," I say. "My friend did them."

"They're awesome," he says.

"Yup."

He hits a timer I hadn't seen, starts playing, so intense that a line starts behind him. All over the room, people are like that, but totally separate, everybody focused on whatever's in front of them. I get a hit of pride for getting Ed's game here. Did what all these people are doing right this second. Kept my eye on the game. Figured it out.

In eight minutes, the bell rings.

The big-eared kid looks up, all bright-eyed. "SirBugUs," he says. "Who doesn't love a play on Greek mythology?" He keeps talking, but a guy with a JersiGame shirt kicks him out. I reset. Another kid sits in the seat, doesn't even look at me, just gets his game on. I check my phone. No news about Jack. More messages from Ma. The day goes on like this, checking for messages, watching my steady line of players. Thinking of Ed. After a few hours, the Bishop bangs a gong, and everything stops.

"Point-and-click contestants—break! Escape room, team one, take your places!"

People jump up, move toward the back of the room, where there's a box the size of a freight elevator, with curtains in front of it. I go, too, bringing Ed's laptop with me. The green girl I saw on the way in walks out in front of the curtain. She's got big pretty eyes and long black hair. She tells us she's the game maker for the escape room. She'll be explaining the scenario in five minutes if we want to participate.

Somebody taps me on the shoulder. It's the kid with the big ears.

"She's really good," the kid says. "I've seen one of her rooms before and the team didn't beat it."

"Yeah?" I say. Check my phone to see a pileup of texts from Ma and Chela, but no news about Jack. Since I've been here, the thought of what might be happening to him's been creeping in my head, getting bigger and bigger. Cops finding him, pulling his hands behind his back. And everything I realized at Ed's grave feels like a part of me now. Jack didn't do it.

"Yeah," the kid says. "So they made her do tips this time. Get people thinking right, so they have a better chance." He points to a homemade poster on the wall, black poster board, big block letters in iridescent green ink:

ESCAPE ROOM TIPS
FRESH PERSPECTIVE MAKES ALL THE DIFFERENCE
ORGANIZE YOUR CLUES

USE YOUR EYES
REMEMBER OCCAM'S RAZOR: THE SIMPLEST ANSWER IS THE BEST

By now, I'm no stranger to gamer rules. Guess they've all got the same playbook somewhere.

"You see how it works?" the kid asks.

My phone buzzes. I give it a quick glance, expecting Ma. But it's worse. Another torture-selfie from Fisk. Him and Diamond, leaving the diner together. Fisk's got his arm around her, pulling her close. His Razer leans against them, I guess so he can have a free hand to take the picture.

"Do you?" the kid asks again, standing next to me, beaming like a stage light. "It's mainly the fresh-perspective rule. You know for a fact that the room isn't escape-proof, right? Because that's the whole point. So instead of asking how you get out, you ask what are the reasons *I think I can't* get out. And you organize your info. Say you start with locks on the door. Too easy, man, they're not gonna be the big thing. So you keep going down your list. Guards at all the exits? Okay, cool, what do you know about them? See what I'm saying? When you get rid of all the obvious shit, you'll get down to the thing you really want to spend your time on."

"Makes sense," I say. The fresh perspective thing isn't so different from what Ed and Diamond taught me about things not being how they look. Reminds me even more of something Ed said, the day he showed me the orange *U*, red *E, YET?* puzzle, the one Guz put on his T-shirts.

Ed'd said, *How I do it is close my eyes and, like, wipe my brain like it's a chalkboard. Then I open my eyes and stare at the puzzle. Don't even blink.*

I check out the rules on the wall again. *Organize your clues.* Had I done that? In my mind, I go backwards, over everything, from the start. What happened the day Jack got arrested. The burner phone. The night we went to Coney Island. The cop at our door and what Jack said when he turned up on the stoop. And, of course, the game clues. I think about the last rhyme, the one I couldn't get past.

"Then, of course, there's Occam's razor," says the big-eared kid. "Simple is best, even though sometimes your mind wants to complicate—"

"'Scuse me," I interrupt. Wanting to try Ed's mind-wiping trick, I open the laptop, pull up the last rhyme, the one I couldn't get past. Then I close my eyes, wipe my brain like it's a chalkboard, open my eyes and stare at the puzzle.

> Please! You think you're nearly there?
> You have no chance of survival!
> You'll be forever frozen here
> 'Less you blaze a trail to your fearsome rival.

"*'Less you blaze a trail to your fearsome rival,*" I say out loud. "Holy. Fuck!"

Was the answer in my face the whole time? I just had to see it different? Ask the right question? Focus on the right word for *this* puzzle?

"You okay?" the big-eared kid asks.

"Couldn't tell you," I say, because my head's all over the place and I've got a racy heart, sweaty-palms thing going, too.

"You wouldn't want to stand in for me, would you?" I ask him. "Take over my place with the game?"

He looks confused. "I have to go to *every* game so I can make an informed choice," he says. I roll my eyes, move away.

Back at the long table, the sound comes out of me as I bend over my phone. *Hmhmhmhmhmhmhm.*

First, I send an email to get backup to rep Ed's game, decline another call from Chela. Then I start hitting websites, checking the theory that's growing clear as hell in my head. I check three different stores, call them to be sure. Check a bunch of sites where people make deals to buy and sell stuff to each other. And it all fits.

Next, I take care of Ed. It's easy, finding Guz online, *gamerguz4_justice* is all over the place. The hard part's asking for his help. I can picture the smugness sliding out his pores when he reads my message. But I also know he'll get it done.

Now, there's just one last question, and only one person can answer it. Breathing hard, *hmhmhmhm*-ing like a fool, I send messages to every one of Jack's social media accounts. Ignore the bounce-backs, just keep going. Because Jack's the last piece of the puzzle. When I'm done with social media, I do his in-game accounts. I remember his YouTube channel, throw the message up there, because he's set it up to give him notifications when he gets messages. I check back on my work. Posted in eleven places, all the same message.

> Meet me tonight at ten any way you can. Outside the gate where my diamond shines. It's important. TRUST ME.

Finally, I call Chela.

Jack and June

The neon sign's turned off for the night, leaving Yard's parking lot to the dull yellow glow drifting over from the streetlamps. I look at the restaurant, the cut-through to Diamond's house, *the spot*. And wonder if it's finally over.

"You're still not gonna tell me what this is all about?" Chela asks. "You got a kid you hate to cover the game contest. Got me to send your parents there after you left. And, whatever this is, your parents better not come for me when it's over." She sounds salty but impressed. It was a stroke of genius, telling her to tell my parents the truth—I was at JersiGame, representing Ed's game. Only thing she didn't say was that I'd be long gone before they got there.

"They'll be all right," I tell Chela. "By the time they get back, I'll be home." Funny, how casual I sound. Because if I called this right, a whole hell of a lot's going down before I see home tonight.

Chela grunts. Starts talking about how cold it is. True, but I know it in my head more than feel it. Feelings can't be a thing tonight. I look down at my phone, at the big mistake I already made from giving in to feelings. The message I sent to Fisk after the ones to Jack and Chela.

ME: Serial numbers don't lie.

Dumb move. But it doesn't matter now. Five minutes before Jack's supposed to be here. Five minutes. Just focus.

"So, listen," Chela says. "I tried to find you when you wouldn't answer your phone. I got Robbie to drive me around, look for you. It might sound weird, but we went to see Junie because you were so into asking her what she knows, remember?"

"I'm done with that," I tell her. "Got what I needed to know."

"We went to where she works," Chela keeps going, like she didn't hear me. "Junie. To one of these big apartment buildings where she does manicures and pedicures for people."

I ignore her. Three minutes. A guy pushes a shopping cart on the opposite sidewalk. He's stooped over, so I can't see his face. I wonder if it's our same homeless guy, got himself some new gear.

"You don't think it's weird?" Chela asks. "That I went to see Junie?"

"It really doesn't matter," I say, getting irritated.

"It doesn't," she says. "Except . . ."

She sounds so freaked-out I turn to look at her. Her eyes shift to the ground. She pulls her lips in.

"What's wrong with you?" I ask. And then . . . "Oh, *come on.* You didn't!"

"I didn't sleep with her, if that's what you think," she says. "But I knew she was queer, Veeze, because of how she was looking at me when we got high. And I wanted to see her again because she's so different. So different from any of the queer kids I know. It's not the biggest deal in the world for her. It's—"

"Do you know how much I don't want to talk about this?" I ask, not even believing she's going there. "We're not having this conversation!" I say.

"Fine!" she says. "I just wanted to tell you I'm not gonna do anything about it. Even if she is cute as hell, she's Singer's kid."

"Stepkid," I say, autopilot. It's so stupid it makes me want to laugh. Right then a shadow falls over us. A hand claps down on my shoulder.

"This better be good," Jack says.

The Game Maker

"Finally," Chela says. "He's here. Let's get this going."

Jack's got on a big puffer coat, hood up. What shows of his face is stressed, but it's still damn good to see him.

"You know what's up?" I ask. I gotta figure he guessed what I'm up to, or he wouldn't've shown up. He looks over his shoulder, checks the street.

"I'm gonna need you to tell me," he says. "And quick, if you don't mind."

"Right now," I say, willing my voice to stay calm. "Here's how it's gonna go. There's something I need to show you. So, we're gonna go look at the thing, but we're not gonna talk, because Ms. Fox might be upstairs, and we don't want her hearing us. So, we're just gonna look and take a picture. Then, we'll go to the diner and talk."

"That's the plan?" Chela asks, disgusted. "Why couldn't we just meet at the nice warm diner?"

"You'll see. Come on." I turn, lead them into the parking lot. Heart's hammering something fierce. I'll feel like the biggest ass in the universe if I'm wrong. But I don't think it's gonna go that way.

Jack grabs my arm. "You sure you know what you're doing?" he asks.

"Yeah, I do," I tell him, shooting up a prayer that it's true. We're halfway across the lot when we all hear it at the same time. Footsteps by the restaurant's back door. *Footsteps.* I go stiff, but Chela steps forward. With the neon sign turned off, and the parking lot between us and the streetlights, it's too dark to see anything.

"Ms. Fox?" Chela calls. "Ms. Fox, is that you?"

No one answers.

"It's just us, VZ and Chela," she says. "Okay?"

The footsteps have stopped. Nobody answers, and I'm not surprised. I turn on the flashlight on my phone. All the rage I've been trying to keep back since I figured this out comes slamming into my throat. I know who it is. I swallow. Raise the light.

Fisk steps out from behind the dumpster. I concentrate on holding my flashlight hand steady. The rage is shaking me for sure. But a part of me's glad he's here, because now I know for sure. He's on foot, not on his scooter. His hands are empty, down by his sides. I wonder if he came ready.

"Look who it is," he says, grinning like he's happy to see us. "What you all doing here so late?"

Beside me, Jack wipes a hand across his face.

"We came to look for something," I tell Fisk. "You?"

"Just meeting my girl," he says. "She's in there being a mama to Ms. Fox, like she does." He waits a beat. "So, what, one of you leave your phone or something?"

I shine the light in his eyes. "My phone's right here," I say. "Go on inside, we'll see you in there."

Fisk doesn't move.

"Veeze, what's going on?" Chela asks. "Why don't we just go inside?"

I don't answer. I'm trying to figure out some kind of plan B. There's probably ten feet between Fisk and me. I know he's not gonna move, and I'm sure as hell not leaving him out here. The only plan B is to get back to plan A.

"It's all about how you figure shit out," I say. "Puzzles and riddles. About finding the answer in the question—or the question in the answer . . ." I take a breath. "It means we shouldn't ask: Who killed Singer? We should ask: How come it looks like Jack killed Singer when we know he didn't?" Even with my heart flipping out, it feels good to say that last part. I've owed it to Jack. He doesn't react, though. The space between us is like a vacuum waiting to get filled. I keep talking.

"I learned all this stuff from Ed and his game. And Diamond. Once I had the right question, I had to look for the simplest answer—that's this Occam's razor thing. I had to look at everything that's happened, from beginning to end. Organize my clues, get it all straight in my head.

"First thing that happened was Jack saying that dumb shit to the cops. Telling them nobody'd talk to them no matter what they knew. So, I asked myself, how come he'd say that? Simplest answer: because it was true." I force myself to keep looking at Fisk, even though I can feel Jack's energy wilding.

"Jack was the person," I say. "He was talking about *himself* when he said no one was gonna tell what they saw." I ignore the little yell Chela lets out. "Because he was here that night, or at least close by, checking out that girl Jasmine who lives over here. Close enough to see the person who did it. That's how come the cops had evidence against him. That homeless guy saw him and told. But Jack wasn't gonna snitch. Not even to me. And he wanted the person who did it to know that. So he said so to the cops right in front of that person."

There's so much adrenaline pumping through me, I can't feel my body. I pretty much just told them who did it, but I don't know if they get it yet. Doesn't matter. I'm the game maker now. I know what to do next.

"But the plan backfired," I say. "The cops took Jack in, and the person who did it got scared. So then, this person who killed Singer? They did some real dirty shit. Planted bullshit evidence that made it look like Jack might've done it. I'm guessing that person wanted to scare Jack into 'forgetting' what he'd seen. To show him that he could make it look bad for him if he didn't stay out of it. Anyhow, once I got all that, a couple of other things made sense. Like Diamond's fancy new Alienware laptop in a room full of old relics. And the whole wrench thing—just because the cops said it was a wrench that killed Singer didn't make it true. Which brought me to the color of Fisk's scooter. . . ."

Every muscle in me tenses, ready to jump his ass when he runs for it. Instead, he comes with his laugh.

"My scooter, dude? You losing it. What could my scooter have to do with any of this?"

"I didn't get it till this morning," I say. "When you sent me the picture. Everything in that diner was dull, and I saw how shiny your scooter is. Realized it's seemed that way for a while. Too bright and shiny. And I put it together with something the homeless guy said—that he didn't tell the cops everything he knew. 'Cause, see, he's the only one that noticed there were two scooters. The one you've been riding around on, and the one that's behind that dumpster right now. That's been there since the night you used it to smash Phillip Singer on his head."

Chela gasps. None of us looks at her. Fisk and I eye each other like hungry rats next to the last crumb of food.

"The cops didn't take it," I say, "when they searched the place in their investigation, because Ms. Fox said it was yours, right? Belonged to one of her employees. So they left it alone. And you thought you'd got away with it. Then you realized something. The simplest solution to stashing the murder weapon behind a dumpster at the scene of the crime? Leave it there. You were too scared to go back and get it, anyhow. Didn't want to risk anybody seeing you pull it out. Not until I was stupid enough to send you that text."

"What text?" Jack asks.

But Fisk's letting out his famous laugh. "You trippin' like this because my scooter's here? At my job? I leave it here all the time. Matter of fact, I was planning on picking it up tonight when I got

Diamond." And then he does it. Leans back behind the dumpster. Pulls out the scooter. It's too dark to see how bright it is, but like I said, serial numbers don't lie. I'd called all those scooter stores, so I knew there's a number on that scooter that's different from the one he's been riding around on lately—the one I'd seen in the pictures he kept sending today. I wonder if this one's still got Singer's DNA on it.

"Right," Fisk says. "You're trippin' so bad, I think I better get on out of here. Tell my girl I'll call her later, all right?"

It's what I've been waiting for. "You're gonna have to go through me," I tell him. Watch for his littlest move. But it's Jack who moves. Turns to me, raises his arms to the hands-up position.

"Easy, buddy," he says to me. "Chill a minute, so we can talk."

But Fisk's putting a foot on that scooter. And I'm not having it. I throw myself at him, and we go down on top of the scooter. Jack jumps on me, tries to pull me off. I hear Chela shout, feel her weight, too. It's a four-body pileup when light breaks over us.

Fisk

"What in the name of Jesus is happening here?" Ms. Fox yells. None of us moves except for Fisk, struggling under three bodies. The padded rubber handle of the scooter juts out from under his arm.

"Fisk?" It's Diamond's voice. "VZ? Not again, you two, come on!"

I feel Jack's and Chela's weight lift off me, but I stay where I am, pinning Fisk and the scooter to the ground.

"VZ, what's *wrong* with you?" Diamond yells, and it stings in spite of everything.

"Victor!" Ms. Fox commands. "Come!"

"The scooter has to come, too," I shout. "I'll let him go if somebody grabs the scooter first." Fisk sends a fierce elbow thrust into my gut. It winds me, but I hold on. Ms. Fox bends over me, and

I wonder if she'll try to pull me off. Wonder if she can. But Chela speaks up.

"I'll get the scooter!" she says.

I trust her. Try to get my feet under me, dead-lift this fool off the scooter. He's fighting against it, but I hoist, and it's enough. Chela grabs the scooter, pulls it out from under. I let go of Fisk, and Ms. Fox hustles us inside. I'm not surprised Fisk comes, too, now that Chela's got the scooter.

The restaurant feels wrong. No food smells, the lights too bright. Ms. Fox stands with her back to the door, checking us out.

"Who wants to tell me?" she says.

I know it's on me. I take the scooter from Chela, hold it out to Ms. Fox. "*This*," I tell her. "It's the—" I break off because it's hard to say without feeling like I'm making shit up, being dramatic. But it's the truth. "It's the thing that killed Singer. And he's the one who swung it."

I point at Fisk. Diamond gasps. Ms. Fox's face crumples.

"It's a long story," I say, to keep them from asking questions. "There're two scooters. This one, that's been stashed outside behind the dumpster all this time. And the new one he bought and's been trying to pass off as his old one. This one's probably got Singer's DNA on it."

Everybody turns to Fisk. You can see it on his face: pain, shame, sadness. Terror. I know it adds up to guilt, but I don't feel relief that it's finally over. Everything on Fisk's face—the scaredness and sadness and pain—seems to be in the rest of us, too. It's heavy and it aches. After too long, Ms. Fox takes charge. Tells us to settle down, as if she could see the thing we were feeling. She pulls Fisk in the kitchen with her, leaving Chela, Diamond, Jack, and me in the empty dining room. Diamond looks like she got flattened by a truck.

"I just figured it out," I tell her. "Just tonight. And I couldn't tell you. It wouldn't've been fair to ask you not to tell him."

She turns her hurt face away from me. Walks across the room, leans against the wall by herself. I know better than to go after her. Chela and Jack have moved closer together, but they're not talking. Chela hugs herself, looks lost. Jack looks . . . pissed? Scared?

"I still don't get why you let it go this far," I tell him. "What were you thinking?"

He eyes the scooter I'm still holding, then the kitchen door. "I was trying to do the right thing," he says. "It had to be me, since I'm the only one who knew. I knew Fisk hadn't gone after Singer on purpose, but I needed him to give up the whole story, and he was too scared to talk. You got that part right. I tried to get him to trust me, so I could help him."

"Help him do what?" I ask. Not snitching is one thing, but this got hella outta hand. Before Jack answers, the kitchen door swings open. Ms. Fox comes out, raises a hand to keep us still. Fisk comes behind her. I stare at him hard. His face is dead serious, no trace of the bullshit grin. Serious and determined and—*grown*.

"Mr. Fisk has something to tell us," Ms. Fox says. Fisk walks over to Diamond. Stands in front of her, but she doesn't look at him. Fisk nods. Fixes his eyes on the same spot on the floor Diamond seems to be looking at. When he talks, I get the feeling he's forgotten the rest of us. He's telling it all to Diamond.

"I was making a buy," he says. "That's how it started, just a regular buy. Because I wanted to get you something extra-nice for your birthday. So I . . ." He trails off as Diamond's head snaps up. Her face is on fire.

"You think you're gonna put this on *me*?"

"I didn't mean it that way!" Fisk says. "Ms. Fox said I had to tell it all, start at the beginning. And that's the beginning."

"Uh-uh." Diamond shakes her head. "Then the beginning is when you decided it was worth it, buying and selling sneakers and who knows what all else. Don't you *dare* put that on me. Like all I care about's money but you can't trust me to care about you?"

Fisk holds up his hands. Turns away. But Ms. Fox isn't having it.

"No, dear," she says. "Keep right on. It's not a thing that's supposed to be easy."

Fisk backs himself against a wall. Looks out into space, this time, when he talks. "I—I found this guy online, selling top-of-the-line laptops for what I could afford. We set it up for the buy to happen here. I'd done buys here before because the lot's off the street, you get privacy. And if you stay over in the corner, it's away from Ms. Fox's windows." He shoots a guilty glance at Ms. Fox.

"I stopped doing it after what happened to Ed," he says. "But that night, the guy wanted to meet in some neighborhood I'd never heard of, so I said no. I just told him to come here, because I'd done it here before. He didn't want to at first. Then he said, fuck it, what's he got to lose. And he said he'd come." Fisk tries a glance at Diamond, goes back to looking at nothing.

"I got here first. I didn't like waiting around, but I really wanted to get it for you, for your birthday. When he drove up, got out of the car, he looked familiar, but I didn't think about it. I'd been there too long, I wanted to get it done with before Ms. Fox came out or something. But he said he'd got another offer since we'd talked, he could get more for it, so he wanted more from me. We got into it. And he . . ." Fisk takes a breath. Starts talking faster. "He kept on looking away from me, over at the spot, you know, where Ed died. And when he got mad, I put it together all at once. How he'd sounded weird on the phone when I told him where I wanted to meet. Why his face seemed familiar. Why he kept on looking at that spot. And I realized he was *that* guy, the guy who'd killed Ed. I wanted to run, but he grabbed me, and he shook me. I thought it would be Ed all over again, except me this time bleeding out in the parking lot. I almost blacked out, I was so scared. He was strong and angry and drunk. We tussled. And then there was this second when I saw the scooter and I grabbed it and I—I hit him . . . I thought it would buy time so I could run. But he staggered back, and I knew it was bad. Then a light came on inside, and Ms. Fox was coming. So I started to run. And . . . and I saw the dumpster, and I threw the scooter behind it. And I just . . . ran like hell.

"I swear it to God, I swear I didn't mean to kill him. I just got scared. It was an accident."

"No." Diamond says it to the floor. "This can't be true." Fisk makes a move like he wants to touch her, but he doesn't. He's gotta know there's nothing he can say that'll matter. Much as I hate him, it's hard to watch. The whole room's like that, too real to look at.

"There's more," Ms. Fox says. "You were to start at the beginning, Mr. Fisk, and end at the end. The end is not until now, this night."

"What do you want me to say?" Fisk's voice is hoarse. "I'm sorry? That's easy, because I am. You want me to say I set Jack up? I didn't, not for him to go down. I wouldn't have let that happen."

"I believe that," Jack says.

"But you didn't give a damn about the rest of us," Diamond spits at Fisk. I've never seen her like this. Breathing hard. Face so set it could break.

"I was scared like hell!" Fisk says. Not like an excuse, I'll give him that. Like he wants us to get it.

All this time, Jack's been by the stage, not saying much. He comes over now, talks quiet. "You see? I knew it was something like that. I knew Fisk wouldn't've hurt Singer if Singer didn't come at him." He's got a righteous look that pisses me off. This whole time, he thought it was Fisk, kept trying to get Fisk to tell him what happened. But he couldn't trust me enough to let me in on it?

He reads the rage I'm shooting his way. "This wasn't mine to tell," he says. "All right? And it's not about you, anyhow. It's about what happened to Ed, and all the demos and protests after. None of it means anything if we just keep letting it go down the same old way. If I have some kind of way to stop it? I'm gonna."

"What way is that?" I ask. "What in hell were you trying to do?"

He ignores me, keeps talking. "Singer was supposed to be so scared *Ed* was gonna kill him that he didn't even get *charged* for what he did, right? Now, think about Fisk. He was scared for an actual real reason. He knew for a fact Singer'd killed a Black kid right on that spot. And Singer put his hands on Fisk. Ed sure as hell never did that to Singer. So, by those rules, Fisk wouldn't get charged, either, right? *Hella wrong. Because Black people aren't allowed to get scared, and definitely not of white people.* You know it's true. Only white people get to get scared. Only white people get to defend themselves. Are we gonna keep letting it be like that?"

I shake my head. Not one thing that's happened is playing out the way I planned. Jack's eyes move from person to person, trying to see what they think. And it hits me. *I didn't plan shit.* I thought I was the game maker at this party, getting Jack and Chela to come here. And Fisk, he thought he was running the show, with his scooter switch, and his bobbing and weaving. But we were both wrong. Jack was the game maker all along. That first day, he lied about where he was when Singer got killed. Said he was home, to protect Fisk, when he was really here. Then, the day Ms. Fox reopened, he told the cops he wouldn't come clean even if he knew who did it—all to get Fisk to trust him. After he got arrested, he knew the homeless guy had seen him. Knew the cops could build a case against him. So he disappeared. But the whole time he was calling Fisk, telling him he wanted to help. He was even gaming me. Got scared that Fisk might lose it if I kept going after Diamond, so he came over to tell me to back off her.

If I weren't so pissed, I'd be impressed. This whole time, there he was, behind it all. Writing the damn code.

Who Makes the Call?

"The phone! *The goddamn burner phone!*" It's Diamond. Eyes flaming, trained on Fisk. "*That was you?*"

Oh, hell. I'd forgot about the burner. Fisk lets out a moan.

"I only did it to get Jack to quit asking questions!" he says. "I had a burner on me, and I thought if I dropped a hint about Jack, you'd tell him and he'd know I could make him look guilty, even though I wouldn't've done it for real. I just needed him to back off, quit trying to get me to talk about it, because talking about it made me want to jump out of my skin."

"That's past stupid," Jack says, finally sounding disgusted. "What were you gonna do if I'd ratted your ass out because the heat was on me?"

"You're no snitch," Fisk says. Like it's that simple. "But I should've talked to you, I wasn't thinking right. I just wanted it to go away."

Diamond lets out a fake laugh. "So you trusted Jack not to snitch, but you didn't trust me to tell me what was going on. I would've helped you. Daddy would've done anything, whatever he could. But instead of asking me for help, you *used* me." Her voice is bitter. She hugs herself.

"You think your dad could really help?" Jack asks, after a minute. "I mean, I was thinking me and Fisk should call him. . . ."

Diamond shuts him up with an ice-cold glare. Turns it on Fisk. Then me. Walks into the kitchen, boot heels clicking. All at once, I'm so tired I can hardly stay standing. I want it over. But everything around me keeps going. Ms. Fox is talking to Fisk. Chela and Jack've got their heads together over Chela's phone. I think about going in the kitchen, trying to talk to Diamond, but I don't have the energy. No point, anyhow. This time, I think she's done with Fisk and me, both.

I go to Jack and Chela. "Time to get outta here," I say.

Jack looks up first. "Yeah? What do you think happens now?" Says it like he knows the answer, and I'm about to get it wrong.

"I don't know," I say.

"Sure you do," he says. "Somebody calls the cops, right? So, who's gonna do that? *You?*"

"What?" The question, the way he asks it, makes me want to smack him. Why is everybody acting like they've got a script and won't let me see it?

"I told you, Jackson," I say. *"I don't know."*

He lets my answer hang in the air awhile. "I know why you did this."

"What the fuck are you talking about?"

"Why you figured out who killed Singer. Because you weren't so sure it wasn't me. Not entirely. And you figured you'd better be, huh? Before accusing your oldest friend in the world."

Oh. I give him a nod, let him know he's right. Suck up the wave of shame that runs through me. But he doesn't even leave it at that.

"You know why you thought it could've been me?" he asks.

"Fuck, Jack! Because you didn't tell me the goddamn truth?"

"I told you plenty of truth. *I told you the cops set me up.* But you didn't believe the guy you've known your whole life. And that's because you had a whole other story put in front of you. *This Black kid did it for revenge. Makes sense, doesn't it? He had a temper. And a motive. And a record.* Sound familiar?"

"I'm too tired for this," I tell him.

He doesn't let up. "You think a system that was ready to throw me under the jail for something I didn't do is gonna give Fisk a fair shot?"

"*Stop talking!*" I say. "Because you're not making sense. Are you saying you want to go down instead of him?"

"I have to believe there's a way none of us goes down. That's what I've been trying to figure out this whole time."

"And there is." Chela breaks in the conversation like she's been waiting to give her line. "Ronnah." She half whispers the name. Her voice shakes a little, but her eyes stay steady on mine. "Restorative justice. We can get Singer's family involved. Do it ourselves, without the cops and courts."

Jack eyes her like she's grown six inches, turned into Barack

Obama. They're serious.

"Che," I say. Try not to jump on her, 'cause I know this stuff's important to her. "We're talking about killing somebody. Not some school shit that was an accident in the first place."

"This was an accident, too!" she says. "And Ronnah doesn't just do RJ in schools. She could talk to Singer's family, Junie and her mom, I guess. See if there's a way to make it right between everyone."

"But there can't be!" I say. "Come on, Singer's family? Why would they do that?"

"I'm just saying we call Ronnah before we do anything else," Chela says. Glances at Ms. Fox, and I know she wants me to side with her and Jack, present a united front to convince Ms. Fox.

"*And not call the cops?*" I ask. Needing to make sure I'm getting this right. "That's what you're saying?"

Chela grabs my hand, squeezes it. "And *not* call the cops," she says. "That's exactly what we're saying."

Don't Tell Ronnah

Dear Ed,

Who knew things would start making sense just because I talked to you? But it went that way last time. So, this is something I do now. Write you letters.

First, your game's in. We repped you through the whole contest, thanks to help from your friend Guz. Whatever happens, everybody who played it loved it. You did good.

And speaking of your game. What the hell was that? Now it's all done, I have to wonder. Clues or coincidence? Jack said it wasn't him by Singer's house that day, just somebody who looked like him. My imagination filled in the rest. Was it doing that with the game clues, too? But come on! Junie's ma's name being a palindrome? The bug truck? Jahvaris having green water in his fish tank? And that last game rhyme where it said I had to get to my rival? And I realized Fisk was my rival!

Were you up in this, buddy? Feel free to let me know. . . .

. Okay, next. What Fisk did. And what Jack and Chela want to do about it. You gotta know, I wanted the whole thing over with for you as much as for me. Everything to do with Singer, done. Finished. But it got complicated. Jack wanted the RJ thing bad. And he called me out on being scared.

You want to think they won't come for you if you play by the rules, is what he said. But you gotta see they're coming for us anyhow. Truth? I didn't do it 'cause he called me out, or 'cause he made a good argument. I did it 'cause I felt the rightness. It's not like I want to see Fisk in jail. I want him to deal, like he should've all along.

So we called Ronnah. Who told us to slow the hell down. We'd have to meet with her before she'd even talk to Singer's people. She needed to be sure we even understood what we were asking. We all went home, met the next day.

What about Fisk, you ask? Couldn't he just run for it while we're dicking around with all of this? Yup. Ronnah said if he did, then RJ wouldn't've worked for him anyhow. Which isn't the point. But the scooter's locked up somewhere only Ms. Fox knows. That's something, I guess.

So I finally got some sleep (after Ma, Pop, and Bennett finished freaking out). And the next day we met with Ronnah. The rules sounded like what we did with Chela, except there'd be more people from Singer's side of things, less from Fisk's. One thing surprised me. She said if we did restorative justice, we wouldn't decide about jail, or try to figure out if Fisk's guilty or not. But in another way, we'd be doing exactly the same thing as people do in court. We'd be a group of people in a room, deciding what happens when somebody hurts somebody else. That's all any justice process has ever been, she said.

In the end, she said she'd talk to Singer's people. It would all be up to them. And if—by some miracle—they said yes, we'd be meeting a lot more before the actual circle. To me, the whole thing's like one of Bennett's gluten-free, sugar-free vegan desserts. A zillionth chance it's gonna work, ten zillion ways it could go wrong. But we all waited by our phones anyhow. Then, when the message finally came, that next Sunday afternoon, it was from Chela, not Ronnah, and it said: Junie's ma wants to meet Fisk. Not allowed to tell Ronnah. Pick you up in 20.

Yup, Singer's girlfriend. Junie's ma. Wants to meet Fisk. I can pretty much feel the shit show we're about to walk into. But since I can't stand waiting anymore, I'm going.

Red Norma

"Get a grip!" Chela jumps out of the driver's seat of Robbie's car, which is parked in front of my building. Robbie's nowhere in sight. In the back seat, sitting way too close together, are Diamond and Fisk. At the sight of them, I turn around, head right back inside. We're supposed to be taking Fisk to see Junie and her ma, which is stupid enough. But nobody said anything about Diamond.

"I woulda warned you," Chela says, pulling me down the sidewalk. "Fisk didn't say anything about her when I called him. She was just there when I picked him up. Who cares, though? Trust me, this ain't no hookup situation."

"It's a ridiculous situation!" I say. "Why are we even doing this?"

"Because Junie's mom won't consider RJ if we don't," Chela says. "I think she wants to see Fisk ahead of time so she doesn't freak out when she sees him at the circle. And maybe she's got questions

266

but doesn't want it too official, like with Ronnah. So I'm gonna do Ronnah's part." She suddenly looks proud. "I'm gonna run down how RJ helps people who got hurt, because they can get something out of it, not just watch somebody get punished, like in court."

"And she's gonna want the punishment plan," I say. "It's bullshit Jack can't go with us. He's the one that wants it so bad." I'd started to call him when I got Chela's message. Then remembered he's still the top suspect, laying extra low at Ms. Fox's cousins' till we can figure something out.

"Just back me up," Chela says, getting in the car. "We're not letting this fall apart now."

I get in beside her, because what the hell. There's no sound coming from the back, and I make myself not look. Chela rolls her eyes, like she knows what I'm thinking.

"How is Jack anyhow?" she asks, changing the subject.

"Good," I say. Buckle my seat belt, get comfortable, like nobody's in the seat behind me. "Too good. He's sure this is gonna work. I don't know how either of you gets there. . . ."

"It's called optimism," Chela says. "Try it sometimes."

Junie's mom opens the door. I recognize her right off from when I followed her that day. Got on red again, red T-shirt, bright-print pants.

"Why are there so many of you?" she asks, instead of saying hello. "I thought it would just be the girl and the boy."

Nobody has an answer. Junie's voice comes from the other side of the door. "It's all right, Ma, just let them in."

Junie's standing by the couch, wearing tight jeans and a shirt that says "Sharpen Your Edges," over a picture of dark purple manicured fingernails. The living room's big for New York, long, with low ceilings. Feels like an airplane—dead air that makes you look for the windows so you can remember there's a world outside. The furniture's got lots of red in it, probably picked by Junie's ma. I'm starting to think of her as Red Norma.

"Sit down," Junie says.

We don't. There's six people and only five seats. "Oh, for God's sakes," she says. "Ma, you sit. And you," she points at Fisk. Her mom sits in an armchair. Fisk on the couch, way to one side. When Diamond sits next to him, I'm not even mad. I can't imagine being Fisk right now. Not feeling being me, either. Now I'm here, I want off the damn plane.

"Can I use your bathroom?" I ask.

Junie looks suspicious but points anyhow. "Back there. Second door."

I turn the lock as soon as the door closes. Feel the relief of being away. Except now I'm in Singer's bathroom. It's regular-sized, blue and brown, plants in the window. Singer's frickin' toilet. The idea of using it feels sickening. So, I open cabinets—Ma'd be proud. Doesn't believe in *not* snooping. There's the same deodorant Bennett and I use. Guy deodorant, I realize. Which means they haven't cleared Singer's stuff out yet—or else there's some new guy, but that'd be quick for anybody. So, if they didn't clean out his stuff, is it because they can't stand to get rid of it, like Ma was when my grandma died? Could anybody really like Singer that much? I open the cabinet under the sink. Behind the cleaning stuff, there's something called . . . holy fuck . . . *Weener* Kleener. *TMI times ten!* I close the door, quick. I want it to be funny—and it is. But it's not. I run hot water, wash my hands. Get the hell out, even though it means going back to the living room scene.

"Oh, good!" Chela says, throwing me a serious stink-eye as she says it. "You're back." She's standing behind the couch, facing Junie's ma, and I stand next to her. "Junie's mom was just asking . . . I mean Mrs.—"

"Norma," Red Norma says. "What I want is for him to tell me what happened." She's zeroed in on Fisk, so no need to ask who *he* is. "Right now, regular talk. Before we do whatever this other thing is."

"But you're going to do it, right?" Chela says. "Because if you have questions . . ."

"I want to hear it in my own living room," Norma says. "Out of his mouth. I got a right to that much." Her chest heaves under the red shirt, and it's not hard to picture her smashing glasses. The room feels charged. Electric.

"Okay," Fisk says. "I'll tell you." He stops, though. Like now he needs permission for every word.

"Yeah," says Red Norma. "Yeah. Go on."

Fisk grips his thighs, keeps his eyes unfocused as he talks. I don't want to hear his story again, but looking away's not easy when somebody's fighting so hard to get every word out. "We . . . Singer . . . Mr. Singer and I talked on the phone, because I'd seen his ad online, that he had stuff to sell."

Red Norma watches him like a wildcat I saw in a video once, tracking prey. Junie has the same kind of look, but she's eyeing her mother, not Fisk.

"He was selling some electronics. And he—we'd emailed each other, but we couldn't agree on the prices. So, we, we talked. And I told him—"

"No!" The voice is a *crack* in the tense room. It's Diamond. "Don't tell her any more, okay?"

Chela shoots me a *What the hell?* look. I shake my head. No clue.

"I already told it," Fisk mutters to Diamond. "I couldn't take it back if I wanted to."

"That doesn't matter," Diamond says. "I grew up with a lawyer, trust me. This isn't right, us being here on our own."

"Jesus!" Junie groans. "You're the ones who didn't want lawyers."

I try to catch Chela's eye. Diamond's right, we should get out of here. Pop may be just a dial-a-lawyer, but he'd say the same. Chela doesn't look my way, though. Red Norma moves to the edge of her chair.

"Somebody calls me up out of nowhere," she says. "And tells me they know who killed my guy? But I'm not supposed to go to the cops. No, I'm supposed to just follow them, do whatever they want. That's not right! Even you kids should know it."

"It's not about what we want," Chela says. "It's a process that's been around for hundreds of years. I can run it down for you, all the reasons—"

"And if I don't agree, then what?" Norma snaps. "This guy runs for it?"

That shuts us up a minute. Till Fisk says, "I'm still here."

I'm glad he said it, let her know it's a choice—probably one he has to make every minute of every day, not to run. But now he has to choose whether to tell Red Norma what she wants to know, or whether to listen to Diamond. Norma can't sit still and wait. She springs off her chair. Starts to pace.

"Diamond's right," I whisper to Chela. "Let's go."

Chela doesn't answer, because now, Norma's at the window. Opening a drawer in the desk underneath it.

Pulling out a gun.

We all freeze. Except for my brain, which is racing. Is this a fake, like in the pizza place? Or is she batshit? About to kill us all? Do we drop to the ground? Jump her?

"It's Phil's gun," Norma says in her calm, pissed-off voice. "The cops said it was still in his pants when they found him. You can't prove he pulled it on him."

"Fisk never said Singer pulled his gun that night," Diamond says, powerful, channeling her dad. She shifts forward on the couch, shielding Fisk—and I can tell it's from the questions, not the gun. Because Norma's still holding the gun flat on her hand. And it hits me.

"That's the gun that . . ." I feel skeeved-out, like maggots are crawling on me, before I finish the sentence in my head. *That's the gun that killed Ed.*

"Why do you have that still?" I say to Norma. Don't care that I'm too loud. "You should burn it! Get rid of it!"

Norma drops her gaze to the gun. For the first time, she looks nervous. "The cops gave it back to me, I . . . I'm just lettin' you know, there's no proof he threatened anybody." She wraps the gun in a cloth, puts it back in the drawer. I'm past ready to be out of here, but Red Norma just looks out the window. Takes a breath.

"Are you gonna tell me, or not?" she asks Fisk, her back still to us.

Diamond whispers something to Fisk. He swallows. Says, "Yes, ma'am. When we do the RJ. I'll tell you everything, I promise."

"Well," Norma says. "Then there's no point in your being here." Since she's not looking our way, it's a minute before we realize she's kicking us out.

"Come on," I say. Before moving for the door, I follow Norma's gaze. Glance out the window. Straight at the cop car that's parked in front of the building. I blink a few times, stare a minute, before I get it.

"It's some kind of setup," I say. "She got him here and called the cops. They're outside."

Red Norma doesn't deny it. Fisk seems to shrink into the couch.

"Why would you do that?" Chela asks. "Why not just say no to the RJ thing, if that's what you wanted?"

Norma doesn't answer.

"Unless . . ." Diamond says slowly. "Were you trying to get some kind of confession out of him?"

"Wait!" Chela shoots a quick look at me. "Are you *taping* this? *Oh shit. Are you?*"

"Relax!" Junie shouts. "He didn't say anything, remember?"

"I'm calling my dad." Diamond pulls her phone out of her

pocket. "He's not walking into cops without a lawyer." I'm reeling from all the twists. The gun. A tape. *More* cops. I get that they set up Fisk, but I don't get why. And I'm not alone.

"It still doesn't make sense!" Chela says. "If you don't want RJ, why are we here?"

"Because!" Junie snaps. "We wanted the damn truth. We needed to know what really happened." She flaps a hand at Fisk. "If this guy mighta set Phil up on purpose. Or if . . . if maybe Phil did something . . . like before. We knew he'd never tell the truth once we got in court, so . . ."

The pieces snap in place for me. They wanted answers, just like I wanted answers about what happened with Ed right before he died. And they figured once Fisk was in court, he'd say whatever his lawyer told him would get him the best deal. Which might or might not be the truth.

"We weren't gonna use the tape," Junie says, "unless he tried to lie later, in court."

Disappointment crosses Chela's face, and I get that Junie was the reason she'd had all that hope.

"Hell no," she says. "Hell, hell, hell no. Ronnah always says that—that nobody tells the truth in court. It's one reason people choose RJ, to get the truth. But you don't get to have it both ways."

For the first time, I feel some of her righteousness. Because, what the hell? No fair, trying to get out of the part where the system sucks but use the part where it's rigged in your favor. I go stand behind Chela. Fisk stands, too, all of us on our feet now.

"She's right," I say. "You want court, you pick court. And you take what goes with it. You want real answers, you pick RJ. But you gotta pick."

We wait. Red Norma finally turns from the window, trains her eyes on Fisk. "If I do this, and you run, I swear I'll fucking find you," she says.

"I believe you," Fisk says.

Norma turns back to the window.

"Put your phone away," Junie says to Diamond. "I'll get rid of them."

And she goes to call off the cops one last time.

Shortcake Shrink

"That didn't happen, right?" I ask Chela. "We were tandem dreaming, or whatever you call it."

We're in her living room, finally. Dropped off Diamond and Fisk, waited for Robbie to come pick up his car. Now we're here, crashed out on the floor in front of the couch.

"Because if we're not dreaming," Chela says, "Singer's weird-ass woman basically pulled a gun on us."

"And had a squad car waiting at the curb," I say.

"And who was that in Diamond's tiny little weave-headed body?" Chela asks. We do saucer eyes at each other, laugh for about ten minutes. And that's before I get to the Weener Kleener. Then Chela remembers her ma made strawberry shortcake and brings it out. We sit up on opposite sides of the coffee table, forks out. Not bothering with plates.

I'm sugar-drunk when I finally say, "I got *zero* love for Fisk. You know that. I wish to hell it hadn't been him, though."

Now it's real, what with Red Norma pulling guns, setting up Fisk, it's a crap feeling knowing I started it. I need Chela to know I did it to get the heat off Jack, not put it on Fisk. *Mostly.* I shove more cake in my mouth.

"I know," Chela says. Leaves it at that.

A few mouthfuls later, she says, "I'd be mad, you know, about Ronnah letting you be in the circle and not me. Except you need it so bad."

Far as I know, she *is* mad about it. Went off when Ronnah told her she could help with prep but there wasn't "a legitimate reason" for her to be in the circle. But I keep listening.

"What you just said?" Chela goes on. "About wishing it hadn't been Fisk. It took you a minute to get there, right?"

"I guess."

"Okay, so RJ helps you figure shit like that out. Remember when Ronnah said you needed to talk about Ed in order to be a part of my circle? Well, this one's even more about him. So, there'll be all kinds of stuff that comes up for you. And it'll give you a chance to . . . see your own perspective, I guess. Maybe see what you need in all this, from yourself or anybody else."

"Need for what?" I ask. "It doesn't have anything to do with me, now Jack's in the clear."

Chela looks unimpressed. "You know that's not true."

"I mean, other than being fucked by what Singer did," I say. Get up to get drinks, hoping to end the conversation.

"That's the thing," Chela says, the second I get back. "Maybe you can be less fucked, now. Maybe it's time." She holds up a hand, takes a swig of the ginger ale I brought her. "Don't answer, Veeze. Just think about it."

How It Went Down

Me: Almost there. How come I'm so nervous?

Chela: Cuz it's a big fkn deal

Me: For Fisk, not me

Chela: For all of us

Me: Fuck

I wipe my sweaty neck. Now I'm almost at the circle, there's no playing it off. It's *too* big an effin' deal. Too much responsibility, too much pressure to get it right. Which is too much to put in a text. I pocket my phone, walk the last few steps.

The place is some kind of community center that Red Norma picked out. There's a glass door. Ronnah sees me through it, waves me in. We're in a big room with linoleum floors, fold-up tables stacked in a corner, and a circle of chairs dead in the middle of the floor. Fisk and Jack are standing by a food table with coffee and a plate of bagels, neither one of them eating. Fisk looks like he's at church, in black pants and a white button-down. Even Jack's dressed up in his polo shirt. I head over, glad I listened to Chela, put a button-down over my T-shirt.

"Ready for this?" I ask.

"Not even a little," Fisk says. Jack drops an arm around his shoulder. I offer up an encouraging nod. And the door opens again. Red Norma and Junie come in with two other people.

"'Bout to be go time," Jack whispers. And then it is.

Ronnah makes us turn off our phones, put them away. We take our seats, go over introductions and rules, pass the talking piece, which is a red enamel music box that Singer gave Norma. I take a mental picture of the circle for Chela. Clockwise from Ronnah, it's Fisk, Jack, then me, then a woman named Judith Park, who's got a strong perfume smell. She's Norma's support, so Norma's on her other side. Then Junie and her support, a girl named Fiona. It's like we're all holding different parts of a giant rubber band—all connected, reacting to each other and the heaviness of what we're about to do. I wish I could text Chela, tell her how intense it already is.

We don't go long before Ronnah asks the big question: "What happened that night at Yard?" Fisk takes the talking piece. His eyes drop to his knees, and I feel him force them back up. I wonder if he'll be able to look at Norma and Junie, and he does, mostly—shifting his gaze between them, Ronnah, and Jack. He says it all, his plan to buy stuff from Singer, how it went wrong. Him realizing who Singer was. Singer grabbing him, and him grabbing the scooter. Norma sits forward on her chair in a way that makes me wonder if she knows she's doing it. She watches Fisk's eyes, his mouth. She doesn't move, and neither do the rest of us.

When Fisk's done, he's got tears on his face. Doesn't wipe them away. After a long minute, he passes the talking piece to me. I know there's nothing I need to say right then, so I give it to Ms. Park, who passes it straight to Norma. She's crying, too, now. Eyes locked on Fisk. She wipes her tears. "I believe you."

The whole circle lets out a breath.

When Norma takes the music box, I don't want to listen. Don't want to feel sorry because Singer got killed. But it's impossible not to listen, the room's so quiet, focused on her.

"I was home," she says, "when I got the call. I knew right off from the voice. They had a woman call, and I could hear right off she was trying to be nice. Gentle, I guess. I knew just from the way she asked if I was Norma Camron." She looks at Junie, who doesn't look away. "It was like I'd been waiting for it. After what Phil did, and we'd got all the hate mail. My first thought was, 'The other shoe. It finally came down.'"

She looks sad, lost, and I can't help feeling sorry for her. But what hits me most is, Singer's own family thought he'd get revenge-killed before it even happened. If the cops'd arrested Jack, they'd've swallowed it, 100 percent, that it was him.

When Ronnah puts out the next question—"What was

happening for you in the days after you heard about Singer?"—Fisk goes quick. Says he felt guilty and scared. Says he prayed a lot, for Singer and his family and for himself. I buy it, since most people would.

Then it's on Jack.

"I felt like the world flipped over," he says. "I'd been wanting Singer to pay all that time, and now he was dead and everything was worse instead of better. Then that shit with the cops went down, and I thought it'd make Fisk talk to me, but that didn't work, either. Whoo, I don't know! I wanted it over, so bad. Except, I was part of it because I had this secret. So it felt like the whole ugly thing was on my skin, inside me. And I had to keep clear of the cops and everybody I cared about till I could get it right with Fisk."

When he puts it that way, I get it. Not that I'd have done it his way. But nothing new there. He hands me the box, and I hold it a minute, decide if I want to talk. "I heard what happened the next day at breakfast," I say. "With my ma. It was good, because we hadn't eaten together in a while. When we heard, she came over and hugged me. I think we both knew he wasn't just gonna die and stay dead. We knew it was gonna be bad for everybody who loved Ed."

I pass the box on, knowing what I said is true. I don't know how I knew it, but I did.

Norma doesn't hold back when the box gets to her. By now, her eyes are as red as her outfit. "I never been through anything that bad," she says. "Everybody telling me they were glad my guy was *dead*. Me crying and can't sleep and trying to figure out what to do, and people telling me I deserve it. I woulda never come out from under that, except I had Junie." She reaches over and grips Junie's leg with the hand not holding the music box. When Junie gets the box, she says it was hard, being with her ma. But she's glad she was there, and same for her support girl, Fiona.

We're starting to get used to each other, like it's a thing we do in the world, telling true shit to the people in this room. After a while, Ronnah pulls over a couple of floor lamps, making the circle feel like its own little island. I think maybe it's gonna be okay, after all. The worst is over. Then Norma takes the music box. She's answering one of Ronnah's catchall questions, "Is there anything else you need to say, before we move on?" Norma wipes her tear-streaked face, gets an excited look. Like she's pumped to say something even though it makes her nervous.

"The thing you have to understand," she says. "Is that I'm not like Phil. I work in a nail salon, and I take care of *everybody*. Phil's brothers would hate knowing I did that—working on Black feet, four outta five customers on a Saturday. But I'm not like them, I do what's in front of me." She gazes around the circle, looking hopeful about our reactions. But something rips open inside me. Not even just the way she said *Black feet*, like they skeeve her out. There's more, and I can't put my finger on it. Jack does, though. He leans forward when his turn comes around, elbows on knees, hands clasped in front of him.

"I don't mean disrespect," he says. "I've lost people, I feel your pain. It's just . . . your family doesn't live off what you make, doing people's feet. So, all I'm saying is, even if you weren't like Singer, you got something out of being with this white man who got away with stuff all his life. The way he made his living doing shit that wasn't legal . . . right up to the day he got away with murder."

Nailed it, as far as I'm concerned. But Mrs. Park, Norma's support person, isn't having it.

"I know what he's trying to say," she says, looking at Ronnah even though she's talking about Jack. "But that young man"—she jabs a finger toward Fisk—"he did the same business as Phil. It's the whole way they met, according to him. So how are they acting high-and-mighty about what Phil did?"

After that, the talking piece flies fast and furious. Jack and me say that selling bootleg iPhones isn't the same as murder, and Ms. Park says, that's right—we're here 'cause Fisk committed murder. On Jack's next turn, things get deep.

"Okay, then! What are we even doing here, if you want to be fair? If both of them killed somebody, why's Fisk having to answer for what he did when Singer never did and never will?"

Before the shit starts flying, Ronnah holds out her hand for the talking piece. "That's a perfectly good question," she says. "And here's the answer. Mr. Singer's dead, and Fisk, right here, is alive. That means Fisk's the person we deal with. On the other hand, the *system* that allowed Mr. Singer the result he got, *that's* also alive. And a system can be held accountable, too."

When Junie asks how that's supposed to work, Ronnah says, "What are systems besides the people who make them up? If we figure out how to hold people accountable for the systems they hold up, maybe Mr. Singer doesn't get away with murder after all."

She lets that sink in, then says, "I think Norma and Junie are holding the system accountable right now, by being part of this process instead of going to court."

When we're done for the day, I write that part down for Ed. I underline *Maybe Mr. Singer doesn't get away with murder after all.*

The Plan

Dear Ed,

We did it. Finished the circle by the second night. And I think you'll be glad how it turned out. A funny thing, first. I redid my room. Put the bed by the window, so it feels different, falling asleep. Bennett even offered to paint for me. We'd just watched Dave Chappelle—apparently bald Black comedians work for him, too—so he was in a good mood. Said he's glad to see I've calmed down. What's funny is, he's got no idea why. From where he sits, nothing's changed with the Singer situation. And damn, has everything changed.

Anyhow.

The final part of the circle started with all of us saying what we want to happen next—even if it's not practical, we had to say it, just to get the idea out.

Norma wanted people to quit talking bad about her, as if she'd done what Singer did to you, and as if she didn't have a right to grieve her man. She wanted to get away from her neighborhood, too. And she wanted—get this—for Singer's volunteer work to keep going "in his name." Apparently, he played piano every week for a kids' cancer hospital because his niece died of cancer. She said it's the best thing he did, and she wants him to be remembered for that, too.

Junie wanted people to know that everybody who looked like Singer or came from his family or neighborhood wasn't a racist ass. And she wanted out—to not go to a New York college, like she'd planned. She wants to go to a place where people don't know about what happened, and they won't ever connect her with it.

Fisk wanted to be able to look at Norma and Junie and all the rest of us and know he's doing what he can. And to do enough over time that his nightmares stop.

Jack wanted to figure out that system accountability stuff, so it doesn't feel like what happened to you will keep on happening.

Me? For a bunch of rounds, I just agreed with Jack. Then I finally came up with something. I wanted you in it even more. I wanted something for you, more than just holding the system accountable for what Singer did to you. Something you'd care about, though I didn't know what it should be, yet. And I wanted that gun destroyed.

Five hours later, we had a plan:

Fisk will work for Ms. Fox full-time and move back in with his parents, so he can make enough money to help with Junie's *college—the difference between the state school she was planning to go to and an out-of-state school. Junie's shooting for California. Means no college for Fisk yet, because he won't have time. Also, he has to help Norma move. And he has to write stuff for social media—anonymously. About how people get fucked when somebody's killed, no matter who they were. And they deserve respect for their grieving. Plus, not everybody who lives in the same place feels the same about things. He's taking over Singer's volunteer work, too. He doesn't play piano, so he's gotta work with them to do some other kind of entertainment for the kids. (I'm guessing Jack'll help with that one.)*

Okay, here's the best part, for you. Junie and Norma are taking accountability for some of the system stuff. They agreed that every time people say bad stuff about you—Ed Hennessey blah blah blah, they'll say it wasn't your fault. What Singer did was wrong. Also—and this is the best of the best—they're gonna start giving away the money people send them. They'll send a letter back, explaining that they're donating it to a place in your name. I got to pick the place. They make computers—including gaming laptops—accessible to kids who can't afford them.

And they're getting rid of the gun. That made me feel good. And feeling good made me remember this thing Chela said, that I could be less fucked when I think about you and everything that happened. Even the hardest parts. Which would be good, right? So, I'm working on that.

Now, the money part's kind of a mindfuck. I mean, Norma and Junie are getting money from Fisk, but giving money away to this nonprofit that helps kids with computers. But it makes sense, too, right? Because Norma and Junie can't be benefitting from what Singer did—that's just wrong. They should be doing something to make up for it—like giving money to the nonprofit. Then, on the other hand, Fisk should be helping Norma and Junie, to help make up for what he did.

So, that's the story. What happens next, you ask? As the circle keeper, Ronnah stays in touch with all of us, checks in to be sure we're doing what we should be doing. She says we'll reconvene the circle if we need to. And we're also supposed to hold each other accountable. So if Fisk quits acting right, we call him on it, call Ronnah in, make sure he stays on his game. Ronnah says that's why RJ's been around for so long. Holding each other accountable is what we've all been programmed for. The bigger the problems we have to deal with, the wider the circle of people you need to help deal.

Before we finally got up to go, I realized Jack was still screwed since we weren't telling the cops about Fisk. He was still their number one suspect. It was Junie who figured out what to do.

"For Christ's sakes," she said. "Just give him an alibi! I'll say he was with me, getting a goddamn manicure."

So that's how it went down. What do you think? About Fisk killing Singer, Singer being dead? All of us doing this RJ thing? I wish you could really tell me. But I'm guessing you feel okay about it. Because I think I'd know if you didn't.

Dear Ed

Bright morning light comin' in around my shade tells me it's late. No idea what day it is. Bits and pieces of yesterday's circle bounce around my head.

Jack and Fisk shaking hands, like there really won't be hard feelings, at least not forever. Ms. Fox weeping as she gave Fisk a list of orders for his first day of full-time work. Junie hugging Chela, and me seeing something there that I still don't want to see. Then Junie and me, coming face-to-face. Tears standing in both our eyes as she moved her pink head in for a hug.

I sit up in bed, get on top of the covers. Open Ed's laptop. Still weird, not having to play. Roll my eyes, thinking of his big fart ending. Diamond was right about that. I should've guessed it. Ed to the core. I wish he could come with us tonight. Jack's dragging me to Coney Island, see if we can meet some girls on the beach. I texted Robbie to come. Him and Jack can wingman each other, 'cause I'm still thinking about Diamond, and being at Coney Island won't help.

There's a noise in the hall, somebody opening a door. At the same time, an email notification pops up on Ed's screen. Heading: *The results are in!* I open it.

A countdown graphic appears, each number exploding across the screen *10–9–8–*

"Veezwee!" Sammy's high-pitched shriek cuts through the house. "Veezwee, I'm up. Get me!"

5–4–3–

"Veezwee!" She sounds so happy just to be saying my name, knowing I can come get her. It cuts through me, how much I've missed that. I put the laptop down, bound out to get her and bring her back, settling her on my knee as I grab the laptop.

There's a whole animated congrats party happening on the screen. Like I knew there would be. I open a fresh doc. Blame Ed for how easy the riddles come. Grinning like a fool, I write:

> Dear Ed,
>   Want to know if you won the JersiGame contest? Here you go, buddy.
>
>   What's the most curious letter in the alphabet?
>   What woolly girl gets naked to keep you warm?

What do you do when you take a leak?

Answer: Y. U. P.

Then I pick up my phone to tell Jack.

Acknowledgments

So much love goes into writing a book. Who knew? Love for my characters, love for the people who inspired them, and love for the people who helped me through the delicious angst of getting it all down in print.

So much love to so many people.

To Andrea Canaan, my writing partner, thanks for writers' camp, for listening to the entire novel read aloud, and for too many bicoastal 5:30 a.m. Zoom calls to count. And thanks to the members of Black Women Writing, my first and forever writers' group: Marcia Gomes, Kathryn T. Hall, A. Iona Smith Nze, and, again, Andrea Canaan.

I am deeply grateful to my fellow writers, beta readers, and critique-group members, Ellen Barry, Caitlin Krowicki, Amin Ahmad, Jacquelyn Ambrosini, Marilyn Fleming, and Annie Kunjappy.

Thank you to my gifted teachers, especially Matt de la Peña and my New School MFA teachers. Love and appreciation also to my wonderful New School cohort. And to my adored niece and literary consultant, Aisha Stith, and extraordinary mentor, Carolyn Tara O'Neil—thanks for helping me over the finish line!

Much gratitude to my movement families, the CJI team—especially George Galvis, Albino Garcia, Mel Motel, and Judy Harden—who introduced me to restorative justice, and to my avid book-support-team: Aleah Bacquie-Vaughn and Trinh Eng. Thank you to Danielle Sered and all of the participants and staff of Common Justice. And to my ongoing RJ support team: Purvi Shah and Erika Sasson. I learned so much from and with all of you.

Along with all of the love and hard work, there's also a healthy dose of luck involved. I got astoundingly lucky with my publishing team: Elizabeth Bewley and Sterling Lord Literistic and Ben Rosenthal and the crew at HarperCollins. Thank you for believing in VZ and me, and for your brilliance, clarity, care, and kindness as we've moved through this process together.

I am lucky, too, to be part of a talented and committed writing community. Thank you to the women of A Writer's Life, including Natalie Devora, Tshego Letsoalo, Sarah Selim, Aidan Kinsella, KJ McCoy, Ayesha Sundram, Brittany Mouton, Denne Dickson, Lisa Clapper, Marisol Lorenzana, Molly Kittle, Nada Stevens, Natalie Bell, Noel Donovan, Wanda Dabkoska, and Kat Whipple.

A huge world of thanks to my beloved family who supported me throughout this journey. To Kwame Allen-Roberts, for teaching me daily about love, life, and video games. And to Carol Allen, Denise

Allen, Andresa Person, and our matriarch, Roberta McCombs, for being there always.

Finally, who gets an analytical reader, copy editor, and giver of exquisite TLC all in one stellar human? Yup, me. Thank you to my partner, Liz Roberts, for being all that and so much more, every step of the way.

Most of all, thank you, readers! You are the whole point of writing a book.